PRAISE FOR *DEFINITELY, MAYBE, YOURS*

"4½ STARS: This book had so many things going for it; I almost don't know where to start. First, there was the cast… They were so perfect for each other, a born problem fixer and a guy carrying an almighty pack of these around, a dark-skinned Englishman of Scottish and West Indian heritage and the blond scion of a Russian-American clan. And if these two weren't diverse enough, there's a bunch of side characters who are just as colorful. All kinds of races, genders, identities, and orientations coexist cheerfully on the pages of this book."

—Prism Book Alliance

"These guys… are smoldering together."

—Joyfully Jay Reviews

"FIVE STARS—Craig Oliver is amazing… from his English mannerisms, to his simplistic views, even his ability to bake with alcohol when his heart gets shattered is amazing. I really love this character."

—Scattered Thoughts and Rogue Words Review Blog

PRAISE FOR *CERTAINLY, POSSIBLY, YOU*

"I am totally having a moment with this series."

—Dahlia Adler, LGBTQ Reads

"I am loving the Sucre Coeur Series as a whole and the fact that we can continue to see characters from *Definitely, Maybe, Yours* not only woven into the narrative of book two, but also supportive and involved in helping Mari and Sarita stay together. I really can't wait to see what happens in the next book *Absolutely, Almost, Perfect*."

—G Jacks Writes Reviews

PRAISE FOR *ABSOLUTELY, ALMOST, PERFECT*

"FIVE STARS—A very funny, romantic, real story about what being a family really means."

—NetGalley review

LISSA REED

CERTAINLY, *possibly,* YOU

SUCRE COEUR BOOK II

interlude ✦✦ **press**™ • new york

interlude ⚏ press • new york

For Angela
You and me against the end of the world!

All the same, she rang the bell,
and then she waited for
whatever would happen next.

—Alice Hoffman

Chapter One

MOST MORNINGS, THE PIERCING SHRIEK OF SARITA'S ALARM doesn't feel quite so much as though it's drilling into her skull. Of course, most of Sarita's mornings aren't preceded by an evening of dancing, yelling conversations over music and drinking.

Oh, so much drinking.

Rolling over, she fumbles for her phone; her head is a water balloon of pain. "I want to die," she whispers as she slides the alarm off, not daring to speak louder in case it makes whatever angry god has taken up residence in her head even more furious. "Die, die, die..."

Blessed silence. She tosses the phone aside. But after several moments of lying very, very still with her hands cradling her poor mistreated head, it is clear to Sarita that Death, whoever he or she may be, is not on duty this morning. *Life it is then, such as it is.* Moving as slowly as she can, with as quiet a whimper as she can manage, she sits up and wiggles her feet down until they're firmly planted in the soft carpet.

So far, so good.

Now she actually has to stand up and walk.

Never again, Alex. Inch by agonizing inch, Sarita pushes herself to standing and wishes that she could direct the poisonous laser of her thoughts across Seattle and into the brain of one Alex Scheff, whose birthday-slash-studio-opening party is directly responsible for the state in which she finds herself at four-thirty this cursed Saturday morning. Well, not the party as much as the open bar, but whatever. Either way, Alex is to blame here.

Sure. Because you're not responsible for yourself at all.

That snarky little inner voice Sarita chooses to ignore. Her maroon bathrobe is draped over the piles of teddy bears and stuffed animals in the one chair in her bedroom, and Sarita snatches it up on her shuffling way to the bathroom. It's not until she's knotting the sash around her waist that she realizes she's wearing nothing under the soft terrycloth but a pair of pink cotton boy shorts.

She frowns. Turning, she sees that the ancient, oversized Sonics T-shirt she usually sleeps in is exactly where she left it yesterday morning, crumpled into a green heap in the lap of her largest teddy bear. *Weird.* It's not as if she gets blind drunk often, but when she does, she still usually manages to at least struggle into her pajama shirt.

I must have really, really had a lot last night.

...wait. How did I get home?

Too much. Too much to consider before caffeine. Mouth first, comb out her rat's nest of hair second—she can see the black cloud of curls on all sides without even turning her head and that's bad—and then get a cup of her strongest tea into herself. *Then* she can tackle the sticky questions of why she slept naked and how she got home and where, actually, her car is, because she knows she drove *to* Alex's photography studio.

Teeth. First. She makes her way over to the sink and bends to her task.

When the very attractive woman pops up behind her with a chirpy, "Morning!", Sarita lets the toothbrush go flying, but she has the presence of mind to clap her hands over her mouth to keep the toothpaste from following suit when she starts to scream.

"THIS IS SO EMBARRASSING. I'M SO SORRY..." SARITA HANDS OVER a mug of spice tea, her face about as hot as the drink. "I can't believe I forgot you were here."

The woman tosses back her mane of hair—a blonde-streaked tumble of waves nearly as dark as Sarita's own hair—and from her perch on Sarita's sofa beams a gorgeous smile that lights up the living room and somehow is confident enough to make her improvised flowery bedsheet toga look like a reasonable thing to wear. "It's a first, but don't worry about it. I'm pretty sure you'll never forget me again."

At this, Sarita can't help but laugh, despite her nearly incapacitating embarrassment. "No, I don't think I will, ahh..." *Oh my God. Do I even know her name?*

Now would be a great time for the ground to open up and swallow me whole.

Unfortunately, whoever's in charge of earthquakes seems to be on the same vacation as Death. Sarita sighs and lets her head drop into the palm of her hand.

The woman's laughter is a peal of chimes, warm and golden. "Maritza," she says, and Sarita hears the tea mug clink as it's set down on the end table, and then Maritza is tugging her hand away so that Sarita has to look into her face, into merry brown eyes and that sun-bright smile. "Maritza Quiñones, if we're being formal." She looks down at her toga and back up again, and her smile is even more elfin. "If we *can* be formal in bedsheets and a bathrobe."

"I think the situation almost calls for it," Sarita replies, a bit surprised at how easy it is to slip into comfortable banter with this girl. This girl she doesn't even remember spending time with last night. *Oh. Oh, boy.* "Um... wait. Did we...?"

"We did not." Maritza squeezes Sarita's hand. "We wanted to, and we sort of tried, but in the end we both passed out and... that was that."

"Oh." It's actually a disappointment. Obviously Sarita is glad they didn't do anything they wouldn't have remembered, but… She looks at Maritza and withholds a groan. Even in a bedsheet, Maritza is gorgeous, about the same height as Sarita's own slight self, but curvier, softer. Her eyes twinkle brown; her full mouth seems permanently bowed into a tiny smile; and her golden-brown skin is flawless. A dimple nestles in her left cheek, making a cheerful appearance every time Maritza smiles, which is, apparently, often. And she's just very, very pretty.

So sure, it's good they did nothing, but also *oh, damn it*.

"You can make it up to me later," Maritza says, and her smile is in her voice. It's as if she is made of sunshine and happiness, and, while it ought to be too early in the morning and Sarita ought to be much too hungover to handle it well, she can't help it, she's charmed to her very core. "Really. I wouldn't mind a second chance at all." Her hand slips from Sarita's and traces gentle lines along the inside of Sarita's wrist. "Now is good for me, if it's good for you."

"I… " *Damn it!* She wants very badly for now to be good, to be able to kiss that Cupid's bow mouth, to run her hands over the full breasts holding up her stupid purple-flowered bedsheet, to do any number of all kinds of everything to the beautiful woman in front of her. Headache and all, she's never wanted anything so badly.

The curving lines that Maritza's fingertip traces on Sarita's wrist are little trails of fire, sparking warm against the soft skin and sending shivers all through her. Desire twists silken cords in the pit of her stomach, and she *wants*, she *needs*…

"I have work," she groans. She takes a step back and pulls her wrist away from that devilishly tempting single fingertip. "God, I am *so sorry*. I wish more than anything I didn't have to."

Maritza's smile droops. "Me too."

"Believe me, really, I want to." Sarita doesn't dare reach forward for a reassuring touch. She knows exactly what would happen then; too much energy sparks between them. "I do. I did last night, clearly, since I brought you here." And that reminds her of something else. "I did bring you here, didn't I? Somehow?"

That seems to restore the missing hint of good humor to Maritza's smile. "You did. In a cab. You mentioned something about a car, but neither of us were fit to drive, so I guess it's still back at Alex's studio."

"Oh." It's not an insurmountable problem, but it's annoying. She'll have to take the bus to work and to get her car. Fortunately for her, work and her car are in the same neighborhood, but she has no idea what Maritza's going to do. "Um, do you live nearby? I don't know how to get you home."

"No. I'm down in Burien." Maritza's chuckle is soft. "Don't look so worried. I take the Metro all the time, I promise. My brother and I are supposed to share our car, not that I ever seem to win the coin tosses. But honest, it's no problem. Really. I have most of the bus schedules memorized. Point me to a bus stop near here, and I'm good. Pinkie swear."

It seems ungallant somehow to Sarita, given that Maritza spent the night with no frisky activity, got screamed at in the morning and got shot down on her second attempt to initiate friskiness. She deserves more than to be shoved onto a bus at five o'clock in the morning.

"Can I get you something for breakfast before you go? I have muffins. I work in a bakery." Sarita has no idea why she tacked that on. "I mean, they're from yesterday, but they're still good. Chocolate cherry almond. Do you like muffins?" And now she can't stop talking. *Help.*

"I should go." When she smiles, the bridge of Maritza's nose crinkles up, and, between that and the dimple, Sarita is about ready to say to hell with the bakery and drag the woman back to bed. "I mean I really should. I've got work today, too, and I probably need to catch a few more z's before I get to it."

"If you're sure." Disappointment floods Sarita. But she won't let this girl get away that easily. She wants that second chance, too. She gropes in her pocket and pulls out her phone. "Here. Give me your number. I'll put it in and text you so you have mine. We should try to meet up for lunch sometime. Or dinner. Or whatever." The knowledge that she is usually much smoother about picking up women makes Sarita want to kick her own ass. Never has she fumbled so much—but then again, never has anyone so disarmed her with a bright smile and a beautiful laugh. "Your choice."

"You're on." Maritza takes the phone from Sarita's hand. "Here, I've got it." When she bows her head over the phone, Maritza's perfectly tousled waves of hair fall around her face, and Sarita is acutely aware that her own hair is still a complete rat's nest. Her face burns as she takes her phone back.

"Thank you," she says; the words are inadequate and soft. "You sure I can't get you that muffin? More tea?"

"I won't even be able to finish this cup." Maritza glances down and brushes a hand over her toga. "I wouldn't say no to you letting me borrow a T-shirt or something, though. I mean, the shirt I wore last night is with my purse, but it's a sequined tank top." She winks. "Nothing says 'walk of shame' more than sequins before dawn, you know?"

Having only worn sequins under duress from her mother, Sarita has no earthly idea what they say at any hour, but she nods as if she does and walks to the clean laundry basket in her bedroom to grab the first thing that comes to hand. Considering the pleasant, but significant, differences between Maritza's figure and her own, Sarita is glad she tends to buy oversized. "Will this work?"

"Anything will work." Maritza drops another wink that makes Sarita go weak in the knees and then sways off toward the bedroom, loosening and dropping her toga along the way. The wicked little half-grin she tosses over her naked shoulder as she closes the bedroom door makes Sarita's mouth go dry. Only the buzz of her backup phone alarm shakes her out of her reverie and gets her moving.

"I'm home." This early on a Saturday morning, Maritza doesn't exactly shout this to the skies when she lets herself into her family's rented home, but she pitches it loud enough to be heard if anyone is awake. And sure enough, as she's hanging her jacket and purse on the rack by the door, her brother Javier emerges from the kitchen, yawning over a cup of coffee with his dark hair sticking up every which way.

"Ay, Mari. Kinda late, eh?" Javi's foot nudges at their cat Coco to shoo the bundle of black fur away from the chair at their shared desk. "It's coming up on seven."

She can't help rolling her eyes. "That's pretty early for morning, and I'm an adult, Javi."

"It's pretty late when you didn't come home last night," he retorts with a smug grin.

She ignores it. She *is* an adult, after all, and older than him by a year. "Did you do a full pot of that coffee?" She points her chin at his mug, hoping the answer is yes. It smells *so good* right now. The spice tea that the girl from last night gave her was delicious, but Maritza has been a certified coffee-holic since she was fifteen. A hard jolt of caffeine is exactly what she needs right now, even if she's planning to go straight to bed after she drinks it.

It's as though Javi can read her thoughts. "Coffee? You don't need to take a nap?"

"Of course I need a nap. I'll have one after I have my coffee." She kicks off her strappy sandals and goes into the kitchen, following the glorious aroma of coffee freshly ground and brewed. "Where's Mama?"

"Still asleep," Javi calls softly, his fingers clacking across the keyboard of their computer. "She stayed late at the hospital. One of the other nurses got sick and couldn't come in."

"Ay, yi. I hope she gets a raise this year for all the overtime she puts in." Maritza slumps down onto the deep crimson sofa with her mug of heaven, inhaling the wonderful smell. "What'cha doing? Physics homework?"

"Always." Javi glances away from the computer just long enough to flash her a smile. "Galileo Thermometers and the Physics of Density."

Maritza's gaze drifts over to their own Galileo thermometer, perched on a shelf by the television with its delicate rainbow of multi-colored glass balls glowing in the gentle morning light. Somehow it had survived their childhoods, Coco's kittenhood and a cross-country move from New York to Washington State. She smiles at her brother's endless obsession with science and tilts her head back on the sofa, resting the bottom of her coffee mug on her jeans-clad leg. "Cool."

Keys clack for a minute or two more before Javi's curiosity apparently gets the better of him. "So? You have a good time at that party?"

"Mm. Yeah." She feels her mouth tilt up into a smile while thinking about last night's girl. She'd been so cute last night, and fucking adorable this morning with her awkwardness and her offers of tea and breakfast. And even if they didn't get very far last night, they got far enough for Maritza to know that her pretty brown skin is so soft and so silky.

Javi clears his throat. "That's it? 'Mm, yeah'? A professional photographer invites you to a bomb-ass party and that's all you got for me? I hope Nicky had fun, at least."

"Nicky wasn't invited." Her smile twists into a frown at the thought of her dance partner. God, if he'd been there he'd have wrecked everything with his schmoozing and gross superior attitude. "I went by myself."

"You didn't leave by yourself." Javier's voice drips with smirking amusement. "Or you'd have been home a lot earlier than seven."

"Eh." She's not ready to share. She wants a few more private minutes of the girl's apple-scented cloud of black curls, of the way their bodies moved together to the bass-beat of Natalia Kills even as the girl protested she didn't know how to dance. *It's okay*, Maritza remembers telling her. *I can show you.*

Oh, she was so pretty and so shy, but maybe Maritza should have suggested they stop after they'd each had three Cape Cods from the open bar. The sigh escapes her before she can catch it.

The couch shifts next to her as Javi plops down with his own coffee and nudges her over to make room. "Okay. What's his name?"

"*Her* name," Maritza corrects automatically. Javi's immediate chortle makes her wince. "Oh, come on, shut up."

"What? I'm being mature, I'm not making any cracks."

"The laughing is gross, Javi." Grabbing a throw pillow, Maritza beats her brother around his head and shoulders, avoiding their coffee cups. "It's not a joke if I go out with a girl!"

"Who's saying it is?" The height and weight advantage Javi has over her is demonstrated as he plucks the pillow from her hand with expert efficiency and tosses it over the back of the sofa. "I would have laughed if you'd gone home with a guy, too. Well, I would have laughed myself stupid if you'd gone home with Nicky, but any other guy, just normal laughter."

"Nicky isn't happening again." Never, *ever* again, and she can't believe it ever happened in the first place. *Whatever.* "Anyway. Yeah. I met a girl."

Javi arches one dark eyebrow. "And her name is...?"

It's not until Maritza opens her mouth to answer that she realizes she has no idea. "Oh my God."

"Is that what she asked you to call her or did it just hap—"

"Shut up, Javi! You're so gross!" Shoving her coffee in her brother's general direction, she scrambles off the sofa and rummages through her purse looking for her phone. "She said she would text me so I would have her number. Maybe she..." Her heart sinks as she pulls her phone out. There is a message, so that's good, but all it says is: *It was great to meet you, can't wait to see you again.* No name. "Oh, no, she didn't leave her name." *How embarrassing.*

Over on the couch, Javi shrugs. "Just reply to her text and ask her for her name."

"I can't do that." Maritza closes her eyes to rack her brain for any moment from last night that isn't clouded in alcohol haze, any moment where the girl might have introduced herself. Maritza knows that they must have exchanged names, they must have, but that moment is apparently gone, and two hours ago she was the only one who gave her name—that much she remembers. "I teased her for forgetting my name! I can't tell her I forgot hers, too."

"So..." Javier seems genuinely puzzled. "What are you going to do? Never text her again? Never see her again?" He gestures with one of the coffee cups. "You're probably going to have to give her that shirt back some time."

"Shirt?" Maritza opens her eyes to look down at the purple T-shirt she forgot she was wearing. She squints and can make out the words *Sucre Coeur* in flowing, if upside-down, white script. "What's that mean?"

Another shrug from her brother. "It's a bakery up in Queen Anne. I go there sometimes with my lab partner because some cute redhead he likes works there. Not that she gives Mike the time of day." He sips at his coffee and his face brightens. "Hey, is that who you went home with maybe? Tall redhead, maybe an accent of some kind? Her nametag said Tash last time we went, I think. Something like that."

"No. This girl was Indian. Like, from India, not Native American." But *tall redhead, accent*, does jog something in Maritza's mind, and she closes her eyes to fish it up from the depths. "I think I met that girl, though. The redhead, she was there, at the studio. Wait, yeah." That image is clear, the way that the girl from last night and the redhead interacted, lively and happy. She can still see her girl's slender brown hands dancing in the air as they talked and see her dark eyes sparkle. "They knew each other. So maybe they work together? Yeah, they have to." More details bubble up from this morning. "The girl I was with, she offered me muffins for breakfast. She said she worked in a bakery; it has to be this one."

"Way to go, Sherlock Holmes." Javi salutes her with his cup. "Anything else coming up?"

Maritza takes a moment to think about it before she gives up. "Nope, *nada*." She shakes her head and rejoins her brother on the couch. Reclaiming her coffee, she sucks down half the cup in a go, with a grimace at how it's cooled. "Ech. Hey, what if I just go up to the bakery and talk to the redhead if she's there? Casual-like and all. I mean, we've met, I could go say hey." It doesn't seem like a terrible idea. The redhead might be there, she might casually drop Last Night's Girl's name, and then everything works out.

It seems like a long way to go to find out someone's name, but Maritza does not mind taking the long way around if it means she can avoid embarrassment.

"Go now? Up into Seattle, when you just came back from there? And instead of your nap?" Javier's eyebrow goes up again. "You're gonna fall asleep at work."

"This is more important than sleep, Javi." It's not as though she's never worked a shift at the pizza place half-asleep. "Anyway, if I go up now, and if you let me use the car, I can still make it back in time for a tiny nap before work."

"You've got dance practice, too," Javier reminds her. "You know Nicky hates it when you show up tired."

"Nicky can go fuck himself." It bursts from her without her thinking, and she pinches the bridge of her nose. "I didn't mean that."

Javier grins. "It's okay if you did."

She shakes her head. "No, it's not, so I didn't. Anyway, I'll just reschedule Nicky for tomorrow, tell him I have to go in to work early or something."

"Yeah, because that always goes over so well." Javier gets up and goes to the coat rack, digs the keys to their shared car from a pocket and tosses them over. "There you go. You'll have to put some gas in it; it was low yesterday."

"Thanks." With a gulp, she finishes off her cold coffee, handing the empty cup back to Javi in exchange for the keys. She hauls herself to her feet and hurtles out the door, stopping only to stretch up on her tiptoes and kiss Javi on the cheek before she goes out into the gray light of a February Seattle morning.

Chapter Two

THIRTY MINUTES LATER, MARITZA IS INSIDE THE WARM, chocolatey-smelling haven of Sucre Coeur facing neither redhead nor Last Night's Girl, but rather a good-looking black guy with dreadlocks tucked under a hairnet who seems vaguely familiar, and who is staring at her with a puzzled expression on his face.

"You don't work for me," he says, his voice a low melodious roll straight out of the British comedies Javier likes to watch. "Or did Theodora hire you? You're late in either case, I'm sorry to say. I'm the manager here, and we have rules about punctuality."

Oh, right. She's still got the shirt on. "Oh! No. Sorry, I'm so sorry. I borrowed this shirt from a girl this morning." Her cheeks flush hot and, she's sure, tomato red as the words emerge from her mouth and the guy behind the counter starts to grin. "I mean, I..."

"I suspect you mean exactly what you say," he says, and his grin broadens. "Which is fine, as this is a non-judging bakery. Can I get you something?"

The array of pastries, cookies and cupcakes in the glass cases before her is nearly overwhelming. All of it looks wonderful, and her stomach growls as she remembers that she turned down the girl's offer of muffins. "Do you have muffins?" she asks. "Chocolate cherry ones?"

"The chocolate cherry ones are baked on Fridays, but I've got double chocolate *chip* today if you'd like," the man offers, leaning over the case to point at a tray of chocolate muffins the size of her head. "I can also offer some really excellent vanilla chai scones." He glances up at her and winks, redirecting to indicate a tray of large pastry triangles drizzled in sugary icing. "Adapted from my family's secret recipe. Any interest there?"

Both sound amazing, and this time her stomach growls loudly enough for both of them to hear it. "I'll take one of each," Maritza blurts, wishing her cheeks would cool off already.

"No problem. That'll be a total of five dollars, unless you want something to drink from the case." He points behind her to a refrigerated case of milk and bottled coffee drinks, then tilts his head. "Hey, didn't I meet you last night? Maritza, isn't it?"

To hear her name from this stranger's mouth is startling. *Okay, I have to cut back on drinking at parties for sure.* "Um..."

"I'm Alex's boyfriend. Craig," he clarifies as he bags up the bakery treats and places them on the top of the display case. "You were at the party last night, yeah? You met Alex at the Pacific Northwest Ballroom Blitz."

"Yeah, he was shooting the event." She and Nicky placed third that day, and Nicky's resulting infantile rage made her stomp off, running directly and quite literally into the photographer at the edge of the dance floor. Once her embarrassment died, they got to talking, and then he invited her to his studio opening. Where she had, in fact, seen him with this guy, rather late in the proceedings. "Okay, yes, I remember you now; yeah, you guys arrived kind of late."

"Alex got nervous about all the people," Craig says and steps over to the cash register to ring her up. "Happens sometimes. Didn't I see you dancing with Sarita?"

"Sarita! Yes!" Now she remembers the girl shouting her name over the thump of the music, with her hand cupped around her mouth and her breath sweet with cranberry and vodka. "Yes. Sarita. This is her shirt."

"You didn't come to... give it back?" Craig's hand pauses over the cash register buttons. "I ask only because you're still actually wearing it."

Again the heat flush to her cheeks and Craig's smile of amusement. "No, I just—"

"Did you want to see her?" He nods toward the back of the bakery. "She's in the back decorating a wedding cake, but I can go get her if you want to say hi. Only a minute, mind. We've got to get that cake done, the wedding's tomorrow."

"Oh. I don't know." Maritza pushes a five-dollar bill across the counter and wishes she'd planned this better. Impulsiveness is not usually a character trait she gives in to, and right now, with painful clarity, she remembers exactly why that is. "Maybe, I mean, I don't want to bother her."

In her imaginary scenario involving the redhead being here, Maritza hadn't thought about actually getting to *see* Sarita, which was incredibly stupid given that, not even four hours ago, the woman told her she had to go to work. Which was here. At this bakery. Right now. In the back, where Sarita is decorating a wedding cake. Maybe she's got a dab of frosting on her nose or forehead, maybe she's wearing a puffy hat thing to hold back her riot of black curls, maybe she is absolutely adorable, and Maritza is standing here with last night's makeup on and Sarita's shirt and she cannot believe she thought a sequined tank top said Walk of Shame more than what she's wearing right now.

"Actually, I really need to get home," Maritza blurts and she bolts out of the bakery door with her bag of pastries in hand. The jangle of brass bells and Craig's puzzled gaze follow her down the sidewalk.

THE SHARP BANG OF THE BAKERY'S FRONT DOOR INTERRUPTS Sarita's reverie and jerks her upright, so she squeezes green frosting from the leaf-tip bag in her hands. She has the good sense to pull away before any excess can drip down over the sculpted scarlet buttercream roses she's been surrounding with foliage. She sets the bag down and looks over at Natasha, whose hands have stopped in the act of twisting dough into cinnamon *bulochki* knots. "What the hell?"

"Don't know," Tash replies, tucking back a lock of red hair that has escaped from her paper cap. She's about as hungover as Sarita, if the purple circles under her hazel eyes and the frown on her pale face are any indication, and the slam-bang of the door probably hasn't done whatever headache she's got any favors, either. "But next time Alex throws a party, do you think we can talk Craig into closing this place the next day?"

"Craig, yes. Theodora, never." Sarita unties her apron, hanging it carefully on a hook. She rubs at her temples. "But maybe we can talk Theo into finally installing that thing on the door so people can't slam it. I'm going to get some Advil from my purse. You want?"

"Please." A smile of gratitude does its best to light up Tash's tired face, and Sarita returns it with one of sympathy as she goes to the front counter.

At the cash register, she finds Craig, a five-dollar bill in his hand and amusement on his face as he turns to face Sarita. "Hmm. Good morning, Sarita."

The expression of smug mirth on her friend's face makes Sarita slow to a stop before taking a step backward. "Good morning, Craig. Again."

"How's the Breville cake coming along?" Craig's grin is much, much broader than Sarita thinks such a simple question warrants. The sight makes her take another step backward.

"Fine," she replies, trying to shake off the unnerving sensation of having wandered into a patch of quicksand. "I just took a break to come get some Advil for Tash and me." She waves a hand toward the cupboard under the cash register. "It's in my purse. Under there."

Craig punches a few keys on the cash register and deposits the five-dollar bill. When he steps aside and makes a slight bow, he's clearly struggling to hold back laughter. "Be my guest."

"Okay, what is your problem?" Sarita doesn't move.

Covering his mouth, Craig starts to snicker. "Sarita," he says through his fingers, "did you sleep with Alex's little ballroom dancer friend last night?"

"I didn't sleep with anyone last night, let alone a ballroom dancer," Sarita snaps, then stops as comprehension hits her. "Wait. Was she here? She's the door-slammer?"

Craig's snicker becomes an outright guffaw before he gets himself under control. "Well, that's not a confusing answer at all, Sarita," he drawls, leaning against the counter. "You didn't sleep with a ballroom dancer, but you want to know if she was here?"

"I didn't—we didn't sleep together. She's a ballroom dancer?" A flash of memory sends a rush of blood to Sarita's cheeks, and yes, ballroom dancer makes sense. She remembers hands on her hips, pulling her close and snug, warmth to warmth, and bright brown eyes shining as Maritza's voice says, *I'll show you...*

That was why Sarita decided to take her home, she remembers now.

"Yes, she's a ballroom dancer. And yes, she was here. Wearing one of your work shirts." Mirth is shining in Craig's eyes. "So I think you can forgive me for drawing the obvious conclusion from the evidence before me, slim as it may have been."

"I don't have to forgive anything. What was she doing here? Did she ask for me?" They exchanged numbers just a few hours ago. Maritza said she was going home to sleep. Why come back into the city—and still wearing Sarita's T-shirt? Did she think Sarita wasn't going to call her? Of course Sarita was going to call her.

As Sarita's brain whirls, Craig opens the cupboard where she and Tash stashed their purses and jackets this morning. He rummages in Sarita's purse and pulls out a bottle of ibuprofen, then tosses it over. "You look like you could use this more than ever now."

"Yeah, thanks." Still trying to work everything out, she tucks the bottle of pills into her back pocket. "Did she say why she was here?"

"I'm afraid not. She bought a scone and a muffin, and when I asked if she wanted to see you, she took off like a shot." Craig shrugs, and his smile now is less amused and more sympathetic. "Sorry."

"She bought a muffin?" This in no way should make a dopey grin spread across Sarita's face, and yet, here she is. *Was it because of me?* She does manage to stop a silly giggle from escaping. "Really?"

Craig laughs. "Yeah, she got a muffin. I don't think I want to know why that makes you look that way." He winks. "Go on, drop her a text or something, let her know I don't think she's crazy. Well, not entirely."

Toying with the pill bottle in her back pocket, Sarita considers the notion. On the one hand, yes! Yes, she definitely wants to contact Maritza. But is a handful of hours too soon? Maybe not, not if Maritza actually bothered to come to the bakery. But then Maritza ran off, didn't stick around. So maybe she wasn't actually interested? Or she was, but then she got scared? But that doesn't square with the calm, confident girl wearing the sheet.

With a shake of his head, Craig closes the cupboard and leans on the counter. "Or don't text her."

"Maybe I should get the cake done first." She can think while she crafts more roses and pipes ruffles around the bases of the four layers. Cake decorating, she has found in the last six years, is as meditative as a good yoga practice. "Then I'll text her, maybe."

"Sure." Craig flashes a smile over his shoulder. "Whatever you decide."

Sarita inches toward the back room. "I should give Tash this Advil before she comes out and commits mayhem for it."

"Right on," Craig says, in quite an agreeable tone.

She's crossing the threshold into the kitchen when Craig calls out, "Sarita? Question?"

"Yeah?" She's glad he's not facing her when she stumbles turning around.

"Did you offer that young lady muffins for breakfast this morning? Maybe those chocolate cherry almond ones?"

What kind of question is that? "Yeah, maybe. I had some leftover from yesterday."

"I see." And he chuckles.

Sarita waits, but when it becomes clear he's not going to explain himself, she spins around again and resumes her trek to the back room, more puzzled than ever now.

CRAIG WAITS UNTIL HE'S PRETTY SURE SARITA'S MADE IT TO THE back room before he pulls his phone out and thumbs the top entry on his speed dial. He grins at Alex's wordless yawn of a salutation. "Morning, babe."

Sleepy mumble, another yawn, this time with a tiny squeak. Craig can hear Alex fumbling for his glasses. "The end table, love. No, the other one."

A crash, and Craig winces. Well, who needs an alarm clock anyway, these days? With patience, Craig waits for Alex to stagger up and out of their bed and to pace their apartment muttering before at last a mumble emerges. "Craig?"

"There you are." Craig does not have a lot of sympathy for his poor hungover boyfriend, since Alex will get to go back to sleep after this while Craig had to open up the bakery with Sarita and Natasha at fuck-off o'clock in the morning. He is, however, very good at faking it. "Feeling a bit rough today?"

"Maybe," Alex rasps. Craig hears the rush of water as Alex fills their electric kettle. "Ugh."

"I've got news for you that might make you feel better," Craig says, looking back over his shoulder to make sure Sarita is tucked well away, around the corner and in the very back of the kitchen. If he strains, he can just hear the women talking. "Somewhat better, at least?"

"You're coming home with a sledgehammer to put me out of my misery?" Alex's question is hopeful, and Craig has to chuckle.

"Sorry, no. I'm just calling to tell you that your little plan worked."

A long, stupefied silence is all that can be heard from the other end. Then, "I had a little plan?"

"You did. With Maritza and Sarita. Remember?" Given all the planning, Craig is somewhat surprised at Alex being so forgetful. Then again, given all the alcohol everyone joyously consumed last night, perhaps he shouldn't be. "Your ballroom-dancing friend, my head decorator? Ringing bells?"

"Vaguely. How many tequila slammers did I have last night?"

Craig thinks. "Two at home after you emerged from hiding in our bathroom and three once you hit the party. Then there was the champagne toast. Toasts. And that's all I remember."

A groan wafts down the line. "And you woke me up because?"

"Because you had a plan," Craig reminds Alex, and he waits.

"Right, the plan. With Sarita." Alex yawns again, and Craig hears the click of the kettle being switched off. "Was it a clever plan?"

"You thought it was when you came up with it, and it seems to be working, so I suppose it was, in the end."

"What was it?"

Grant me strength. "To put my decorator friend together with that charming ballroom dancer you met a few weeks ago."

The clink of a stirring spoon rings through the connection, then stops. "Oh, yeah."

"I thought you'd be interested to know that they apparently went back to Sarita's together last night, and they're acting like nervous birds this morning. It's precious, really." The memory of Maritza in Sarita's shirt with her dark eyes wide and puzzled, then that of Sarita with nearly the same expression on her face a scant moment later, it's not just adorable, it's funny, and he laughs. "I thought you said Maritza was a spitfire? She was as indecisive as a kitten, until she decided to run out the door."

"Dating isn't ballroom dancing." Alex yawns yet again, with the scratch of a kitchen chair being scraped across their battered linoleum to accompany him. "She's a force of nature, I promise."

"Well, she must be quite impressive. Sarita offered her breakfast this morning." Craig is still amused to the hilt at the idea.

Alex seems less so. "That means something?"

"Only in that I distinctly recall having a conversation with her just last year in which she informed me quite clearly that she did not offer her, ah... what's the word I want?"

"Assignations?"

"Good one. Yes, she hadn't met any lady assignation who had made her want to offer her breakfast."

"And now she has. Ah. Cute. She's taking a leaf out of your book." Alex laughs softly.

"Can't blame her for going with something that has a proven history of working, can you?" Craig lets himself drift back to their first morning together, to the sweet memory of pancakes and spice tea and ten or fifteen minutes of monkey business that are still top-ranked on his list of peak relationship moments. He gets so lost that Alex must repeat his name several times, in increasing degrees of amused irritation, to pull him back to the present. "Sorry, what?"

"I asked you what was next," Alex says, and Craig can all but see him shaking his head. Gently, so as to not disturb the hangover, of course. "You said Maritza left? Is Sarita going to call her or something?"

"Hope so, couldn't tell you." Footsteps and a pair of female voices behind him are his split-second warning. "Love you. Got to go." He clicks off before Alex can say anything in return.

"Checking in on Alex?" Natasha asks, and when Craig turns around, she's pinching the bridge of her nose. "I hope he feels better than we do."

"Not really, but don't feel too sorry for him. He doesn't have to work today." He casts an eye over his employees, noting that they look slightly less pained, but still exhausted. "Am I to take your appearance to mean you'd like to take a coffee break?"

Sarita nods. "Please. We'll go and be right back, and we'll bring you a latte."

"Be my guest. Here." With a flourish, he opens the cash register and pulls out a twenty. He hands it over along with a small bag of brownies for them to give Cliff, the manager of their favorite coffee shop. "Extra whipped cream, please?"

"Sure. Can I get past you there?" Sarita accepts the twenty and tucks it into her pocket, sliding past him at the same time to get to her purse. She's very surreptitious about it, but he sees her palm her phone and shove it into her other pocket when she gets her and Tash's jackets out. "Thanks."

Of course she could have grabbed her phone for any reason at all. It's the twenty-first century; they all carry their phones around all the time. But as the women walk out the bakery door, Sarita pulls her phone out, and her face lights up when she clicks it on. Giggles shake her shoulders as she tugs at Natasha's T-shirt sleeve and shows her the screen.

Craig is pretty sure that Alex's plan is proceeding very nicely, indeed.

"Guess you know I showed up at your bakery and made an ass out of myself," Sarita reads aloud for the third time as she and Tash cross the threshold of the Java Stop. "Don't know what I was thinking! Can we meet up tonight? I have to work but I can take a dinner break."

She hasn't stopped giggling for the entire four-block walk. What kind of morning *is* this? She's hungover, she smells like frosting—that's not bad, just a touch on the cloying side of sweet when her head still aches a bit and her stomach is still quietly churning—she's exhausted, but she's absolutely delighted by this girl she took home with her last night. "I should say yes, shouldn't I?"

"Uh, *yeah*." Tash grins at her as she lifts a hand to wave at the coffee shop manager. "Hey, Cliff. Three lattes to go? Brought you a couple of Craig's Big Bite Brownies."

"And that's why you're my favorite ladies." The grizzled musician-cum-coffee guru behind the counter makes a courtly bow. His gray-streaked ponytail falls over one shoulder before he looks up at them and winks. "I'll have you set to go in ten minutes or less."

Tash hops onto a stool at the counter and slides the bag of brownies over to Cliff. "Thanks." She bounces a glance at Sarita. "So. You are going to say yes? She's cute. You really should say yes."

"I'm going to." She thumbs out a quick reply on her phone.

Yes, I'll be done at two if that's okay.

The message zips off, and Sarita lets out a happy sigh. "She's super cute, right? God, she's cute."

"All this and you two haven't even slept together, amazing." Tash winks to take any possible sting from the tease. "I didn't know that was possible."

"Last I checked, you were of the opinion that sex wasn't the most important part of personal relations." Sarita arches an eyebrow and returns Tash's sunny smile.

"It's not, to me. But I know how the rest of the world is. I have a television. I watch romcoms just like everyone else. How many times have you and I watched *In Her Shoes* together?" Tash's shoulder lifts in a shrug. "Besides. I know how *you* are. We've been friends for how long? I'm not knocking it. I'm just pointing out that you're kind of a smitten kitten right now."

Sarita squirms on her perch and can't stop a silly grin from spreading across her face. "She's *really* cute. And funny, I think, if I remember correctly. And she can dance."

That last captures her imagination for a good several ticks of the clock. Those *hips*.

She shakes herself out of it. "Anyway, yeah, she's cute." Her phone buzzes on the countertop.

Meet me at the West Seattle Trabucco's sometime tonight? I can get them to let me take a break at 7, and I'll save us a table.

Sarita's eyebrows go up. "Huh. She works at a Trabucco's. I thought Craig said she was a ballroom dancer."

"You work at a bakery. It doesn't mean you're not a grad student," Tash reminds her, hopping down from her chair. With another smile across the counter that makes Cliff melt, she takes the cardboard carrier of coffees. "We can be lots of things at once. Okay, back to work. My ex keeps texting to remind me that I need to pick up Katerina soon. I'll go grab her once I get the *bulochki* into the oven, and I still have another four dozen knots to make. You can get them out of the oven when they're done, right?"

The phone buzzes again.

I think our special tonight is quattro formaggio, if you like cheese.

Sarita might eat cardboard if it means she gets to spend time with this woman.

I do like cheese.

She hits send and slides off her chair. "Yeah, I can do that, no problem."

Also not a problem: finishing her decorating project before the next Saturday shift people come in so she can go home and get ready to meet Maritza tonight.

Problem: What the hell is she going to wear?

Chapter Three

"THIS WAS A TERRIBLE IDEA." THE CLOCK ON TRABUCCO'S kitchen wall reads a quarter to seven. Maritza scrapes at her apron and gray T-shirt, her fifth failed attempt to scratch out the ghostly blot of tomato sauce left from a collision with her coworker Zach in the kitchen. "God, why have I been doing the impulse thing all day? I should have waited. I should have asked her out to dinner on my day off or something."

"Day off?" Zach asks, his voice loaded with mock innocence as he heaves a stack of boxed pizzas onto the delivery rack. "You have those? You know what they are?"

"Sometimes!" She resists the urge to disappear into the restroom and check her hair and makeup again. They're as fine as they're going to be after working in a pizzeria kitchen for four hours, which is to say her hair is a puffy wreck wrestled into a ponytail and her makeup, apart from peach-flavored lip gloss and what's left of her mascara, no longer exists. She glances at Zach instead, and droops in the face of his blatant skepticism. "Kind of?"

"Last night was your first night not slinging pizza or holing yourself up at the dance studio in like, weeks. Possibly months," Zach points out. "When would you have ever had the time to see this chick again? Bringing her here was totally your best bet." He winks. "Besides. Better you bring her here than to the dance studio. She should meet us first; we're way less scary than Nicky."

At the cash register, her friend Grace nods her head. Her silky black ponytail swings in a way that evokes shampoo commercials and makes Maritza instantly envious, not for the first time. "It's true," Grace says, turning to lean back and rest her elbows on the counter. "We're nice. We're practically family. And we will only tease you a *little*." Her black eyes twinkle and her cheeks dimple as she smiles and raises two fingers in a salute. "Scout's honor."

"She can't make promises for me," Zach says. "But, lucky for you, I've got these deliveries to make. It's fine. You'll have to bring her back here again sometime anyway; it's the only way you'll get to see her."

Maritza's jaw drops as he waves to the two of them with jaunty good humor, picks up his pizza bags and saunters out the pizzeria door. "I know how to take time off," she calls after him, but it's futile as he's already gone. She slumps down on the counter next to Grace. "Well, I do."

"You do," Grace agrees as she picks up a towel and sets to wiping down the counter. "He's right, though, it's been a while. When are those auditions again?"

"April eleventh." The answer is automatic, the date of *Dance Nation's* Seattle tryouts having been scorched into her brain for months now and the entire reason why last night had been her first free night in much too long. "So close now."

Grace smiles. "You're going to be fine. More than fine, we all know you're the best dancer in Seattle." The team at the West Seattle Trabucco's had, for the last three years, made it a point to have at least one person at every one of Maritza's competitions, joining Javier or Maritza's mother Susana to give moral support. "Bad timing to start dating though, I think. Although on the other hand, at least it's not Nicky again."

"Never again," Maritza groans for the second time that day. Today sure did seem to be a day for everyone to remind her of her not-very-past mistakes! "And I only need him to get me through the audition."

"Does he know that?" Grace raises an eyebrow. "Eh, never mind, I don't care if he does or not. Come here." She tugs at Maritza's arm until they face each other, and her fingers fly nimbly as she uses a paper napkin to blot sweat from Maritza's cheeks and forehead, then brushes stray waves back from her face. "There. Now, don't freak out, but a really cute chick just walked through the door and she looks like she's looking for someone, so I assume it's show time."

"What?" Adrenaline is an electric surprise through her veins. Maritza turns, and, sure enough, there Sarita stands by the front door: slight and shy, and, as Grace had said, really cute. The long black halo of untamed curls hangs in better-behaved long ringlets now, nearly down to Sarita's waist. There's a small, nervous smile on her face, and, as she twists her fingers together, a pair of silver bracelets chimes softly on one slender wrist. She's wearing a black coat over a long black sweater and jeans with black ankle boots, all simple and clean, and Maritza feels like a frump in her work clothes.

What a terrible idea this was; how unimpressive Maritza is next to Sarita. Well, too late now.

"Hi," she says, putting on her brightest smile as she comes around the counter with her hand outstretched to catch Sarita's. "You came. I'm so glad."

"You came to my workplace; I thought the least I could do was return the favor." Sarita's mouth quirks into a half-smile. Her voice is soft and her eyes sparkle with teasing light. "Although I wish you'd stuck around to say hi to me."

Maritza chuckles even as her face heats up. "Eh, sorry. It was a weird, crazy morning, wasn't it? I shouldn't have gone barging in on you like that. And yeah, I should have stuck around to say hi. I don't know what I was thinking." She takes a deep breath to put a halt to her babbling and tugs Sarita toward a table in the back corner. "Here, let me get you something to drink. Do you want a salad, too?"

"I've had the big house salad at one of the other locations, I love it. That would be great. And a Sprite is fine." Sarita smiles as she pulls her chair out and sits down. "You said you were going to take a break and join me, right?"

A glance at the counter shows Maritza that Grace is pleased as punch, smiling as she waves at Maritza to sit down. *I'll get it*, Grace mouths and her waving increases in intensity. "Um, yeah, looks like they're going to let me do that."

"Great." Sarita tucks her bag under her chair. "Did you like your breakfast this morning?"

"Huh? Oh." Right, the muffin, the scone. They had been slightly worse for wear by the time she got home, because she hurled the bag into the car in a careless panic after she raced out of the bakery. But they were still so, so good with a second cup of morning coffee. She'd split them with her mother, who'd woken up by the time she got home. "God, yeah. They were so good! I should have taken you up on your first offer this morning. Did you make them?"

"Me? No." Sarita's chortle is a smoky, dark thing of beauty from low in her chest. "I strictly decorate. I'm the head decorator there. The only thing I really know how to bake is this pistachio and cardamom shortbread my mom taught me. I'll have to make it for you sometime." She rests her chin in her hand. "Craig and Natasha did the baking today. You met Tash at the party with me, right?"

Before Maritza can answer, Grace is at their table with two Sprites and a big bowl of the house salad. "Ladies, here you go." She has everything down on the tiny tabletop in quick order, hands flying as she pulls two silverware rolls from her apron pocket and plunks them down too. Then, to Maritza's horror, she's turning to Sarita with her hand outstretched. "Hi, I'm Grace Nguyen, I work with Mari. You have to be the cute Sarita chick she's been talking about all afternoon."

Sarita seems at a loss, but she's giggling. "Um, well, I'm *a* Sarita, at least."

"Grace," Maritza protests, hands flying to her cheeks. "What the hell, Grace?"

"Sorry, Mari. Zach's not here, I have to make up for his absence." But she winks, and her teasing expression softens. "Kidding. Sorry about that. Do you guys want a medium *quattro* to split?"

"Whatever gets you out of here faster," Maritza mumbles, unable to look at either of the other women. What had she been thinking to bring Sarita here? She *should* have brought her to the studio first, even if Nicky would almost certainly have been a jerk about it. At least in the studio, she'd be wearing cute dance gear and could show off. Sure, she'd be sweating just as she is now, but at least she wouldn't smell like pepperoni and cheese. "God, Sarita, I'm so sorry."

"For what?" The touch of a hand on hers does get her to look up, and, when she does, Sarita's eyes are big, dark and concerned, and Grace is gone. "What's the matter? You were so confident this morning."

"This morning I wasn't wearing frumpy clothes, and my hair smelled maybe like tequila and my perfume," Maritza says as she pulls her hand away. "Not like a pizza joint. I was cute this morning! I was flirty! I shouldn't have brought you to work. It's just that I wanted to see you."

The words had come out of her in a rush, and Sarita sits back with wide, surprised eyes as if the sentences had stampeded over her. "Oh."

Maritza claps a hand over her mouth. "Oh, shit," she mumbles through her fingers.

"You wanted to see me?" Sarita's eyes brighten. "Really?"

The rush of blood to Maritza's head is so fast, she's surprised it doesn't knock her out. "Yes," she says, still muffled behind her fingers and hoping her cheeks aren't as red as they feel.

Sarita's mouth curves into a pretty smile, and she leans forward to pull Maritza's hand away from her face. "I have a suggestion. I would like to propose that we start over. Wipe out this morning, this whole day. I'm starving, so let's eat this salad and let's just talk. Because you are absolutely cute, and I wanted to see you, too."

"Really?" Maritza answers Sarita's beautiful smile with a grin of her own.

Sarita props her chin on her hand and nods. "Really."

THE ENTIRE NIGHT SEEMS TO PROCEED ON AN EVEN KEEL AFTER that: None of Maritza's fellow employees bother her again, their conversation bubbles and sparkles, and it's as if the morning hadn't happened at all. "Although I am not likely to forget it," Sarita says when she picks up her second slice of pizza. She pauses with it dangling in her hand so cheese stretches down to her plate as she pretends to ponder. "I mean, when a cute girl scares the crap out of you at four-thirty in the morning, that's memorable."

"Stop." Maritza giggles and buries her face in her hands for the fifth time.

"Why are you embarrassed? I'm the one who threw my toothbrush at you," Sarita reminds her, and her cheeks flush with a touch of red as she laughs. "Okay. Back to you. You're a ballroom dancer! That's so cool. How long have you been doing that?"

Maritza has to think about it. She's been dancing so long that it's natural as breathing, as if she's always done it. "Let's see, I'm twenty-three now, so, fourteen years? I think so. Yeah. Since I was nine."

The slice of pizza still droops from Sarita's hand, and her mouth hangs open. "Seriously? Fourteen years?"

"According to my bunions, blisters and a wall of trophies, yep," Maritza replies and she's surprised how pleased she is to be the focus of Sarita's astonishment. It's such a complete one-eighty from Nicky's usual arrogance and disdain and it's very welcome.

"I was a tomboy and a half when I was a kid, and Mama didn't mind it, but she thought I needed a girly influence sometimes. So when a dance show tour came through New York, she dragged me to see it, and, well, that did the trick, actually." She smiles as she remembers the rainbow of chiffon and sequins, the music that thumped and flowed by turns as dancers demonstrated different styles, the graceful way the women were whirled across the floor and how they smiled. "I wanted lessons right away and I didn't shut up until Mama found a school for me."

At last, Sarita takes a bite of her pizza, and there's a thoughtful look on her face as she chews. "So," she begins after she swallows. "You're from New York. I watch a lot of movies—all of them say that New York is where dance is. Like, people go *to* New York to dance."

Maritza has to nod. "That's true."

"So what are you doing here?" Sarita's brow furrows. "I mean, don't get me wrong. I was born and raised in Seattle, and I love it here. But this is not exactly a dance mecca, is it?"

This makes Maritza smile. "Ballroom is everywhere," she says, using her fork to push the remains of her salad around. "I mean, all dance is everywhere, but you're right, a lot of professionals go to New York. But mostly for Broadway or ballet. Ballroom does better out here on the West Coast."

"In L.A.," Sarita points out. "Not here in Seattle. Our worldwide claims to fame are Starbucks, the Space Needle and our constant rain. And the Seahawks, sometimes," she adds as an afterthought.

"Here is where my partner is." *Whether I like him or not. Never mind. Only a few more months.* "Nicky saw a YouTube video of me dancing in a competition in Newark a few years ago. He was connected to a studio here that's run by a retired pro, one of the greats. He liked my style and was in the market for a new partner. I was looking to push myself to the next level. I saw his videos and I knew we'd dance well together, so I begged my mother to move us out here."

This makes Sarita's eyes pop. "Seriously? No way. That's crazy."

"Yeah." It took a year because Susana insisted they wait for Javi to finish high school. Maritza could have come on her own; she was eighteen then, but she couldn't face that kind of move alone. She was always conscious of the sacrifice her family made for her. "It was crazy, but Mama agreed. So here I am, five years later."

Slowly, Sarita shakes her head. "That's amazing. I mean, all I've done the last... mmm, eight years? Is go to school."

Maritza can't help the surprised yelp of laughter that erupts from her. "Eight years! And you think I'm nuts for moving here?"

"From New York? A little." Sarita grins and takes another bite of her pizza. "I mean, it's just school. I'm getting ready to submit my qualifying paper to enter the PhD program at the university."

"Dr. Sengupta, I like the sound of that." Maritza smiles.

"Me too. So do my parents." She blushes again, and, oh, that's lovely, the way her golden cheeks bloom into something like roses. "But mostly I really like studying philosophy, and I haven't come across a reason to stop yet. It's fascinating to me."

"Eight years." Maritza can't imagine going to school so long. She'd barely had the patience to finish high school. There was nothing *wrong* with school as such; it just cut in hard to her dancing time. "I mean I guess it's rich for me to be surprised when I've been dancing almost twice as long."

"Maybe, but I can't dance without tripping over my own feet," Sarita says. "As you saw last night."

Both of them blush at the memory of that. Maritza's throat is as dry as paper as she remembers how she pulled them together, thumbs slipped through belt loops and her hands guiding Sarita's hips in a slow, sensuous back and forth motion. She remembers the tickle of Sarita's soft black hair on the skin of her neck as they swayed together and the music thrummed through both their bodies and she remembers the whispered invitation. *Do you want to go back to my place?*

She squirms in her chair. *I do, yes, I do.*

Across the table, Sarita's left hand flaps in a fanning motion, and Maritza would bet all her tips of the night that she's thinking about it, too. "You danced just fine to me," she says, forcing herself to smile at the pretty, pretty woman she wishes she'd been able to touch more last night. "You didn't trip at all."

"With your help, anyone could be a good dancer." There's a tremor in Sarita's voice that matches the flutter of Maritza's heart in her chest. "Maritza..."

"Mari," Maritza interrupts, her heart speeding up.

"Sorry?"

"Mari, it's what everyone calls me. Call me Mari." She wants to take a drink of her Sprite to soothe her dry throat, but she doesn't dare pick anything up right now; she can't trust her hands. "I'm sorry. I interrupted, that was rude."

"No, it's... no problem." Sarita's face lights up with a quick flash of nervous smile. "Mari, I... I am so sorry I fell asleep on you last night. Please, you have to know I really wanted to... I... " Pale roses bloom hotter into fiery dark red on Sarita's cheeks as she seems to search for the right words. "You're *really pretty*, and it was not you at *all* that was the problem. I don't usually drink so much but you made me nervous and..."

"Weren't we starting over?" Maritza asks. *Adorable. Too adorable.* "We can... " She puffs a breath into her cheeks, she can't believe she's about to say it. "We can definitely try it again. Believe me, I am not opposed."

Sarita's cheeks are still bright as she says. "We can?"

"Yes! Absolutely, but..." As her schedule crashes down on her, Maritza sighs and feels it as if it's an actual weight on her shoulders. "I don't know when. When I'm not working, I'm at the studio. Last night was my first night off in months."

"I don't get nights off either, not really." Sarita looks a bit deflated herself. "Between school and work, I hardly have time to see my family. Valentine's Day is next week; it's our busiest time outside of wedding season. I barely have the first page of my paper written. I skipped working on it tonight so I could come see you."

Maritza falls back in her chair, resisting the urge to pout. "Damn it."

"I mean, I don't want to just sleep with you, though." The words tumble from Sarita's mouth in a rush. "I'd be happy to spend more time with you. Maybe I can see you dance. Maybe you can come to the bakery. We can have coffee at school sometime."

"I could drive up with Javi sometimes on class days." The idea has merit. "I don't work until the afternoons, and it would be quicker to get here from there than from my house. I could even get the car sometimes. Fred gives us a day off once or twice a week so we don't burn out."

"Fred?"

"My dance coach." Maritza spins the ideas around in her head and nods. "We could at least see each other, yeah. I want to see you again. Is that okay?"

Sarita chortles. "That is more than okay. I definitely want to see you more than once. It's not every girl who gets a toothbrush thrown at her and comes back for more. I need to hold on to you."

There's a shout from the kitchen. "Mari, time's up," Grace's voice calls. "Sorry, we got a big order."

"Be there in a second." Maritza reaches across the table to grab Sarita's hand. "Saturday nights, am I right? Go home and work on your paper. I'll call you tomorrow?"

Sarita nods, and her curls bounce around her beaming face. "Yes, please. In the afternoon? I need time to work."

Maritza mentally scans her schedule. She managed to push Nicky off that morning by the simple expedient of texting him *Sorry can't make it today, stomach bug* and turning her phone off while she slept. He texted back a terse direction to meet him at the studio Sunday morning. She'd be a good four or five hard hours there, race home, shower, nap, work. But work wasn't until six on Sundays, so, "Yes. I'll call you at four? Four-thirty," she corrects. She needs every minute of sleep she can squeeze in.

"Mari," Grace calls again and this time when she emerges from the kitchen, she has a harassed look on her face and a pair of to-go boxes in her hands. "Sorry, honey, we have *got* to get moving. Zach's going to have to take this order in two trips."

"Oh my God." Maritza looks back at Sarita, and her heart sinks into her stomach.

"Go. People are having major pizza emergencies." Sarita waves. Her smile is still bright as she accepts the empty boxes from Grace and stands up. "I'll box up what's left and leave your share on the counter, okay? Do you want any of the salad?" Without waiting for an answer, she picks up the salad bowl and begins to divide the greens between the two boxes, wedging them into corners to leave room for the pizza slices.

Maritza sits, ignoring Grace as she stands by and wrings her hands. "I'm so glad you came," she says. The words come out on a thread of breath so softly, she doesn't know if Sarita hears her over the clank of utensils and the blare of an old Soundgarden song from the restaurant speakers.

But she does. The spoon and fork drop, and Sarita moves to stand in front of Maritza and tugs her to her feet. "I'm glad too," she says, with a squeeze of Maritza's hands. In the next instant she's got Maritza's face in her palms and pulls her forward for a quick kiss. "So glad. Now go. Grace is going to pull her fingers off if you keep making her nervous." She points Maritza toward the kitchen and pushes, delivering a surprising hard slap to Maritza's ass as she does it.

Maritza is still rubbing the sore spot on her behind as Grace drags her into the back of the kitchen. "Ow!"

"I like her," Grace says as she pulls out balls of pizza dough and lines them up on the counter for tossing. "I like her a lot."

Glancing toward the front counter, Maritza sees Sarita flash a quick smile as she drops off one of the to-go boxes and walks out of Trabucco's with a jaunty farewell wave. "Me too," Maritza says, her eyes still on the door. "So much."

IN HER CAR, SARITA LEANS HER HEAD BACK ON THE HEADREST AND thinks about Maritza—*No, Mari, she told me to call her Mari*—her smile and her laugh and the graceful, sure way that she moves.

If she tilts her head, she can see through the glass door into the restaurant, through to the kitchen where Grace and Maritza stand side by side and toss pizza dough into the air. They're laughing over some shared joke and trading their pizza doughs back and forth as easily as breathing.

If she doesn't start the car, she'll sit here until the place closes, and that would be creepy. Sarita twists the key in the ignition and sets off, casting one last look into her rearview mirror and catching a glimpse of dark ponytail. It's Grace's ponytail—the flick of hair is straight, not twisted in soft dark waves. She lets out a sigh and punches on the radio to break the silence and to help her clear her mind so that she can do as instructed and get some work done.

Home isn't much better on the silence front. Her keys clank in the bowl by the door, and she wishes for the thousandth time that her landlord would allow her to have a pet. It has always seemed a crying shame to have a brother who breeds tiny, adorable Yorkshire terriers and be unable to take advantage of the fact. Then again, she's in school or at the bakery most hours of the day. It wouldn't be fair to subject a tiny dog to endless hours alone just so she can be a little less lonely when she gets home.

Sarita checks her phone for the time: nine-thirty p.m. Damn it, not as late as she'd hoped. There's still time to get some work done on her paper before she has to go to sleep. Or she can go to bed now and wake up early tomorrow. She can go to bed still fizzing with the excitement of her semi-date and dream of Mari. The bakery isn't open on Sundays; waking early is an option, an option that never works. She never does the waking up early part on a day off.

So. Work for an hour tonight it is, then. With a grind of her teeth, she puts her box of pizza and salad in the fridge, shrugs off her coat and sits down at her laptop to get to work. There's a battered copy of her favorite comprehensive collection of the works of Baruch Spinoza near the mouse, and she picks it up. She shuffles through the pages until she finds the quote she's been kicking around as her focus statement.

I have labored carefully not to mock, lament, or execrate, but to understand human actions, she types with one hand on the keyboard while the other holds open the book to source her quote. She's always liked good old Spinoza, optimist that he was. Tonight, though, he rather grates.

She reads the lone sentence she's just copied. *I have labored carefully… to understand human actions.* "You've been dead for a few hundred years," she says to the empty air of her apartment as she reaches into her shirt to remove her bra and then tosses it aside. "What do you know?"

Leaning forward, she taps her fingers on the desktop and re-reads the sentence. Not to mock, lament, or execrate… God, why had she chosen this as her PhD focus? Hell, why was she thinking of doing a PhD?

Because you don't know what else to do.

She frowns. That's… ouch. True. She shoves the thought aside and focuses on her laptop, thinking about her grumpy outburst. Reworded appropriately, that could be a good lead-in. She tilts her head and considers, then bends to her task.

In analyzing Spinoza and his contemporaries, she types, *it can be argued that perhaps it was simple for him to make such a statement and to believe it. His was a simpler time altogether, not necessarily because it was easier, but because ignorance, as the proverb says, is bliss. In the society of today, with greater awareness and comprehension of society's ills*, with the lightning-quick reach and tone-deafness of the Internet, it can be much more difficult to set aside both laughter and loathing in favor of understanding.

Case in point, my relationship with my sister.

No, self. No. She erases the last sentence immediately. That is a can of worms that does not need to be opened in the middle of her paper. Sarita pushes away from her desk to rest her hands on top of it, lets her head hang down between her arms and stretch her neck out. *Should have gone to bed with my happy thoughts. Damn it.*

She tries to summon back the elation with which she'd walked through her apartment door, but it dances just out of her mental reach. *Come on. You kissed her, you slapped her ass, you remember the way she laughs and how she couldn't win a bet to talk for one minute without using her hands.*

She remembers, but it doesn't set off a flock of butterflies in her stomach. *Enough.* After closing her laptop, Sarita picks up her phone to flash off a quick text.

Hey, you still up?

Her brother's reply is fast.

For now. Stuck on your paper again?

She winces. It's only been a month since she started the semester and already she's made this a habit Devesh can identify. Oops.

Another message pings through.

Sunil says hi and get back to work. ☺

With a roll of her eyes, she hits the dial button and waits for Devesh to answer. "I don't want to get back to work," she says in lieu of a proper greeting. "That would require thinking. Thinking is hard."

Her older brother laughs at the whine in her voice, and she can hear his husband chuckling in the background as well. "You're the one that wanted to pursue higher education in philosophy. Too late to change to basket weaving now, Reeti." His laughter trails off. "What's the problem?"

She fires off her customary answer. "Don't know." But she does know, she knows for sure now, and she doesn't know what to do about it.

What's the point of what I'm doing?

It was a question she could always push aside before—before she met Maritza, a woman who had picked up and moved her entire family across the country because she knew exactly what she wanted and how to pursue it. Before determination and self-knowledge smiled at her from across a tiny pizzeria table, Sarita had been able to ignore the question, even when she'd begun her paper and the little voice that asked it started to pipe up louder.

After tonight, the question sits heavy in her stomach where there had been butterflies, and, wow, it sucks. "I met someone."

Devesh makes a happy humming noise. "Reeti, that's great."

"Yeah. It is. She is. I mean, so far. I met her last night." Not for the first time, Sarita wishes she'd had a land line put in. She could use the coiled phone cord to fiddle with right now. "We had dinner tonight."

"That's really fantastic." Devesh has a smile on his face, she can tell, and she hears him put a hand over the phone to tell Sunil. "Sunil says that's great, too. Tell me about her?"

"Um." She plucks at her laptop cable, winding it around and between her fingers. "Well, her name is Maritza. She's hot, and she's funny, and she's a ballroom dancer who seems to actually know what she wants to do with her life, and now I've got a complex."

"Reeti." Devesh sighs and he *tsks*. "Come on, don't think like that. You're great. You don't need to have a complex."

"Eight years of college and I don't know what I want to do with my life. *You* come on." Shaking the twisted cable from her fingers, she picks it back up and starts twisting it again. "She's known what she wants since she was nine. When I was nine I wanted a Tamagotchi, which I couldn't even manage to keep alive for more than a week at a time."

"Okay, the only person we knew who was successful with their Tamagotchi was that Brian Michaelson kid from down the street," Devesh says. "The rest of us all sucked at it. I wouldn't go around using it as a yardstick to measure your life's ambition." His voice softens. "Don't worry about it, Reeti. You're doing fine. You want to study philosophy, so you're doing it. You like it. Do what you like and figure everything else out later. And Jesus, don't judge yourself by someone else you just met."

Sarita leans on her hand and runs her fingers into her hair. "I'm just tired of my life being a puzzle I can't quite put together. All the edge pieces in this pile, and the sky pieces over there, and maybe there's some pieces missing."

"We switched from Tamagotchi to puzzles?" Devesh asks. There's a strange, soft sort of scraping noise. When Devesh speaks again, it's muffled. "No, Sunil, I don't know where she's going with the metaphors."

Sarita sighs. "Never mind. It's been a long day."

"I guess so." Devesh's voice is clear again, and the sounds of him settling against a pile of pillows rustle down the line. "So. Funny, hot and a ballroom dancer, huh? She sounds like a keeper."

He's trying to distract her. It's working. Sarita leans back in her chair, and suddenly she's smiling again, her paper and her existential crisis forgotten. "Early days, but, you know, I definitely want to see her again. And again..."

The butterflies take flight.

Chapter Four

"NICKY, IF YOU DON'T WANT ME TO ZIP YOUR HEAD INTO MY bag, you're going to give me five minutes off my damn feet." Maritza flops down on the studio floor next to her open bag and waves her hand over it toward her dance partner. "Mm, smell that. My Capezios are, like, particularly ripe after yesterday."

"You're disgusting. Fine." Brushing from his face a lock of blonde hair that had come loose from his ponytail, Nicky pouts and picks up his water bottle from the floor near her, then moves well out of her reach. "We still have two more hours to go."

"I'm aware, Nicky." She tugs her oversized pink T-shirt away from her sweaty skin, hoping Fred will return to the studio soon. He is the only thing in the world prevents Maritza from outright killing Nicky. *Two more months,* she chants to herself, closing her eyes and grabbing her own bottle of water. *Well, two months and three days. But who's counting?*

Who was she kidding? She was. Every second.

Taking a long drink of water, she sets the bottle aside and inspects her feet. A new blister popped up on the side of her left big toe and then broke while they danced. That triggered her insistence on a break after three hours of nonstop samba. She has never been so tired of listening to the Gipsy Kings, and her feet have never hurt so much. She digs in her bag for her first aid kit and begins to tend to the blister, wincing as she cleans it with an antiseptic wipe.

She can feel Nicky's hard gaze crawling over her skin, and it is easy to imagine the dismissive contempt in his blue eyes. "You keep getting blisters there because you're going too hard on your turns," he says. "You're too flashy. If you'd just let the turns happen—"

"If you didn't drag me along, isn't that what you mean?" She makes her tone as sweetly poisonous as possible, tossing back her heavy ponytail as she lifts her head to bat her eyelashes at him in false innocence. "I've told you a million times that you pull me into spins faster than I can go. I'm not flashy. I'm keeping up."

"Maybe you should finally learn to go faster," Nicky snaps.

"Maybe you should finally learn the meaning of *tempo*."

"Can't I leave you two alone for any amount of time without this starting up?" The despair in Fred Corbett's voice precedes his entrance into the studio by a good ten seconds. He walks in, black hair sticking almost straight up where he's combed agitated fingers through it. He looks as harassed as Maritza feels. "Two months and three days to auditions. Can we please keep it together? You're both excellent dancers, and when you keep your mouths shut, you make excellent partners." As both dancers open their mouths to protest, Fred raises his hands, eyes resolute. "Not a word. Nicky, fix your hair. Maritza, get your foot fixed up. We've got one hour left."

"We've got two!" Nicky yelps, pausing with his hands stuck in his hair. "Two hours! It's in my phone calendar!"

"It's Valentine's Day, Nicholas." Fred sticks his hands in the pockets of his blue jeans. "I have a wife who would like to go out to dinner without me smelling like a locker room and dressed like a hobo. Maritza's hurt and she has a date besides."

Maritza closes her eyes tight. Usually Fred was better about keeping his mouth shut. She pries an eye open to see him looking at her, horrified. *Sorry*, he mouths, just before he pulls a hand from his pocket to cover his face. Across the room, Nicky is glaring at her in icy blue fury, with his fingers twisting in the hem of his black tank top. "So we're allowing personal lives to get in the way of our work now? Or wait, just hers, I suppose."

Fred draws his shoulders back and raises an eyebrow at Nicky. "Well, do you have a date?" Of course, he knows as well as Maritza does that the answer is *no*. Nicky hasn't dated anyone since Maritza dumped him before Christmas. And she and Fred both know that's because he's waiting for her to "come to her senses," as he put it one tipsy, margarita-filled night that Maritza spent fighting off his advances.

As far as Maritza is concerned, the act of coming to her senses took place the night she dumped him. Not that she'd been able to convince him of that, if the petulant rage on his face was anything to go by. "Fred, I can stay here with Nicky. You don't have to stay with us, you can go home and we'll get our two hours in. You know we can lock up." *And sometimes I can throttle back the urge to murder him, when it's important.*

Fred looks at her in exasperation, and she knows it's because he's fed up with her placating and babying Nicky. "Mari—"

"It's okay. Really." Giving Nicky the full allotment of his expected rehearsal hours was the least she could do after Fred dropped the bomb of her date on him. Yes, she placates and babies Nicky. As much as they snipe and shout at each other, Fred was right: they *are* good partners. They make each other look good. No, great. For the most important audition of her life so far, she needs him. Dumping him romantically caused enough damage; she wasn't willing to risk more. "Two hours. I can shower in your office bathroom, right, Fred?"

The exasperation doesn't fade from Fred's face. "You know you can."

"What about me?" Nicky asks, still angry as he ties his hair back into a sloppy bun.

"You live ten minutes away; she lives an hour away by bus. You can go home and shower." Fred waves a hand, turns away from Nicky and kneels next to Maritza. "How's the foot?"

Maritza smooths a fresh Band-Aid over her blister, then checks her shoe. "The foot's okay. I need to replace the moleskin in this thing, but then I'm ready to get up and get moving again."

She puts on a fresh pair of thin socks and tapes a new piece of moleskin into the strap of her dance shoe, where it will protect her new blister. Nicky is standing over her, impatient, but her placating only stretches so far, and she refuses to be hurried. After she straps her shoe on, she waves off his reaching hand and gets to her feet under her own power, brushing off her leggings-clad rear end as she stands. She takes one deep breath, then another and, when she feels steady on her aching feet, she nods and holds out her hand. "Okay. Let's go."

He pulls her into the middle of the studio immediately, making Fred scramble to start the music. Guitar music jangles out over the speakers, and Maritza fixes her brightest smile on her face, tosses her hair back and reaches out her free hand to beckon Nicky with a wink.

Spin in, back out, release, twirl, twirl, twirl, stop. She sways her hips in a motion counter to the shimmy of her chest, waits for Nicky to grab her and move with her in a sinuous slow body roll before he lifts her from the floor with her legs bent into a stag position and her toes pointed.

Sweat and movement, short breaths and spins, lift, drop, catch, pace around each other with alternating steps—they wink and smile as if nothing's ever been wrong between them. Maritza executes a sharp turn and kicks her leg into a long straight line for an instant before she allows her knee to bend over Nicky's shoulder and he slides his hand up her thigh, slow—too slow.

Maritza drops her smile, just one quick second of flatline, but Nicky sees it and he smirks, clearly pleased to have gotten a reaction from her. She sucks in a sharp breath and sets her resolve to not react again. *Smile on, shoulders back!*

Open hold, close hold, open, close, her hips roll as she follows Nicky's steps. She gives extra little shimmies that will look great when she's wearing a ruffled skirt on audition day, if they choose this piece. And she smiles, smiles, smiles the entire time, even when she's hanging from Nicky's arm at the tail end of a complicated maneuver that ends with her doing the splits—between Nicky's legs as he stands over her.

"If you do that pelvic thrust you're thinking about right now," she says through her gritted teeth, "I will head-butt you in the dick. Got it?"

Nicky knows full well she will follow through, so he rolls his eyes and pouts, but does not thrust his crotch into her ear. He simply hauls her to her feet and shoves her to her starting position. "Again," he growls, pointing a sharp finger at Fred to start the music, and oh, aren't the next two hours going to be a treat.

One hour later and Fred is gone, as promised, but not before making the two of them swear they would spend the next hour practicing and not speaking a single word to each other that's not dance-related. "I want you two alive at the end of this, got it?" he says, bouncing a narrow-eyed gaze between the two of them. "And I want you both to call me when you separate, just to be sure."

They nod, too out of breath for words. Fred's promise is moot since they can barely catch their breaths, but Maritza suspects it's probably wise that he errs on the side of caution—a suspicion that is proven correct as soon as they hear the alarm on the front door of the studio beep, signaling Fred's departure. "A date, huh?" Nicky asks, spinning her out and back in, stroking the back of his hand down her arm. "Who with?"

Maritza keeps her mouth shut, concentrating on precise footwork as she shimmies out of his arms.

"Do I know him?"

She allows one side of her mouth to quirk up and shoves her hands up into her hair, gripping either side of her ponytail while she sways her hips.

Nicky's mouth presses into a nearly straight line. "Who is it?" he demands. His hands are rougher than they need to be when he grabs her waist. He tries to pull her close to stare her down, but, with a deft twist, she's prancing across the studio floor and away from him. This is more fun than it probably ought to be. When she turns to face him, Nicky's normally attractive face is red and twisting into a distinctly unattractive expression of thwarted petulance.

Her name is Sarita. She's funny, and pretty and a better kisser drunk than you ever were sober.

Maritza wraps one arm over her chest and the other around her waist and takes dainty steps forward and back, her hips rolling, and Nicky is absolutely furious and there is nothing he can do about it, because she's not saying a goddamn word—not even goodbye. She gives him nothing more than a too-bright smile and a tiny wave when she locks him out of the studio at the end of the hour.

Asshole.

She stands there, one hand on the lock and one hand on the door bar, eyes closed as she catches her breath and settles her mind. She concentrates on emptying out her thoughts, on the feel of her sweat-soaked ponytail straggling down her back, on the ache in her feet, on the smell of air freshener and years of dance sweat that permeates the very walls of Fred's studio. Maritza thinks about how she knows every inch of this studio, that there are sequins caught between floorboards, a rainbow of strings loosened from fringe in every nook and cranny and, under the reception counter, a box full of abandoned dance shoes: pairs and singles, women's, men's and children's.

At last, calm and conscious that anyone passing by the studio can see her standing motionless in the glass doorway, Maritza opens her eyes and pulls down the shade. *Time for a shower.*

She's in and out of the shower in record time and bopping along to her favorite going-out playlist as she grabs her fresh change of clothes from the hanger on the back of Fred's office door. A glance at the clock tells her that, as fast as she's going, it's still going to be a tight race for the bus.

She squirms into the skinny jeans, ducks under the wide neckline of her artfully cut-up and sequin-dotted gray T-shirt, wiggles feet into high-heeled wedge sandals that look painful but are actually the most comfortable shoes she owns. Body taken care of, she tends to her face with a dusting of powder, a few swipes of mascara and eyeliner, and deep-plum lipstick. The hair… She winces as she takes it down from the towel and looks in the mirror. The hair could be a problem. She can only hope it will dry on the bus ride.

She fluffs damp waves out around her shoulders and digs her jewelry from her purse. Bracelet on, earrings in, and another glance at the mirror tells her she will more than do. If she's not quite as knock-your-socks-off hot as she was at Alex's party, she's still a vision. Slapping her own butt, she blows herself a kiss, grabs her coat and dance bag, sets the studio security alarm and hustles out the door with her heels clacking as she goes.

Free at last.

It's a briskly breezy, gray day, and she's got to catch the Metro pretty quickly, which means a brisk trot on aching paws, but Maritza's still got a smile on her face that she can't shake. It seems to be contagious, too, she notices with delight as she swings onto the bus and everyone she makes eye contact with smiles back at her. There's Jackson 5 on someone's radio—"I Want You Back," always an upbeat, get-your-feet-moving good old classic—and usually that would be grounds for everyone on the packed bus to grumble and slant icy glares toward the offender, but today the bus driver starts singing along, and that gets a couple more people near the front going, and Maritza can't help but join in, hanging on to one of the poles and dancing in place.

The guy holding the radio is grinning as the Jackson Five segues into Earth, Wind & Fire, and everyone is *still* singing along. Nobody wants to be the first to drop out of the infectious fun, and everyone who gets on the bus at a new stop is swept up immediately. By the time the bus drops Maritza off in front of Sucre Coeur, there's got to be thirty people of all ages and ethnicities with smiles on their faces, and they're agreeing with Donna Summer that they'll never find that recipe again, oh no.

Sarita stands outside of the bakery, covered in frosting splats and with an expression of naked astonishment on her pretty face as the bus pulls away. "Is that a bus full of people singing 'MacArthur Park'?"

"Sure is." Maritza sticks her hands into the pockets of her purple coat. She's pleased with how this day has transformed itself into something a great deal more awesome than it was just an hour ago. She hopes it's a good omen for the night ahead. "And wow, do I ever want a piece of cake right now. Do you guys have anything left?"

VALENTINE'S DAY, ALWAYS A BIG DAY FOR SUCRE COEUR, HAS exploded in the last year since they were written up in a couple of local magazines for their innovative event cakes. Sarita is pleased about that, of course, always pleased because she is name-dropped as the bakery's head decorator and who doesn't love a little acclaim? And yet today it's the most inconvenient thing ever, because it's kept her busy piping people's names onto enormous heart-shaped sugar cookies and mixing buttercream to cover a pair of last-minute sheet cakes for a spontaneous elopement party.

"I feel awful," she hisses as she sidles over to Craig while she sweeps the kitchen floor and keeps an eye on Mari, who sits at Sucre Coeur's lone café table playing games on her phone and looking ever-hopeful at the prospect of escape from the bakery. Guilt floods Sarita's chest. "She got here two hours ago."

"We're almost done," Craig hisses back while he wipes down the marbled countertops. "Will should return from that wedding cake delivery any time now, and we've got the place all but clean. I'm sorry, Sarita, any other day you know I'd let you go early but it's Valentine's Day!" He scrubs at a spot of dried chocolate, maybe with more force than is strictly required. "I'm going to be late for my Valentine's dinner too, you know. Alex got us reservations at some new Korean barbeque place. We haven't been out in weeks, but do you see me complaining?"

"I'm not complaining." The implication that she is stings a bit. Craig has been mysteriously short-tempered this week, even more so than would be accounted for by the clusterfuck that is Valentine's Day in a bakery. He's also apparently forgotten the art of the apology. Sarita bites back the snapping retort she wants to make, bows her head and wedges her broom under the counter to get at the crumbs that always collect there.

Mari's phone beeps and blips, and Sarita's shoulders droop farther. *What a great first real date.* In just over a week since the pizza semi-date, they've had countless phone calls and texts, and once they snatched fifteen minutes for coffee at the Java Stop while Mari waited for Grace to pick her up for work. This, their first night that they'll get to spend time together sober, is not going the way Sarita hoped.

They shouldn't have made Valentine's Day the date of the occasion because, now that Sarita thinks about it, there's a lot of pressure involved, isn't there? And of course it was going to be busy, and of course she was going to be sweaty and covered in frosting and of course Mari was going to have to wait for her to finish. Sarita closes her eyes. *I just wanted to see her again!*

The tap on her shoulder startles her, and she spins around, opening her eyes to see Mari, gorgeous and beaming the same sunshine smile she danced off the bus wearing. "Hi."

Sarita swallows. "Hi."

"So, I think you might be a little upset," Mari announces, bright and cheery, sequin-sparkly under the kitchen lights. "And I wanted to tell you to calm down, because it's not that late, and I don't mind waiting to spend time with you, and if you want any help cleaning up, I would be happy to lend a hand."

"Oh, we don't need—" Sarita begins, but she's swiftly interrupted by Craig leaning over to thrust his damp rag into Mari's hand.

"Wipe out the display case after I remove the trays, will you?" And without so much as a please or thank you, Craig starts pulling the trays out and, with his arms swiftly laden, he marches off to the dishwasher in the back of the kitchen, leaving Sarita and Mari staring at each other.

Sarita breaks the startled silence. "He's usually better behaved."

"I remember him being so, yes." Mari nods with a single eyebrow raised as she stares over Sarita's shoulder into the depths of the kitchen. "Boy troubles?"

"I don't think so. He said he and Alex had a date tonight." Movement outside of the bakery window catches Sarita's eye. "And here's Alex now."

"Good. We can question him before letting him go find Craig. Hi, Alex!" Mari's smile takes Sarita's breath away again, leaving her standing still as Mari drops her damp rag and spins to greet Alex with a hug. "Happy Valentine's Day, jerk."

"Happy Valentine's Day to you, brat." Alex hugs Mari back, and the twinkle in his gray eyes belies the mild insult. He lifts the strap of his camera bag over his head and lowers it to the floor along with his Yorkie-toting dog carrier. He nods and smiles at Sarita. "Nice to see the two of you. Is Craig in the back?"

"Yes, but we need you first." Curling her arm through Alex's, Mari grabs Sarita's wrist and pulls both of them out the front door of the bakery. "Just for a quick second. Well, Sarita needs you. I'm just here for moral support."

"I don't—" Sarita starts to protest as she's shoved in front of Alex. "Hey!"

Maritza nods toward Alex. "Go on, ask him. Inquiring minds want to know, and Craig'll be out here any minute. I bet he heard the jingle bells on the door."

Alex looks down at the two of them and runs his fingers through dark brown hair that's already disheveled from just this action; his freckles seem to stand out more than usual, as if his face has somehow gotten paler than it naturally is, which Sarita would have thought was just about impossible, really. "Ah, ladies..."

A poke to Sarita's ribs makes her jump. "Hey, listen. Craig is being... not-so-Craig today." Another poke tells her to hurry up. She shoots a glare over her shoulder at Mari, only to be greeted with an unrepentant smile. "Okay, he's being kind of a jerk, and Mari and I—" Damn if she's going down on the good ship *Nosy Meddlers* alone; she didn't start this— "were wondering if something was going on that we needed to know about?"

"He didn't say please *or* thank you when I volunteered to help with closing," Mari points out, and Sarita is surprised when warm arms wrap around her waist. "I don't mind helping, but he was way nicer the night of your party, Alex."

Alex, face twisting a little as he thinks, glances through the glass front of the bakery and slips a hand through his hair again, then plucks at the black and white plaid of his shirt and at last allows both hands to slide into the pockets of his jeans. "Oh. Yeah. We've got a lot going on. The studio and all. You know. And Valentine's Day. Theodora bailed on him three years running now..." His gaze shifts between them and the shop, and his smile is crooked. "Sorry. I'll talk to him."

"No, wait, don't do that—" Too late, Alex is already through the bakery door. He picks up the dog carrier and hustles to the back. Sarita disengages herself—reluctantly, she admits—from Mari's snug embrace and whirls to face her. "What the hell, what are we doing interrogating Alex?"

"Getting answers from someone who won't bite our heads off." Mari lifts her chin and grins, clearly very proud of what she has accomplished. She opens the bakery door, gestures for Sarita to precede her and drops her voice to a whisper. "Someone who will go back there and soften Craig up, who might then come out and let us go already, or who'll at least apologize for being a crabby asshole." She pauses. "Wait. Oh, that was just wrong, that didn't come out right."

"Yeah, thanks for that mental image." Sarita picks up the broom she dropped when Mari dragged her outside and resumes sweeping. She doesn't quite believe Alex's answer, but she doesn't know why, except that it takes an awful lot to get Craig angry enough to be absolutely rude, and the reasons Alex offered didn't seem like enough. Her train of thought is derailed when Mari picks up her damp rag and bends down behind the counter to reach in and wipe out the display case.

She sweeps her way back behind the counter and is not, no, she absolutely is not going to stare at Maritza's ass in those blue jeans, she is an *adult* and she has *dignity* and *grace* and a *job* to do...

...and that is a *really great* ass. If that is what ballroom dancing can do for an ass, Sarita is on board. Sarita may want to take lessons, so long as Mari is the teacher.

Maritza, shoulder deep in the display case, looks back and grins. "See something you like?"

She knows her cheeks are red and she is going to die of embarrassment, but Sarita manages to nod and say, "I do, yes."

A quick shake of her behind and a wink from Maritza make Sarita weak in the knees and make Maritza's grin broader. "So the question is," Mari says, continuing to wipe down the display case, "If I keep doing this, is it motivation for you to help get us out of here sooner, or does it just slow you down?"

I am an adult, I am a graduate student, I am... at a loss for words.

Fortunately, before Sarita has to try to remember how to string words together into a sentence, Craig and Alex emerge from the tiny office in the far reaches of the bakery with the puppy nestled snugly in Craig's arm. They seem somewhat disheveled and a lot happier than they had been. "Right, you two, out," Craig says, and this time he smiles when he orders them around. After disengaging his non-puppy hand from Alex's and handing Fitz over to his boyfriend, Craig grabs Sarita in a hug, broom and all, before she has time to think. "And I'm sorry," he murmurs, all but squeezing the breath out of her. "I was rude. My mother would have my hide. Got a lot going on."

She pulls back. "Are you going to tell me about it?"

"Not today." He glances over to where Alex is laughing uproariously at an impression Maritza is doing. "Today I want you to take that very attractive woman wherever you plan to take her—may I suggest your apartment?—and spend a very nice evening with her."

Sarita holds up her broom. "We haven't finished the cleanup."

"You have." Craig snatches the broom and tosses it aside, then reaches into the cupboard under the register for Sarita's purse and jacket. "It's almost done, Sarita. Will really should be back soon, and Alex has reminded me that he's helped me close up on many occasions. He's happy to help me out now. Get lost, will you?" He loads her arms and points her toward Maritza. "Or was it someone else who pointed out to me that her Valentine's date has been waiting for *two hours* to get out of here?"

Sarita shrugs into her jacket. "So you're saying get while the getting's good."

"And before the penny drops." He gives her a gentle shove. "Out."

After a scruff of the puppy's ears and a whisper into Maritza's, they're out on the street, arm in arm and laughing together within three minutes. Butterflies take flight in Sarita's stomach again as she asks, "Do you want to come back to my place, or do you want to try to find somewhere for dinner?"

Maritza's breath wafts warm against Sarita's ear as she says, "Yours, please," and a shiver ripples down Sarita's spine.

Chapter Five

As soon as Sarita secures the locks on her apartment door, Maritza pounces.

She manages to wiggle out of her coat and somehow get Sarita out of hers at the same time and drops bags and jackets to the floor without ceremony. Then Maritza's got Sarita against the door with her hands on that slender waist and her lips kissing the taste of frosting and coffee from that sensual mouth. "I have an idea," she says against Sarita's mouth, letting her hands roam over the softness of Sarita's purple Sucre Coeur T-shirt. "Want to hear it?"

"If it's anything like your current demonstration, I think I can follow along," Sarita gasps. Her head falls back to allow Maritza access to the smooth curve of her neck.

"Not quite. Well, not yet." She pulls back, smiling at the dazed expression on Sarita's face. "I thought after your long day at work, you might like a nice hot shower."

Bleary dark eyes brighten. "Take it with me?"

"No, I took one at the studio after practice." Maritza tugs Sarita away from the door by the belt loops on her jeans and steers her toward the bedroom. "But what I will do while you're in there is make dinner. Take a good long shower and it will all be ready when you come out."

Sarita pauses in her dreamlike walk. "Hmm, dinner," she says, and her face appears to be interested in the concept of food, but her eyes are fixed on Maritza's mouth. She takes a step back toward Maritza.

"Go," Maritza says, her own growling stomach the only thing keeping her from tackling Sarita into the bedroom and down onto the flowery bedspread. "Go, go, I've got cooking to do."

She waits until the bedroom door is shut and she hears water running in the bathroom before she turns toward the kitchen. It's always a crapshoot messing around in someone's kitchen for the first time. She never knows if she's going to find a stack of frozen pizzas, or a pantry full of rice cakes and almond butter, or a dizzying array of canned soups or *what*. She's particularly plagued by the memory of Nicky's apartment, which seemed perpetually stocked with nothing but bananas, protein powder and whole grain bread. A shudder rattles her spine at the memory.

So it's a pleasant surprise when she finds a fresh package of chicken breasts in the refrigerator along with a green pepper and a bunch of cilantro, and then in a cupboard she locates an onion, rice, a can of tomato paste and a bulb of garlic—pretty much everything she needs to make her mother's *arroz con pollo*. She checks the spice rack. Never mind, there's *everything* she needs. Pleased with herself and with Sarita's kitchen, Maritza gets to work.

By the time Sarita emerges from her bedroom in a loosely draped pink top and a pair of black leggings, Maritza has filled the apartment with the smell of deliciousness in the form of *arroz con pollo* bubbling away in a big pot. She turns from stirring to smile at Sarita. "Hey. How come your kitchen is perfectly stocked for Puerto Rican cooking?"

Sarita's hands are gently rubbing a towel over her hair. "It's not. It's stocked for Bengali cooking. Well, for when I'm in the mood for it, like this week. I've just been too tired."

"Trust me, I am making a Puerto Rican dish right now, and it's from stuff I got from your cabinets." Maritza turns back toward the pot and sniffs. *Yum.* "Do you like chicken with rice?"

"Since that was basically what I was going to make with that chicken, sure." A towel hits a chair with a *flomp*, and then Sarita is at Maritza's shoulder standing on her toes to peek into the pot. "Mmm. That smells amazing. I'm so hungry. Is it almost done?"

Maritza checks the clock, trying to not be distracted by the warm, pliant, citrus-scented woman draped across her back. "Almost. I think just a couple more minutes. Do you want to get out some bowls?"

"Sure." And then Maritza's back cools as her dampened T-shirt is caught in the gentle passing breeze caused by Sarita and all of her hair spinning around toward wherever the dishes are kept. There's a bit of clanking in the cabinets and drawers of the island that divides the kitchen from the living area, and then, "Okay. Ready when you are."

Grabbing a knife, Maritza pokes and peers into the pot, then slices into the biggest chicken breast. "Done. Do you have one of those things to sit a pot on?"

"Already out." With oven-mittened hands, Sarita leans around and grabs the pot and carefully moves it to a trivet on the island. Two heavy, burnt orange ceramic bowls are lined up on the faux-marble countertop along with a big spoon and some silverware. With deft hands that don't spill so much as a grain of rice, Sarita spoons dinner into each of the two bowls and, her brow furrowing, hands one to Maritza. "I don't have a dining room table. The dining room is a little..." She waves a bemittened hand, and Maritza turns toward where the niche for an apartment-sized dining room would usually be to see a nook lined in tall Ikea bookshelves, with a small desk and laptop tucked into one corner. She blinks at it as Sarita finishes with, "...full."

"Wow. Moving must be a complete bitch." Picking up a fork, Maritza wanders with her bowl toward the dining-nook-cum-library and peers at the spines of some of the books. "Oh, you like science fiction. You'd get along really well with my brother."

"And he'd get along with mine. Most of those are gifts from Devesh, trying to convince me that I *would* like science fiction." Sarita walks up with her own dinner in hand. "They're not bad. I've read them all, and Dev has good taste. They're just not my favorites." Popping a bite of chicken into her mouth, she points her fork at the next bookshelf. "I like those. Grown-up retellings of fairy tales from around the world."

Maritza leans down for a better look. "*Sleeping Beauty*?"

"Not those! Those were an accident." Sarita chokes as if she's tried to swallow her dinner sideways. After a brief coughing fit, she shakes her head. "Those are not actually about Sleeping Beauty and I have been too embarrassed to bring them to sell at the used bookstore." She taps on the blue and green spine of another book. "This one *is* a retelling of Sleeping Beauty. And this one's young adult; it's One Thousand and One Nights retold. Actually, you should borrow this; it was amazing." She gets back to her feet and passes the book to Maritza. "They're fun to relax with. Escapist fiction at its very best."

"I didn't realize there were so many retellings. I've only ever read the Wizard of Oz story, the one from the Wicked Witch's perspective." Maritza stands up straight and looks over the shelves. "Oh, yeah, there it is; you have it."

"That guy's written a few more, too. He's why I got interested in the whole genre in the first place." Sarita smiles and leans against the nearest bookshelf. "And yes, back to your first comment. Moving is, in fact, a bitch. I guess it will be a bigger one when I get around to moving out of here. There are more books in my bedroom closet—the ones that don't fit out here. I outgrew these bookshelves a couple of years ago."

Maritza looks at how crammed full the bookshelves are—there are stacks of books on top of each of them, piled almost too high—and lets out a low whistle. "Nice." She glances back over her shoulder to the living room. "So. No dining room table, can we snuggle up on the couch and watch a movie?"

"I like the way you think." Sarita leads the way to the flowery, overstuffed couch and plops down with her bowl in hand. "I've got a whole bunch of streaming movie subscriptions and one of those thingies so I can watch them on the TV."

"Thingies are awesome. I love thingies." Maritza pauses mid-sit as her face flushes hot. "Shit, that didn't come out right."

"You've been having that kind of day." Sarita's fingers tuck into the waistband of Maritza's jeans and tug her downward. "Come on. Help me pick out a movie to go with this amazing dinner you made. What's it called again?"

Maritza curls her legs under herself and snuggles into Sarita's side. She'd forgotten how nice it was to have a date compliment her cooking. Lord knows Nicky never did. "Aw, thank you. It's *arroz con pollo*. Rice with chicken. It's one of the very few things I know how to cook, thanks to my very patient mother."

"Oh, I'm the same. I only know a few of my mom's recipes. We should do a recipe swap one day." Sarita grabs the remote from the end table. "Stop me when you see something you like."

"Stop," Maritza says almost immediately. "Stop! I see what I want to watch."

Sarita stops, remote dangling from her hand, thumb hovering over the right arrow button. "*Strictly Ballroom*? Don't you get enough ballroom dancing in real life?"

"Please?" Maritza leans harder into Sarita's side, bats her eyelashes and makes her eyes as big as she can. "It's one of my favorite movies. You loaned me one of your books; let's trade. It's like we're getting to know each other." She bats her eyelashes again. "Besides, this is one of Baz Luhrmann's only romantic movies that doesn't involve someone dying in the end."

"Well, it is Valentine's Day. I guess we don't want death putting a damper on things." Sarita plants a kiss on the top of Maritza's head that leaves her stunned and fuzzy on the inside as the movie begins. "The Blue Danube" spins from the television speakers. "Are those... are those *feathers*? Are those women wearing feathers?"

Maritza lets out a giggle, still dazzled by the little kissy moment. "Shh."

"No, seriously, Mari, I need to know, do you *dress* like this for competitions? I can get down with sequins, but *feathers*!" Sarita begins to giggle as well, bending her head over her bowl. "Please tell me you don't wear feathers."

"I don't wear feathers... I don't wear *many* feathers," Maritza amends, remembering last year's turquoise number for the rumba. "I definitely promise you I do not wear ostrich feathers at all. Waltz dresses are more streamlined these days. This movie is from the 90s; ballroom fashion was... something else, then."

Sarita's eyes are glued to the television as she spoons food into her mouth. "No kidding," she says, gesturing toward the male lead, who is dressed from the waist up almost entirely in large, yellow-gold sequins. "It's a good thing he's a good dancer. It distracts from his terrible costume choices." She glances aside. "He is a good dancer, right? I mean, he looks like one to me, but I don't know anything about ballroom. I just know I like watching him."

"That's the point of the movie. Watch." Maritza settles against the back of the couch; she balances her bowl on her knee as she eats. "But yeah, he's good, the guy playing him is a professional dancer."

Sarita leans forward and squints. "His partner looks familiar."

"It's Nikki from *My Big Fat Greek Wedding*," Maritza volunteers.

"Oh, my God, it is; it's Cousin Nikki. Look at that *hair*! I hardly recognize her!" Sitting back, Sarita laughs, clapping her hands. "Oh, I love that movie."

"Me too." Forgetting the movie, Maritza shifts on the sofa to face Sarita. "What other ones do you like?"

"God, loads of them. My friend Natasha—remember, the redhead from the party—comes over when her ex has their little girl, and we do the ice cream and romantic comedies thing. Between the movie services and my DVD collection, I am covered in the romance department." With a flash of a smile, Sarita sets her bowl aside, slides off the couch, crawls to the cabinet by the television and opens it. "It's a little lacking in the lesbian section, is my only problem."

"There aren't many, are there?" Maritza joins Sarita on the floor. "My mom tried to be the cool mom and buy me movies for Christmas when I told her I liked both girls and boys, but she couldn't *find* anything, nothing she felt comfortable giving to a teenager, anyway."

She's flipping through the movie collection when she realizes Sarita has gone stock-still, her only movement breathing. She slowly turns her head to face Maritza. "You're bi?"

Uh-oh. Maritza's heart turns into an icy lump in her chest as she looks at Sarita, trying to read a face gone completely inscrutable. "Um. Yeah. I, uh, is that a problem?"

Please don't let it be a problem. Not again. She's never liked that unreadable face that so many women get. But it's been so long since she's found a woman to go out with that she'd forgotten her bisexuality could be an issue. *Please let it be not an issue this time.*

Sarita's gaze shifts to the open movie cabinet, but she doesn't seem to be seeing anything. Maritza holds her breath and waits. *Please, please, please.*

At last, Sarita shakes her head and the softest chuckle puffs from her mouth. "You know what? No. It's not a problem." Raising her head, she locks her wide, dark eyes directly with Maritza. "I had a stupid moment. God, I'm sure you know the moment."

Maritza laughs and can't help the tinge of bitterness in it. "Yeah. I would say I know the moment."

Sarita shuffles around until she's sitting cross-legged and facing Maritza again. "I like you. I like you a lot, even if I hardly know you. You're here, so I guess you like me. And that's all that matters. Right?"

Relief floods Maritza's chest with warmth, melting away the icy lump. "Right."

"La Cumparsita" is streaming from the television speakers so a sharp pulse of tango fills the air when Sarita bends, slowly, with hesitation. Maritza holds still, her breath trembling in her lungs, as Sarita moves closer and brushes a lock of hair from Maritza's cheek with unsteady fingers.

It starts with a brush of their lips, a quick feather-light pass, before Sarita, with a sharp inhalation, presses her lips more firmly to Maritza's; her fingers comb into Maritza's hair to cup the back of her head and hold her close. Soft lips, warm lips, moving with an increasing, melting sureness. Light sparks behind Maritza's closed eyelids as she reaches for Sarita, whose hands envelop her waist just as they collapse backward to the floor.

"Sorry." Sarita laughs, her position on top of Maritza making the good humor shake through them. "I got a little carried away."

"You are *welcome* to keep doing that," Maritza says a split-second before she lets her own fingers twine through Sarita's cascading curls and tugs her into a second kiss. "Please," she mumbles against Sarita's lips, "get as carried away as you want."

Sarita props herself up as she tosses her hair over her shoulder. "And what if I want to get *really* carried away?"

"If you do, we should either get on the couch or head for your bedroom." Maritza grips Sarita's hips and shifts her own in a way that makes Sarita gasp. "This ass is not padded enough to get carried away on the floor if there are other options."

"Oh, but it's such a *great* ass." Sarita is on her feet and pulling Maritza up after her in the space between heartbeats, and they're halfway to the bedroom before Maritza can say another word.

They crash through the door and collapse onto the bed; lips come together again as hands roam and tug articles of clothing off and away. With a squeak, Maritza arches as her bra comes off. "Cold, too cold," she babbles. The air conditioning is blowing directly onto her nipples and making them tighten up.

"I can fix that." Sarita tosses Maritza's jeans aside, and in the next instant her warm mouth closes over Maritza's left nipple. Her hand covers the right one; the soft skin of her palm rolls against the already-sensitive peak. Ripples of arousal spread out and down through Maritza's stomach, rushing like warm water to her clit and making whimpers catch in the back of her throat.

Sarita's tongue and fingers work gently, not in tandem but alternating, a flick here, a rolling pinch there. Maritza's hips press up again; she traps Sarita's thigh between her own thighs and rocks the warmth between her legs against Sarita, chasing the orgasm that's already building. Her fingers curl around Sarita's shoulders and press in a way that's sure to leave marks.

"No... uh-uh." With a last lick, Sarita wriggles out of Maritza's grip, and the cool air of the room rushes over Maritza's nipples again. "If you want to come, I'm doing it."

"Please?" is all Maritza can get out, as she bunches handfuls of soft bedspread into her fists. "Please..."

There's a rustling noise from the bedside table, and then Sarita is nipping and kissing her way down Maritza's stomach. Her fingers tug Maritza's panties down and off. The fabric hits the floor with a whisper and Sarita nestles herself between Maritza's thighs and blows a thin stream of cool air directly over Maritza's clit.

Maritza's lost all faculty of language now; English and Spanish both desert her except for one word. *Please... please...*

Something soft drapes over Maritza that she is dimly aware must be a latex dam, held firm by Sarita. Then mouth, lips, tongue, soft and mobile and warm even through the latex, are on Maritza; fire traces up her spine as she arches her back with her fingers tight around the folds of blanket.

The room is dark; the movie is a murmur from the living room, and Maritza's toes curl every time the tip of Sarita's tongue teases at her clit just before her lips close around it, sucking so soft and so gently. Maritza bites her lip and twines her fingers through Sarita's hair, winding curls around her fingertips and trying not to tug too hard, but she *wants*; she's reaching and needing the release that's just there, waiting just out of reach; it's close and she *wants*...

She cries out; the sound breaks the gentle quiet, and her fingers clench, holding Sarita close and hard between her thighs. Sarita's mouth still gently works Maritza over as an electric thrill rolls through her, over and over, as she arches up hard and then slumps, all at once weak, so weak all she can do is try to catch her breath and gently bat Sarita away with one helpless hand.

Tickling fingers and a low chuckle precede Sarita's ascent back up Maritza's body until her palm comes to rest on Maritza's stomach, where it rises and falls with Maritza's gradually slowing breath. "Mm. Well, happy Valentine's to us both."

Maritza laughs, turning her head to catch Sarita's lips in hers, tasting fake strawberry and latex. "That's a hell of a first present."

"Well, you made dinner." That sets them off, curled around each other as their bodies shake in a fit of laughter. Sarita tucks her face into the curve of Maritza's neck and nuzzles her nose against the skin. "Okay, but speaking of food, I'm actually still hungry."

"I'm even more hungry than I was." Maritza stretches out across the bed, wiggles her toes and enjoys the pops as her spine loosens. "I don't want to get dressed."

Sarita licks across her collarbone. "I don't want you to get dressed."

Boneless and happily fuzzy-brained, Maritza curls around Sarita. "We could take the big blanket out to the couch and, like, wrap up in it and watch more movies and finish eating."

"You're smart. I like you. I like your ideas." Rolling away, Sarita scoots off the bed, grabbing Maritza's hand as she goes. "I have some ideas, too."

Maritza snatches the comforter as she's hauled to her feet and wraps it around them. "Tell me?"

A kiss to the tip of her nose. "Show you. After we finish dinner."

Maritza grins and allows herself to be pulled out of the bedroom in a shuffle of flowery blanket. Definitely the best Valentine's ever.

Chapter Six

"YOU ARE LATE." SHANTI SENGUPTA'S VOICE, LIKE THAT OF nearly every Bengali mother in the world, is a mixture of affection and exasperation as her youngest child enters the kitchen. From her position at the stove, as she stirs something that Sarita identifies from the delicious smell as spicy fish stew, she points a slender, bangle-wristed hand at a box of salad greens on the counter. "Quickly, find things in the refrigerator and put the salad together."

Sarita tucks a dishtowel into the front of her jeans as a makeshift apron and gets to work. She waits until she's bent over looking in the refrigerator to make her protest. "Not late," she says, picking an orange bell pepper, celery, and a red onion from the crisper drawer. Hands full, she kicks the fridge shut with her heel and walks over to kiss her mother on the cheek. "It's a quarter to six. You're still making dinner. You haven't even made the naan."

"By your usual standards, you are late, yes. You are usually here by five-thirty." Sarita blushes at the admonishment—she spent too long on the phone with Maritza, and ran into traffic on the way out to Bellevue as a result—and a frown creases Shanti's smooth brow as she glances at Sarita's hands. "Not celery. It upsets Jayani's stomach."

A groan twists up from Sarita's stomach at the sound of her niece's name. "Ma, no, tell me Anjali and her family aren't coming."

"Be nice to your sister," is all Shanti says, turning back to the stove to tend to the pot of stew.

I would if she would be nice to me, Sarita thinks as she returns the celery to the crisper drawer, selects a cucumber and takes it to the cutting board with the salad greens. So much for her good mood. The one thing in the world absolutely guaranteed to put her in a foul mood is the presence of her oldest sibling. When she could, she avoided coming to dinner when Anjali was going to be there—undoubtedly why her mother had failed to inform her ahead of time that it was going to happen, even though the last dinner with all of the Sengupta children present back in December had ended in tears for Sarita. Anjali's nasty jabs over the course of the evening about her job, her degree work and most of all her being a lesbian had finally become too much, and Sarita had left without even saying goodbye to her nieces, nephew and brother-in-law, all of whom she liked a great deal more than her sister.

"Your father asked me to have you all come for dinner, *shona.*" Shanti's voice is quiet, and when Sarita turns from her vegetable chopping to protest, her mother is carefully not looking at her as she puts a lid on the pot of stew and turns the burner low. Still avoiding her daughter's gaze, she uncovers a towel-covered tray, revealing garlicky naan ovals ready for baking. She tosses her long dark braid over her shoulder and bends to put the bread into the oven. "We haven't seen you all together since December."

Sarita observes her mother, as she bends and stands and moves and the whole time avoids eye contact. Sure, it *could* be that Shanti felt guilty about tricking Sarita and Anjali into being here at the same time, but it seems extremely unlikely. Putting down her knife, Sarita grabs her mother by a sleeve of her orange and gold *salwar kameez* as she flits by. "Ma, hey, what's going on? Is something wrong?"

"Not at all!" But Shanti's smile looks more strained than what Sarita is accustomed to seeing when all of her children are expected for dinner. She deftly twitches her sleeve from her daughter's hand and pats Sarita's arm. "I got you a new shirt. It's on my bed. Why don't you go have a look at it and wear it for dinner, hmm? I'm afraid it might be a bit long for you." Still with that strained smile, she moves her attention to Sarita's hair and pats the curls, fluffing them out. "It's that deep purple that always looks so nice on you, though. And it was the only one with embroidery instead of beads. I thought you might like that. Go. I'll finish the salad. Thank you, *shona*."

Sarita finds herself stripped of her apron towel, herded toward the stairs of her childhood home and pushed upstairs before she can think of another word. Puzzled by her mother's odd behavior, she pushes open the door to her parents' bedroom and goes inside.

The purple shirt, a kurti-style tunic top, is there, just as Shanti said, along with another one in rose with silver beading that has to be intended for Anjali and a pair of smaller blouses in pale green and dusty blue for Anjali's daughters. "We're going to be a rainbow at dinner," she mumbles to herself as she picks up her shirt up.

"You're telling me," comes the voice of her older brother from the bedroom doorway, and Sarita sends the purple shirt flying as she hurls herself into Devesh's arms.

"Dev!" She squeals as she finds herself picked up and twirled around. "Put me down, I'm not a toy."

"You sure? Because seriously, sis, I saw a doll that looked just like you at FAO Schwarz when Sunil and I were in New York last week." Devesh sticks out his tongue with laughter in his dark eyes.

"Shut up, ugh, you're such an ass." She punches him in the arm as he sets her carefully on the floor.

"Maybe they didn't look like you after all," Devesh says, "they're actually taller than you. Anyway!" He steps neatly out of the way of her next swing at his arm and gestures at his own shirt, a closely fitted men's kurta in maroon. "Check me out, I'm a fashion model, hey? She got Sunil one in saffron."

"You can call it yellow," Sarita replies, rolling her eyes. "It's just yellow."

"And lose my gay card? Perish the thought." Wandering over to the bed, Devesh brushes his bangs from his face and inspects the other tops. "She's got Bimal in dark green; he and Anjali will look like a flower together. You aren't kidding about the rainbow."

"What about Dad?" Sarita asks, picking up her shirt. "What's he wearing? I haven't seen him yet."

"He's in orange and gold to match Ma." Devesh sits on the bed as Sarita goes into the bathroom to change into her new top. "Ma's going all out, isn't she? I saw she's making *macher jhol*. Dad's favorite. And she got all of us here, including the littles. You know something's going on."

"Yeah, but she wouldn't tell me. She sent me up here before I could ask more questions." She smooths the purple top over her hips and sighs when she glances in the mirror on the back of the door. She barely tops five-foot-two, making most long tops too long for her. This one's not too bad, though. The golden embroidery is only on the three-quarter sleeves and at the neck, so it will be easy for her mother to take up the hem, which was probably another reason she picked this one. "Do you have any idea?"

"She chased me up here with a knife," Devesh says. "What do you think?"

"I think you made a smart-ass remark and you earned that outcome." She opens the bathroom door and walks out, showing off with a twirl. "Well?"

"You look cute. Did you look this cute when you went to that party?" Devesh flops across the bed, avoiding the tops spread out on the bedspread, and props his chin in his hands. "Is that why you have a new lady friend?" He laughs when an unstoppable smile pops out across her face. "Ha! Tell me everything; last I heard from you was right after you met her."

"Shut up!" She covers her face when she realizes she can't make the smile stop. But that just makes her giggle. "Oh my God, Dev, she's amazing."

Coffee dates, phone calls, text messages and their one night together is all they've had so far, but that is more than enough to make her grin like an idiot as she pulls her hands away from her face to look at her brother. "I have the worst crush."

"Look at you; you're a giggling mess. That's hilarious." Devesh chuckled. "You said she was a ballroom dancer, right? Tell me more." He winks. "Does that make her good in bed?"

An instant flash of memory, of Maritza's soft dark waves of hair tickling Sarita's inner thighs in the deep dark hours before the morning after Valentine's, makes her blush like fire. "Disgusting. You don't ask your baby sister things like that." Sarita shoves him off the bed and grins at his grunt of surprise when he hits the thick red carpet.

"Yes, please refrain from discussing your perverted lifestyle choices in front of my children." Anjali Bhattacharyya sails into the room with her two daughters in tow. She tosses her short curls away from her face and regards her siblings with an expression that Sarita has seen far too many times in the last decade: contempt. "Whatever you two must do, do it and discuss it in the privacy of your own homes. Bad enough Devesh has to bring his so-called husband here."

"It's not so-called; it's legal in Washington State, Anjali, remember?" Devesh gets to his feet smoothly and with a poise Sarita can only envy. She balls her hands into fists and shoves her hands into her jeans pockets as she watches him calmly interact with their detested sibling. "You have a bad memory for a paralegal. My marriage is as legal as yours, and it'll be legal nationwide by the end of the year, I guarantee it."

"Perish the thought. Ugh." With a snap of her fingers, Anjali walks over to her daughters. "Jayani, Priya, go take your kurtis and change in the bathroom there. Hurry up; dinner's waiting."

Priya wanders off as instructed, but Jayani sidesteps her mother to throw her skinny arms around Sarita's waist. "Hi, Auntie."

"Hi, baby. I'm happy to see you." She gets down on her knees and tucks locks of her niece's black hair behind her ears. She sees so much of her small self in Jayani, in her knobby knees and big eyes and wild hair. "How's school going? You're going to finish third grade this year, right?"

"It's okay," Jayani begins, only to be halted by her mother's hand on her arm.

"I said go change, Jayani. Go." Anjali glares down at Sarita. "Please, you're the last person to talk about finishing anything when it comes to school."

"Yeah, Devesh is the only one who gets to pick on me about that," Sarita snaps, getting back to her feet and stretching as tall as she can make herself. She cranes her head and pretends to think. "I wonder why? Oh, right. It probably has something to do with him not being a hateful monster."

"Okay, we're going downstairs now. Bye-bye, Anjali." Taking Sarita's arm, Devesh all but drags her out of the bedroom and down the stairs. "Well, I see we're off to a great start for tonight's festivities. Try not to throw your dessert at Anji this time, maybe? It upsets Ma."

"I make no promises. If Ma made mango *kulfi* instead of pistachio, it's fair game." Tugging her arm from her brother's grip, Sarita stomps off into the kitchen and despises her sister to death.

IT DOES ALL START FAIRLY WELL. SARITA HAS TO ADMIT THAT IT'S nice to look around the table at all of her family, brightly clad, smiling and chattering with each other. Devesh's husband Sunil in his burnished yellow is in close conversation with Shanti about the most recent litter of Yorkshire terriers he and Devesh have bred. Anjali and Bimal's son Ramendra, all of three years old, is in indigo, sitting soberly between his mother and father on a booster seat. Sarita wiggles her fingers at her nephew, eliciting a dimpled smile. Bimal grins at her and nods in approval. "You're always so good with the children, Sarita. Ramendra's missed you these last weeks, haven't you, hmm?" Ramendra giggles and shrieks as his father tickles him.

"Don't get him excited, Bimal, he's already going to be up past his bedtime, and I don't need to have a fight on my hands when it's time to put him down." And there's Anjali, a cold splash of water as usual. She's lovely with the rose of her top against her golden skin and dark green eyes, but the beauty of her face is marred by her frown of disapproval, which softens only slightly when she looks at her husband. "Please."

"Sorry." Bimal's grin is sheepish now, and there's an apology in his eyes as he looks back at Sarita. "Well, anyway. We haven't seen you in a while. How are things at the bakery?"

"Oh, you know, Valentine's Day was just last week, so we've been busy." She takes a bite of her *macher johl* before going on, savoring the flavors. Her mother has really outdone herself with this evening's dinner. "Mostly wedding cakes. One couple asked us to do a galaxy cake for their Valentine's wedding. I think that one was my favorite."

"What's a galaxy cake?" Jayani asks from Sarita's left, having fought for and won the right to sit next to her Auntie, much to Anjali's annoyance. "Like space?"

"Exactly like it." She bumps foreheads with her giggling niece. "It was three tiers, and we had to do the frosting in gradients of blue, like Ramendra's kurta there, and white, and lighter blue like your shirt, and some lavender. Then I drew on lots of these really tiny stars and I got to use edible glitter and silver luster spray to make it sparkle."

Jayani's eyes grow wide. "It sounds beautiful, Auntie."

"It sounds like something dreamed up by one of your flaming gay friends." Anjali rolls her eyes.

"Anjali," Shanti warns, clanking her spoon on the edge of her bowl.

Sarita rolls her eyes back at her sister. "Not that it matters, but it was for a straight couple. She's an astrophysicist, and she helped design the cake. Would you mind pulling the stick out of your—"

"Sarita!" Shanti hisses. "You stop right there. Not in front of the children."

Fair enough. With an apologetic pat to Jayani's hand, Sarita returns to her conversation with her brother-in-law. An environmental lawyer, he's always been intelligent and tremendously kind, and she has no earthly idea why he chose to marry Anjali. "How's life at the firm, Bimal?"

"Good, it's good. We're fighting against a company that wants to start fracking in Wenatchee. I can't give you specifics, but it looks good for our clients." He beams, clearly proud of his work. "You know me. I like to stick it to The Man, I'm having a great time."

"How does that work, exactly, when as a lawyer you're kind of also The Man?" Sarita winks as her brother-in-law lets out a hearty laugh. "Okay, no, seriously, that's great. Fight the good fight. Good for you, Bimal."

Bimal turns to Anjali and squeezes her hand. "My only regret in the case is that I'm not allowed to get your sister working with me on it. Her research skills would be invaluable. I'm making do, but I know we'd be done already and with a good settlement if I had her on board."

Because she does like Bimal and her nieces and nephew, and because she doesn't want to get into another quarrel with Anjali, Sarita refrains from suggesting that divorce might be an effective way to get around nepotism concerns. She manages to paste on a smile as she says, "That's true, Anji always was really good at research. She can organize a binder full of information like no one else I know. You actually are missing out there. Isn't she your firm's best paralegal?"

Her smile broadens as she spots her sister glaring at her, trying to find an insult in Sarita's statement. Anji wouldn't be able to find one because there *wasn't* one. Sarita had meant every word she'd said. Sometimes there was nothing more satisfying than killing your tormentor with kindness. Sarita takes an oval of warm naan and dips it in her stew, entirely pleased with herself.

Her joy is short-lived. At the end of the table, her father Sandeep stands up. "I hope you have all enjoyed the delicious dinner tonight," he says, his first words of the meal since thanking Shanti for making it. "I asked your mother to make it especially for us all, because I have some very big news for you. If you'll all quiet down."

"I knew it," Devesh says, reaching to take Sunil's hand. When he spots Anjali switching her glare to focus on him, he sticks his tongue out at her, a brief moment of childishness before he frowns. "Something's wrong, isn't it, Dad? Are you sick? Is it Ma?"

Sandeep waves off his son's concern as he sits down, spreading his napkin over his lap with care. "No one is sick. You worry too much, Devesh."

"Then is it your job?" Anjali asks. "What is it?"

"It's not my job, well, not exactly. Could you all be quiet so I can get a word in edgewise? Stop guessing." He glances around the table; his eyes touch on each of his children in turn. "All right, then. Thank you. I wanted you all to come to dinner today so I could tell you my news all at once, so that we could celebrate it." He pauses, reaching to grab Shanti's hand and smile at her. He's looking at her when he says, "Your mother and I are going to sell the house this year and move home to Kolkata."

Chapter Seven

Sarita stares at her father, not sure she's heard him correctly. "Sorry, Dad, what?"

Sandeep's smile doesn't fade as he glances away from his wife. "We are moving home."

Gasps and shouts fill the dining room, each Sengupta child trying to shout over their siblings, with husbands and grandchildren joining in the cacophony. Even Ramendra gets into the spirit of the shock when he grabs his ears and lets out a piercing siren of a wail.

The noise makes a headache rocket through Sarita's head, and she rubs her temples, waiting for the rest of the family to wear themselves out. Her father sits at the other end of the table, calmly spooning food into his mouth and using his free hand to hold Shanti's. The Sengupta parents are supremely unperturbed by the aftermath of their bombshell announcement, and Sarita wonders how long this has been in the works, how long they've been planning this night.

At last, Shanti and Sandeep's calm seems to diffuse around the room, and one by one the rest of the family falls silent, bending their attention to the head of the table. Sandeep looks around. "Now. Is everyone ready to hear why we are doing this?"

Nods around the table.

"It's very simple," Sandeep begins, reaching for the basket of naan for another round and dipping it into his dish. "When I agreed to marry your mother, it was with the promise that one day I would bring her back home."

"It's not home to you, though, Dad," Devesh says. He squeezes his husband's hand; his face is pinched. "Is it? You've basically been here your entire life."

"Yes, but my family is from Kolkata, like your mother's. I have been back and forth many times. I married your mother there. I'm not without roots."

Sarita pushes her plate away. "What about work?" Her father had been with Microsoft for as long as she could remember, working his way up to Senior Software Development.

"I can work there. I can develop software anywhere in the world, and we did open an office there last year." Her father is very calm and very sure. "Global telecommunications are a great innovation. The arrangements have all been made. Microsoft has been very accommodating."

Anji's turn. When she speaks, her voice is tinged with the hysteria Sarita had only just managed to fight off. "But you're selling our *home!*"

Shanti makes a soft clucking sound. "You are all adults. You don't live here anymore. We would have sold the house eventually anyway to get something much more reasonable for two adults, had this opportunity not come up." Her voice is chiding as she faces her eldest child. "You should be pleased for your father. That we are able to do this is a testament to how highly they think of him at Microsoft."

"But India." Sarita's throat clogs, and she can't get her voice above a whisper. "You'll be on the other side of the world." *You'll miss everything,* she doesn't say. Ramendra's first day of school. Devesh's first child, if he and Sunil ever decide to have or adopt one. Her own eventual possible graduation with her doctorate. "You won't be here…"

Shanti is still calm and she projects an aura of reassurance and tranquility. "There is Skype, and of course we'll come back to visit you when we are able. But I miss India. I always knew I would miss it when your father and I left. It was wonderful of him to promise that we would go home one day in the future, when we could." She gets up from her seat and moves to stand behind Sarita, bending down for an embrace. "And you can come, all of you can come visit. You should know your roots better. Know where you came from. We haven't been back since you were children. Haven't you been even the least bit curious?"

Sarita exchanges glances with her siblings, the three of them united for the first time in years. Anjali is squeezing her husband's upper arm, while Bimal sits, stoic and quiet. "Ma, please," she says, her face paling. "You'll be so far. We'll worry about you."

"As your mother said, we'll be in constant contact with you," Sandeep says, his black eyes still and calm as a lake at night. He sits up straight, drawing back his shoulders. "At any rate, the deal is done. This is happening, children. We hope to sell the house and go before summer. Your uncle Vijay will let us stay with him while we look for a place of our own." With a smile, he looks at Sarita. "And don't worry. The sale of the house should give us enough that we can leave you money to help you with your doctorate. We won't leave you stranded."

Before Sarita can begin to process this, Anjali gasps and releases Bimal's arm. Her hands slap down on the dining room table so hard their drinking glasses sway and clink. "Is that why you're doing this?" she demands as she flexes her fingers into fists. "Do you need money because of that dykey little spoiled *brat*? Are you leaving the country because her endless refusal to join the real world and get a real job is bankrupting you?"

Shanti frowns. "Don't be ridiculous, Anjali."

"Ridiculous? Me?" Anjali's snort of contempt is poisonous, and Sarita flinches from it as her sister glares at her. "No. What is ridiculous is that Devesh and I both had to pay for school ourselves—"

"Sarita paid for her undergraduate schooling, just as you did, with loans and scholarships," Sandeep says, the calm in his gaze giving way to steely disapproval as he stares his eldest down. "She also paid for half of her master's program by working at the bakery. Your sister works hard in school and at her job."

Anjali breathes hard through her clenched teeth; her furious gaze bounces between her parents and Sarita. Sarita clenches her fingers into a knot under the table and tries to draw strength from her mother's hand on her shoulder. This is worse than that last dinner by a mile. "Sure she works hard," Anjali hisses. "For what? What are you going to do with a degree in philosophy, *Doctor Sengupta*?" Her laugh is bitter. "Why does she get to hide away in school as long as she likes? And why for *that* degree? I could have gone to law school! Devesh could have gotten a master's in economics!"

"I didn't want a master's, Anji, just like you didn't actually want to go to law school," Devesh snaps. "God, can you lay off Sarita just for *one night*? Our parents are leaving the country! Literally! And no, not because of Sarita. If anything, I'm sure they're leaving to get away from *you*!"

This stops Anjali in her tracks, and her eyes grow large and sound as she inhales a sharp, shocked breath. In the next instant, she's on her feet and tearing out of the dining room. Bimal looks around, apology all over his face. "I'll go calm her down," he says, dropping his napkin on the table and following after his furious wife.

Sarita sits, trembling and shaken, still tying her fingers into knots. She jumps when she feels Jayani's small hand curl around her arm. "Are *didima* and *dadu* leaving because of Mom?"

All over guilt, Devesh beats her to the answer. "No, baby. I shouldn't have said that. It wasn't nice of me."

"Uncle can speak before he thinks sometimes," Shanti says as she leans down to hug her granddaughter. "He's right. We are not leaving because of your mother or because of anyone here. We are simply going home."

"Speaking of going home, I think I should," Sarita says. She puts her hand on her chest where her heart is beating so hard she wonders if it will burst out and away. That was the worst Anjali has been in some time, almost as bad as when Sarita came out. "I have work to do, and anyway Anji won't calm down as long as I'm here."

"It's not your fault, Sarita." Sandeep is outwardly calm, but Sarita can see from his eyes that he's furious. "You don't have to leave. You haven't finished your dinner, and there's dessert yet."

"It's okay, Dad. I know it's not my fault. I just don't know..." She sighs. "I don't know what it even is anymore. But please, I'm tired and I do have my paper to work on. It's been a really long weekend." She does manage to muster a smile, but it's weak. "Don't worry about me. I'll come visit you guys again later this week, if that's okay."

"If that's okay," Shanti scoffs. "Of course it's okay. And if you must leave, you must. But come into the kitchen with me so I can send you home with some food for that friend of yours."

This makes Sarita perk up. She doesn't have to go *directly* home. If she has food, that means she has an excuse to stop by Craig and Alex's, and she could really use a cup of tea and some friendly non-family faces right now. She gives her father a quick hug, follows her mother into the kitchen, and surreptitiously sends a quick text.

Can I come by? Got food.

Craig's response is nearly immediate.

Of course. See you in thirty?

Sarita pockets her phone. "Thanks for the leftovers, Ma. Craig always appreciates them."

"And I appreciate that about him! Such a lovely young man." Shanti flashes a quick smile over her shoulder. "You should bring him over again sometime before your father and I go. I'll make that mutton *biryani* he likes. Have him bring his boyfriend. I haven't met him yet."

"Anjali will have a fit." Sarita tries to keep the bitterness out of her voice, but her mother's affection and understanding is so at odds with her sister's rage that it loosens any control she can muster.

Shanti puts down the plastic container and embraces her. "Then we won't invite her," she says simply, stroking a hand over Sarita's curls. "I would have spared you tonight if I could."

Squeezing her eyes shut helps Sarita keep back the tears. "I wish I knew why she hated me so much. I mean, she doesn't much like Devesh either, but God, Ma, she's so awful to me, and I don't know... she wasn't always like this. And you're really not selling the house just to pay for me to screw around in school a few more years, right?"

"You know better than that," Shanti says, the gentlest of rebukes in her voice. She pulls away and uses her thumbs to brush a few escaped tears from under Sarita's eyes and offers a soft smile before turning away to finish packing the leftover stew. "Don't fret, *shona*. Everything will be all right. And Anjali will calm down one day. She will have to. All fires eventually go out."

And Sarita smiles, and smiles, and smiles at her mother as hard as she can, all the while not asking, *But what about the people who get burned?*

When the knock comes on their door, Craig is setting out the tea mugs and sugar on their tiny kitchen table. "Could you get that, babe?" he asks Alex, as he turns to snag the milk jug. "The kettle's about to boil."

"Sure." Alex puts down his paperback and glasses and slides off the bed to amble the two steps to the apartment door with Fitz yipping at his heels. He swings the door open, pretending to look around as if he can't see who's there. "Weird, I thought I heard—oh hey, there you are!" he says with a chortle, hopping back out of the way of the wild punch Sarita aims at his arm. "Sorry, Short Stack."

"I let you get away with the short cracks because you're pretty, you know," she says while she glides past him with a plastic bag in her extended hand. "Be nice. I've got dinner for you, but I can just take it home."

Alex lifts his head and sniffs. "I smell... fish stew? Excellent." He pulls a chair out for her, deftly lifting the bag from her hand at the same time. He's just handed it over to Craig when Sarita falls down hard into her chair and lets out a sigh that seems much too large to come from her. Alex raises an eyebrow. "Rough night?"

"Let me guess," Craig says before Sarita can respond. "I'm good with putting clues together. You've brought us fish stew in a container and I'm sure if I look on the bottom of it..." He pulls out the container and peers at the bottom. "Yep. Just as I expected, there's an address label for Shanti Sengupta stuck here. So you've been to your mother's, and you've come here instead of going directly home and you're actually here rather early *and* you're clearly in quite the foul mood." He looks at Alex and clucks his tongue. "That means one thing: Anjali."

The name doesn't ring a bell for Alex at first, and he has to think about it, casting about in his memory for faint details. "Oh, wait, your sister, right?"

"Unfortunately." Another too-big sigh, and Sarita wrestles out of her jacket before she bends forward over the table to rest her head on her crossed arms. Her hair spills all around her, completely concealing her face and helping to muffle her voice. "No one breaks up a dinner party quite like Anjali."

Craig pours the stew into a pot on the stove to warm before he brings the electric kettle to the table. "I've never liked her, not for one minute," he says, tossing tea bags into each of the three mugs and pouring boiling water over them. "Sarita, love, do you want a bit of bourbon in your tea? Help you unwind a bit? You've got to be tense."

"Tempting, but no, thanks. I just wanted to stop in for a sort of sanity check before I had to go home and be alone with my thoughts and my paper." She raises her head slightly, pillowing her cheek on her arms. "And right now, you two are as close to sanity as I'm going to get."

Craig snorts, and Alex harrumphs in mock outrage. "I resemble that remark," he says, sticking his chin up in the air and pretending to be hurt. "How very dare you."

He watches her closely, and even he, a casual acquaintance of Sarita at best, can see that her responding smile is strained and thin. She looks weighed down, as if the world is pinning her by her slight shoulders to their kitchen table. And that is a feeling which he has known all too well the last two years. Despite all the therapy he's been in, it's not a distant memory yet, and his heart contracts with sympathy. He reaches over, cautious, and touches her hand. "Do you want to talk about it?"

She sits up with hesitation in her eyes as she looks between the two of them. "It's not a long story," she says, and the words emerge with reluctance. "But I don't know, I didn't come here to dump my problems on you guys, I just needed some breathing room."

Craig seems to be at a loss for words as he pats Sarita's other hand, so Alex figures it's up to him. "You don't have to tell us, but you can if you want to." He offers a smile. "My therapist is really big on airing out your feelings. I have to say it has made me feel better to put my stuff out there. If you want to. I can leave if you'd rather just have Craig; he knows you better than I do."

Her smile brightens, and she slips her hand out from under his to squeeze his fingers. "You don't have to leave, Alex. And thank you, you're right, I would feel better if I talked about it. It would make it more real." She glances at Craig. "It's not actually Anjali, exactly. I mean, she didn't help at *all*, as usual, but honestly the whole problem I'm having with tonight is that my parents just dropped on us that they're selling the house and moving back to India at the end of the summer."

Craig's jaw drops. "They what!"

"Yeah, that's about the size of all our reactions, too. Multiplied by, you know, five. Six or seven if you count my nieces, who are just exactly old enough to understand what's going on." She pulls her hands back and starts rubbing her temples. "Oh, man, my head."

Alex gets to his feet; his chair scrapes over the linoleum with a screech. "I'll get you an Advil."

"So where does Anjali come in to all of this?" Craig asks, getting to his feet as Alex goes to the bathroom. "Don't mind me, sorry. I just want to check the delicious whatever-it-is you've brought us."

"Oh, well, that's the best part." Sarita lets out a sigh. "According to my darling sister, my extended higher education is bankrupting my parents, and they're having to sell the house to bankroll my collegiate malingering."

"That is the dumbest thing I've ever heard," Alex blurts out as he returns and hands over the pill bottle. Craig turns to aim a dirty look in his direction, and blood rushes to Alex's cheeks. "Sorry," he mumbles and slinks back into his chair, where he hides his embarrassment in his tea mug.

"No, you're right; that's really dumb," Sarita says. "I mean, it's dumber that I actually believed it might have been true for about thirty seconds there, but yeah. Yeah, it's dumb."

At the stove, Craig inches up the heat and stirs for a moment or two before grabbing his tea. "What I've never understood is *why* she's so hateful. Difficult sibling relationships I get. I haven't spoken to my older brother since we were teenagers. Of course, we're in different countries, that does make it easier... but you haven't got that luxury. And besides that, you don't know why either, do you?"

Sarita shakes her head and leans down to pick up Fitz for a quick ear scritch. "I've never known. It's one of the great mysteries of my life that she refuses to explain—of course, she'd have to stop screaming at me for more than ten seconds at a time for that to even be a possibility. But no. All I know is that I came out when I was fifteen and she was nineteen, and suddenly something she didn't mind when Devesh did it mattered a very great deal when I did, and that was the end of that." One slender shoulder tilts up in a shrug. "Maximum homophobia ever since, inexplicably."

Alex considers. "Is she religious?"

"No. She doesn't go to temple any more regularly than I do." She sets Fitz back down on the floor, and, when she comes up, her hands spread out, and she shrugs again. "Literally no one in my family, including Bimal, cares about Devesh and me being queer except for Anjali, and she cares to a degree that seems very personal to her, and she makes it very personal for the rest of us."

"Pity she's not the one leaving the country," Craig says as he turns again to check the curry. He winces. "Ah, sorry, Sarita. My turn to be the thoughtless one."

"Well, you're not wrong. I would miss her kids and her husband, because he's really cool, but I wish she was the one going. I can't lie." Sarita slumps back in her chair, small and upset in a way that makes Alex's heart squeeze again. He desperately wants to cheer her up, to not let her leave his and Craig's home without being somewhat more cheery.

His options are limited. Casting about, Alex tries to think of something, anything, to help. He realizes he only has to go as far back as a couple of weeks ago. "Okay, well, subject change: What do you think of Maritza?"

For a moment, Sarita's delicate face contorts comically at the non sequitur; her dark eyes narrow and then they widen with realization. "Oh, oh, I get it, you did that, didn't you? You set me up!" Craig, from his station at the stove, chuckles, and her hair whips out in a cloud as she turns to stare at him. "And you! You were in on it!"

Ladling the stew into a pair of blue pottery bowls, Craig raises a hand to waggle a finger at her. "I knew about it. I wouldn't say I was in on it except to agree with Alex that the two of you made a cute pair on the dance floor. And you did."

She laughs, a helpless little *ha!* "Wow."

"Sorry," Alex says, not really repentant except that he might have meddled, and he's always hated it when his cousin Samantha does that, but seeing Sarita's face light up at the mere mention of Maritza is pleasing in a way that makes him get why Sammi does it. "I met her a while ago when I was doing the event photos for a dance competition she was in. I thought she was a lot of fun, and very cute, and she told me she'd semi-recently broken off her romantic relationship with her dance partner—"

Sarita's eyes get even bigger. "Nicky? She was dating that Nicky guy she talks about?" Her nose rumples in a puzzled frown. "I've only known her for a couple of weeks, but in that entire time I've never heard a good word about that guy."

"Wait till you meet him," Alex advises. "You'll see why. Nicky, he makes things difficult for her. He is... really something." *A toddler trapped in the body of a twenty-six-year-old man. No, toddlers behave better.* "I'm glad you like her, though. I know you and I don't know each other well, so I was really kind of guessing as to whether or not she'd be your type, but she was nice, and funny, and cute and into girls, and I figured it was a good place to start?"

"It was actually a really great place to start, so thank you." Sarita surprises him with a kiss on his cheek. "I like her. I'm looking forward to spending time with her. She's a great antidote to my sister, that's for sure."

"She's apparently breakfast-worthy," Craig says, all innocence, as he sets the bowls of fish stew on the table while carefully not looking at Sarita. "Can I get you a bowl of this, Sarita? There's plenty left; your mum was really generous."

Sarita looks slightly confused as she turns to take her jacket from the back of her chair. "Um, no, thanks, I actually had plenty at the house before Anjali started in on me. It was really good tonight. My mom outdid herself." She slides her arms into her jacket sleeves. "No, I better go. I'm on the early shift tomorrow; there's that birthday cake to do."

"Oh, yeah, that green robot beastie," Craig says with a nod as he sits down. "Yeah, I finished cutting the shapes for you today, they're in the walk-in, just to your left when you go in. Theodora's in tomorrow morning, not me."

"She's back from Bali?" Sarita looks surprised, and no wonder. In the last year, Alex has seen her and Craig's boss maybe a handful of times. The woman has many business interests and a savvy way of picking managers for all of them that allows her ample time to go globetrotting, which she does with relish. "I thought she was due back next week."

"Mmm, no, she wanted to come back early." Concentrating instead on his food, Craig is once again not looking at Sarita. "Good Lord, your mother really has outdone herself this time. Please let her know?"

"Sure, she loves how much you love her food, you know that." Her eyes brighten. "She wants you to come for dinner before they leave, by the way. She says she'll make the *biryani* you like, and that you need to bring Alex so she can meet him."

Craig smiles, reaching to grab Alex's hand. "That's fantastic, yes, absolutely, just let us know when."

"I'll walk you to the door." Alex untangles his hand and stands up, but Sarita waves him off.

"It's like, two feet. I can see myself out and down the stairs." She grins and bends down to fluff Fitz's ears before she opens the door. "See you guys later. Thanks for the tea and the talk and all."

"Anytime." Alex follows her to the door and locks it behind her. Turning around, he leans back and raises an eyebrow at Craig. "You still didn't tell her."

Craig shrugs. "It's not really my news to tell," he says around a mouthful of food. With a guilty half-grin about his bad manners, he swallows before going on. "Besides, it's not finalized until I get the business loan and sign the contract with Theo and the lawyers. Theo doesn't want to say anything until we know for sure I'm going to get the buy-in money."

"Your people will guess something is going on," Alex points out as he wanders back to the table.

"Sarita already does think something's going on, or have you forgotten Valentine's Day?" Craig is all over calm as he takes another spoonful of stew. "Oh, this is just so excellent."

Alex knows Craig wants to drop the subject, but he's been holding this secret for weeks and he's *tired*. "Yeah, and eventually she's going to start asking you questions. She said it herself: Theodora came back early from her trip, and I'm gathering she doesn't do that often."

"She doesn't," Craig allows, setting down his spoon with a sigh. "But the bank said we'd know this week, and she's really eager to sign the paperwork and get me officially established as co-owner as soon as possible." Propping his chin on his hand, he casts Alex a rueful smile. "Two self-employed wankers in one household. We're going to eat nothing but beans on toast for years. You sure you don't want out now?"

"I wouldn't leave you if we had to live in cardboard boxes and make Fitz dance for pennies," Alex says, and he kisses Craig as Fitz snuffles around their feet.

Chapter Eight

"**...I** DIDN'T MEAN TO DUMP ALL OF THAT ON YOU." THREE days after what Sarita has decided was absolutely the Worst Dinner Ever, she's parked at the Java Stop, cuddled up in a booth with Maritza. This is the third time she's explained the debacle to anyone—Tash sat wide-eyed through the recitation just yesterday as they worked on a pair of cookie cakes for a kiddie party—and she notes with an almost detached interest that she's already getting better at it, more concise. It's good practice for her eventual thesis defense, maybe. It's still depressing. She shakes her head clear of the gloom. "I just wanted to see you."

"Well. Here I am." Gently, her hands are pulled away from her hair, and Maritza's fingers twine through hers. "And I can I can bring the mood back up." Maritza leans over and brushes the tip of her nose against Sarita's before giving her a sweet kiss. "Because... " she breathes between kisses, "I love... your smile..." This time, she bites down a little on Sarita's lip, and Sarita's breath skips out in a gasp. "I love... making you... smile."

A pleasant fog overtakes Sarita's brain, and she does indeed feel a smile coming to life under Maritza's continued kisses. "I'm so glad I met you," she mumbles and she inclines her head to let Maritza nibble down her neck. "You are... mmm... so much fun... and..." The blissful sigh slips out to interrupt her before she knows it. "... such a great distraction."

"I am..." Maritza gives one last gentle bite right at the soft curve at the base of Sarita's throat and pulls away to lean on the table with her chin in her hand and a twinkle in her eyes, "...so very, very glad to be of service."

A cough startles them out of their drifting, goofy-grinning reverie. "Ladies," Cliff says, very polite as he lifts up a full coffee pot. "Can I interest you in refills? Fresh pot."

Maritza puffs out her cheeks. "Sure, why not, Gracie'll be here any minute to take me to work."

"I had chai, but if you're offering coffee I could use it. I have a meeting with my bosses," Sarita says and holds up her cup.

Cliff takes the paper cup and lifts it to his eyes for closer inspection; his brow wrinkles at the bite marks and picked-off bits. "How about I give you a fresh cup with a lid, Decorating Lady? I don't think this one'll stand up to a whole lot more abuse."

"Fab," Sarita says, grateful that she won't have to walk to Sucre Coeur with a half-nibbled, lidless cup in her hand.

"I'll bring you a fresh one, too, Tiny Dancer." Cliff snatches up Maritza's equally battered cup. "What you ladies do to my go-cups, I should look into something a little more indestructible. Be right back."

"Thanks, Cliff." Maritza smiles after him before returning her attention to Sarita. "So. Feel better?"

"I feel a *lot* better. God, I wish you could go with me to this meeting and home with me afterward." Just over three weeks into this, and sometimes Sarita's heart races when she thinks about how much she likes Maritza. *Too much* is what crosses her mind most of the time when she's alone, and she worries about the intensity. But then she gets another snatched afternoon or evening or just a handful of stolen minutes with Maritza, and it's fun and comfortable and a veritable island of happiness in the constant anxious road race of Sarita's life, and it's not *too much*, it's fantastic, and she wonders why she ever worried about it.

"Actually…" Maritza draws up her shoulders, and her smile is just a touch too broad and bright for full sincerity. "Not tonight, but what are you doing tomorrow?"

"Something I might regret, if that smile on you is any indication." Sarita raises an eyebrow.

Maritza wobbles her hand. "Maybe yes, maybe no. Mom's off tomorrow night and she wants me to bring you over for dinner." She bats her eyelashes. "I get it if you've totally had enough of family dinners to last you a couple weeks, but I can promise you that there's nothing more exciting planned than my mom's cooking. Although it is really good cooking."

Sarita considers the option. She doesn't mind putting off work on her paper another night. She got an entire three paragraphs written last night after work; that was progress. She even got to flip to the next page in her Spinoza text. "You know, I think I might like to see what it's like having dinner with a normal family," she says, nodding. "I didn't even get to tell you about my terrible sister."

"I would love to hear about your terrible sister," Maritza assures her. "Does it sweeten the pot if I tell you that you can take me back to your place for the night afterward? And that I finally got my test results back from Planned Parenthood and they're all clear, so bye-bye, dental dams?"

"Same for my tests, too. And your mom is going to cook for me, *and* I get to take you home? That *is* kind of a bonus." Sarita's mood is considerably better now, a vast improvement over the slumped-shoulder grump she trudged into the Java Stop wearing. "You have rehearsal the next morning, I take it?"

"Yes, but your apartment's convenience to the studio is not the big draw," Maritza says, up and leaning in again for more kisses. "That'd be you."

"I'm gonna need an insulin shot." Grace's bright amusement makes them both look up to see her standing over their table with a huge grin on her face. She flicks her ponytail over her shoulder.

"Okay, seriously though, you two are way too cute, and that should be outlawed."

Maritza sticks her tongue out. "We are putting much needed positivity and joy into the world, Grace. This is a public service."

"Yeah, you're totally altruistic." Grace responds with a raspberry of her own and rattles her car keys. "I want to get a green tea to go. You have as long as that takes to say your goodbyes. Sorry to take her away, Sarita." She offers a one-shouldered shrug and a repentant smile. "I got a text from Zach on the way over; we've got orders for three parties tonight. I need this girl's pizza-tossing skills ASAP."

"I'm going to be late for my meeting if I don't jet now anyway." Sarita grabs her bag from under the table, gets to her feet and tugs her favorite slouchy rainbow wool hat down over her ears. With a quick skip, she's around Grace and leaning down to kiss Maritza goodbye. "See you tomorrow?"

"Can't wait." Maritza beams.

It's a smile that warms Sarita from the inside out, makes her dance her way over to the counter to grab her fresh coffee and plant a kiss on the cheek of a surprised Cliff. As she hits the sidewalk, it's almost as if her feet don't even touch the ground.

"So. That looks like that's going well." Grace lifts one slender black eyebrow as she slides into the other side of the booth. "What's tomorrow? You going to introduce her to Nicky?"

"I am trying very hard to get through life without *ever* having to introduce her to Nicky." Maritza can't help her shudder. "Like, seriously, my goal is to get through auditions and then ditch him forever, with him not even knowing what she *looks* like. Or that she's a *she*, actually."

Grace's mouth twists as she mulls this over. "Yeah, that's a really, *really* good idea."

"I have them sometimes." Maritza manages to flash a smug grin at Grace before she softens it into a nicer smile for Cliff as he brings over her new coffee. "Thanks, Cliff. Can Grace get a mid-size hot green tea with honey to go, too?"

"Can do, five minutes." With a salute, Cliff ambles off back to the counter.

"Thanks," Grace calls after him. When she focuses on Maritza again, her gaze is sober. "Okay, so this is going really well, and I'm happy for you. I am, really, especially after that train wreck you had going with Nicky."

Maritza takes a sip of her coffee. "But…"

"But, reality check: What are you going to do when you make it onto *Dance Nation*?" Grace props her head on her hand. "March is next week, and April's going to be on you before you know it."

She can't help it; Maritza feels her bottom lip push out in a pout. "I was doing really well not thinking about that, thanks, Grace."

"I live to be the splash of ice cold water right down the back of your neck." As pragmatic as she ever is, Grace keeps a steady gaze on Maritza; her eyes are clear with the challenge for Maritza to stop sticking her head into the ground. "Come on, Mari, seriously. I'm not looking to ruin your fun, but you're getting a ticket to skip town in less than six weeks."

"There is every chance in the world that I won't make it into the top twenty," Maritza shoots back. "I might not even make it to the Los Angeles callbacks. It's my first audition year, and I'm going up against every dancer over the age of eighteen in Washington, Oregon and probably British Columbia! My odds are maybe even."

Grace lets fly with an undignified snort. "Please. *Nicky's* odds are maybe even, and that's me being generous and not taking his shitty attitude into account. I don't know anything about any kind of dancing, but I know you're good, Mari. I know you're as good as anyone who's been on the show, because you've made me watch the last three seasons with you. Plus, you've got that whole single mom, dead dad story, and they *love* that. So be real, okay? You are *at least* going through to callbacks. And then what? You come back here and do regional competitions forever? No way. If you get to L.A., you're good enough to stay there."

The unsolicited praise puffs up Maritza's ego even as the reality check deflates her generally sunny outlook. "Grace, come on, I don't want to be real," she whines and she knows it isn't particularly adult or attractive and she *definitely* knows Grace is right. She's been dodging having to think about this for weeks. "I want to keep seeing where this is going to go. I know it's selfish."

"Maybe a little," Grace says as she wrinkles her nose.

"But I like her, and she is so amazing, and all I want to do is spend any free time I have with her." It spills out in a rush, words tumbling end over end. "I can figure something out, Grace. I'm not trying to screw with Sarita. I just barely have any time to think from one day to the next and all I want to do is make the most of what we get. I'll work it out, I am totally going to work it out, somehow. Eventually."

"Before it's too late?" Grace lifts one straight black eyebrow, somehow able to keep her eyes on Maritza as she accepts her drink from Cliff and hands him a five-dollar bill.

"Well, no," Maritza admits, and oh, isn't it funny how guilt can feel just like the urge to throw up?

This is *exactly* why she has been avoiding this entire issue, and, as she follows Grace out of the Java Stop, she wonders how she can cram it back into the little box she's been keeping it in so she can stop thinking about it again.

"What do you suppose her response will be?" Theodora leans against the single tiny window in the tiny office that she and Craig share and blows a stream of cigarette smoke out into the alley behind Sucre Coeur. She taps off the ash and turns to raise one expertly groomed blonde eyebrow at Craig. "Hmm? Any guesses?"

Craig, seated at the desk, has to hold his knee down so that he stops compulsively tapping his foot. "Keep telling you, I've no idea, Theo." With his free, non-knee-clutching hand, he shuffles paperwork and pens around on the desktop; he picks things up and puts them down again. He looks up at his employer—no, *co-owner now*, he corrects himself, still trying to come to grips with his new reality. It's been twenty-four hours since he signed all of the paperwork that bought him a half share in the bakery he's worked in since he was in college, and grasping that is still a struggle.

The bottle of cheap champagne he and Alex consumed the night before probably didn't help matters. Craig rubs at his temples, trying to get the lingering hangover-ache to go away. One good thing about sinking all of one's meager savings and some substantial loans into a pair of businesses within a matter of months is that he and Alex will no longer be able to afford even cheap champagne for quite some time. He's got that going for him.

It doesn't do much to stave off the mild panic over the financial hole he and Alex have just dug for themselves, but he supposes that will wear off eventually as well.

Two personnel files sit in front of him on the desk. *Natasha Collins. Sarita Sengupta.* He shuffles them together while Theodora continues to defy Seattle's indoor smoking ban, and, as near as Craig can guess, she's mulling over the pair of conversations they're about to have with their most senior employees. One of them is going to have to fill the managerial gap he's just left behind, and neither of them is sure which might be the better for the job.

Or if either one of them might even *want* it.

A tentative tap at the office door lets them know that their time is up. Theodora hastily stubs out her cigarette as Craig pulls the first folder, Sarita's, from the desk. "Come in," he calls, not trusting his wobbly nervous knees to hold him up for even the two long steps it would take him to get to the door. Despite his best efforts, he can still hear a thready tremble in his voice and he takes a deep breath as the door creaks open.

Sarita's already big eyes are even larger than usual, dark and full of concern as she edges into the office clutching a slightly crushed-looking Java Stop cup. "Hi?"

"Hi, come on in, have a seat." He waves at the chair wedged into the corner opposite the door. "Hey, what's this, you didn't bring enough coffee to share with the class?"

It should be impossible, but her eyes widen farther. "I'm sorry, I didn't think—"

"It's a joke, darling." Theodora slides the window shut and smiles, and Craig marvels at her aplomb. She's not ruffled by this in the slightest—but then, he supposes she has no reason to be. She's been doing things like this for years; he's the one who's got a lot to learn. Theo picks up the file on the desk. "Go on, have a seat. Craig's comic timing is lacking today; don't worry about it."

Sarita drops her purse on the floor and nudges it under the indicated chair before taking what seems to be a very nervous seat. Her fingers are already tying themselves into white-knuckled knots around her battered cup. "Is everything all right? Did I get an order wrong? I know I was late Monday. I'm sorry; my advisor kept me late—"

Theo waves off the excuse and shakes her head, tossing back her blonde shag. "Nothing's wrong, darling. Honestly. Craig and I want to have a talk with you; we've got some news about the bakery."

Sarita's intake of breath is sharp. "The bakery?"

Craig squeezes his eyes shut. Theodora is a very kind and compassionate woman, but calming the agitated has never been her greatest strength. She has always, during their acquaintance, expected people to just calm down when she instructs them to do so, to banish worry at the drop of a hat. But the demand serves only to make nervous people even more nervous, and it's doing a bang-up job now, as Sarita's gaze bounces between the two of them. Her bottom lip is caught between her teeth and already looks a bit ragged.

Theodora opens her mouth, presumably to deliver more well-meaning but ineffective reassurance, but Craig can't take it anymore. *Better to get this over and done with.* "Listen, Sarita, I've bought into the bakery. It's all fine, I just own half of it now."

Behind him, Theodora clucks and sniffs, while Sarita's jitters still, and her eyes lock on Craig. "You did what?"

"Bought into the bakery," he says, with a nod that he can only hope is reassuring. "Me and Theo, we both own it now."

"Okay..." Sarita's head bobs in a slow nod so her messily piled hair slips forward. "You bought half the bakery."

His own nod is more emphatic. "I did."

Her gaze shifts to Theodora. "So what's that mean?"

"It means that Craig now quite rightfully has a very large share in a business he spends much more time actively running than I do." Theodora leans against the office wall and crosses her arms. "It was the least I could offer him for his years of dedication. It also means that there's a managerial position that's suddenly opened up, and that's where you come in."

The blood drains from Sarita's face. "You want me to be the manager?"

"We want to consider you for it," Craig interjects as Sarita's fingers begin to twist again. "It's a lot to ask of you, I know, but you have seniority, and you've been indispensable in your role as head decorator all these years."

She nods, a single, half-formed bob of her head, and her eyes take on a thoughtful, distracted cast. "And what would happen with that?"

"If we offer you the managerial position, we'll move Will up to head the decorating team." Theodora tosses it off quite matter-of-factly. "If we don't offer it to you or if you turn it down, you'll remain our chief frosting wrangler, and Natasha will be the manager."

Another of those slow not-quite-nods. "So it's me or Tash."

"You've each got unique qualities and strengths to bring to the position," Craig says, scooting his chair forward to rest his hand over hers. "But you also share the ability to stay firm yet flexible under pressure. You know how important that is, especially now that we've spent the last year developing the event baking side of things."

Sarita's fingers still, and she draws herself up, sitting very straight in her chair as she sucks in a deep breath. "Okay. This is a lot to take in."

"We can give you a couple of days to decide if you'd like to be in the running or not." Theodora slides the window open a crack. "If you both say yes, then starting Monday, we'll let each of you run the bakery for two weeks. For one of those weeks, you'll run it under my or Craig's supervision—to be terribly honest, probably Craig's—and the next week you'll run things alone. And then we'll compare and decide. Whichever way it goes, of course, we'd still want both of you to stay on board with us."

"Of course, no, that's fine." Thoughtful distance gives way to surprise and then something Craig has a split second to decide might be elation before Sarita leaps out of her chair and wraps her arms around his neck in a hug. "Oh, my God, Craig! Congratulations! This is amazing!"

The exuberance and velocity of the hug leaves Craig quite literally breathless, but he does manage to get out something that resembles a laugh as he squeezes her back. "Thanks, love. I'm personally finding owning a business to be rather terrifying, but Alex assures me that will eventually pass." He snorts. "Which is a bit rich coming from him, he's *still* terrified. I assume he's passing along someone else's advice."

Sarita pulls back, her smile bright. "You're going to do such a good job running this place. I mean you basically do it all anyway—" Her face flushes pink, and she slides guilty eyes over to Theodora. "Ah, sorry, Theo, I didn't mean—"

"No, you're exactly right, darling, that's precisely why all of this has happened." Apparently having decided she waited long enough, Theodora shoves the window open, leans out and lights a fresh Gauloise, but not before she casts a reassuring smile over her shoulder. "And so you know, your candid way of expression is one of your unique qualities that's helped put you in the running for this job. You won't sugarcoat and hedge and get us into schedule trouble with that way of thinking and speaking. That's very important."

Sarita toys with the ends of her hair; her smile is small and bashful now as her cheeks pink further. "I appreciate that. And your consideration. Really." Another long breath pulls her fully upright with her shoulders back and head up. "I'll let you know in a couple of days if I want to stay in the running."

"That would be grand. Thanks, Sarita." With Theodora half out the window smoking and Sarita looking far calmer than when they had started the meeting, Craig figures it's a good time to wrap things up. "Listen, I know it's a bit early for your shift, but the Farrells called and they'll be wanting another dozen cookie sandwiches for their party. I've made the cookies; do you think you could..."

"Oh, sure. No problem. Time is money, even if it's only thirty minutes. I could definitely use every extra bit of cash, thanks." Sarita grabs her bag and stands, bouncing a little on her toes. "I'm on it."

"If it's helpful," Theodora drawls from her window perch as a plume of smoke streams into the increasingly clammy air outside, "the managerial promotion does, of course, come with a fairly significant pay raise. Just so you're aware."

Sarita nods. "Great. Great, thank you."

She's out the door in a flurry of coffee fumes and wild hair; the office door clicks shut behind her. Craig turns to Theodora, trying not to wrinkle his nose at the smell of the smoke. "Well, that's one down. One to go."

Theodora's eyes are fixed on the door Sarita's just exited, and one sandaled foot taps out a tattoo on the concrete flooring. "You're sure we need this to be a multiple choice sort of thing?"

Craig thinks back to Sunday night's dinner conversation and gives a slow nod of his own. "Like I said, they both have different skills to bring to the table. Either one of them would be great. I can't pick between them myself; I've worked beside them for years. I gave you the two best candidates, but you're the tiebreaker; you've got to be."

With a frown rumpling her usually smooth brow, Theodora heaves a sigh and pitches her cigarette out into the mild rain that's just begun to fall. "Well, all right, darling, if you insist. I suppose it won't kill me to spend a month or two in one city for once."

Chapter Nine

"**G**ET YOUR FEET OFF THE COFFEE TABLE, JAVI. GOD, SHE'S going to think you're a savage." Using the orange and gold striped throw pillow that Javier has just chucked to the floor, Maritza delivers a hard blow across her brother's shins that makes him yelp and recoil. "And these pillows belong on the sofa!"

"They take up too much butt room! There's no squish to them!" Javier snatches up another pillow and throws it at Maritza, hooting when it bounces from the top of her head. "Find some other place for them, shove 'em in a closet or something; we're not gonna have any room to hang out on the couch otherwise."

Maritza tucks one pillow under her arm and rubs at the spot where the other pillow connected with her skull. Javier was right, the pillows were neither comfortable nor useful, but she and her mother had gone to way too much effort making sure they coordinated with the sofa and the rest of the living room, and she wanted everything to look its best when Sarita arrived. "Deal with it, Javi. Go sit at the desk or something if the sofa's so uncomfortable." She picks up the other pillow, brandishes it at her brother and bumps at his knees with her own until he gets up with a grumble and moves to the desk.

"The sofa's fine; it's totally comfortable once you get those pillows off it," he says as she tries to fluff the unfluffable pillows while she arranges them on the sofa with care. "And it looks fine without the pillows."

"It looks better *with* them." Stepping backward around the coffee table, Maritza stands in front of the television and tilts her head to squint at the couch. "Like right now, it looks great."

Javier rolls his eyes and turns to his laptop. His fingers fly across the keys to pull up Minecraft. "Yeah, okay, just try not to let her sit on it. You'll ruin the illusion."

"No! No video games!" Maritza vaults the sofa and skids across the hardwood floor to jab her brother in the side with her elbow. "Take a night off!"

"She's not here yet; she's not due for thirty minutes. Cut me some slack," Javier howls.

The click of heels on the floor signals Susana Quiñones' entrance into the living room before her voice rings out over those of her squabbling offspring. The authority in her steps cuts right through the bickering. She needs only one word to silence them completely: "Children."

Maritza looks at her mother and winces with guilt. Susana's face is calm and smooth, but her dark eyes glitter, and her chin is raised; she's got her take-no-shit aura firmly in place tonight. She can't even be a little offended at being twenty-three and called a child by her mother. She's totally earned it. "Sorry, Mama."

"I don't know what your friend would think if she were to come in to see the two of you acting like babies in a playpen. Nothing good." Susana glides through the living room to straighten the throw pillows, brush an invisible speck of dust from the television, and adjust the position of the Galileo thermometer on its shelf. Somehow, she spots a microscopic thread of cat hair on the sleeve of her soft cantaloupe-colored sweater, plucks it off and deposits it in the small trash can by the desk. Her hand absently brushes Maritza's hair as she passes by. "Dinner's almost ready. Come help me set the table, both of you."

She glides back out of the room, a vision of stateliness to which Maritza can only hope to aspire. "Why can't I be that calm?"

"It works for her. You'd be boring if you were calm." Javier closes his laptop and gets to his feet, jostling Maritza's elbow. "Come on, Mari. Chill. The house looks great, Mama's making a great meal, and I promise not to tell all your embarrassing kiddie stories in front of your friend. It's gonna be fine, hey?"

"Ha," Maritza gets out, the one syllable as shaky as the jittering hamsters that seem to have taken up residence in her belly. She can't help but repeat her mother's actions in reverse as she walks to the big, light kitchen—a twitch of the Galileo thermometer, another quarter-inch clockwise; a brush of her hand across the television; a nudge at the pillows. She would have gone on looking for more imperfections had Javier not rolled his eyes and grabbed her wrist to pull her into the kitchen.

She handles the distribution of silverware, napkins and hot pads across the wooden expanse of their big kitchen table, not trusting her hands to manage the breakable dishes. It seemed like a great idea to invite Sarita for dinner, and her family was being amazingly helpful and supportive. Granted, they would be supportive and helpful of just about anyone who wasn't Nicky.

A knife shakes in her hand as she puts it down on a folded napkin. However great the idea and however supportive her family, she can't calm the crawl of her nerves or the hopping of the stomach hamsters. To introduce anyone to her mother and brother for any reason is a big, big deal, and the last one had gone *so* badly. She knows Sarita won't be anything like Nicky, and thank God for *that*, but the disaster still lingers in the back of her mind. It's hanging out with yesterday's conversation with Grace and it is doing its best to make her absolutely miserable.

Maritza circles the dinner table, willing her hands to be steadier as she sets out the salt and pepper shakers. Her feet ache from rehearsal this morning, another reminder that she's *got* to tell

Sarita about the *Dance Nation* auditions. She's not as confident as Grace in her chances of making it to callbacks, let alone onto the show, but she has to admit Grace is right: If she gets out of Seattle and free of Nicky, once she's got even five minutes of national television exposure, she might be able to parlay that into some kind of gig, at least into an audition or two. The likelihood of her coming back to Seattle isn't zero, but it's definitely in the very low double digits. She's not a nervous teenager anymore; she's ready to move up to the next level. It's an inevitability, much like the end of the coziness of this new relationship with Sarita. From here on out, assuming Sarita wants to deal with a long-distance love affair, it's all hard work. *What if she decides I'm not worth it? What if she doesn't like me as much as I like her?*

Damn it, why did I have to meet her now?

Deep in thought, she jumps when Susana rests a hand on her shoulder. "Doorbell, *mija*. Showtime."

Maritza nods and smooths her T-shirt over her hips. She hopes she looks okay. Apple green isn't really her color, but she likes it a lot anyway, and she's taken scissors to this shirt so that it's strategically ripped but also closely fitted, and her jeans are supposed to be casual but they're her good jeans and they fit just right, and she's wearing heels but a low heel, a very simple sandal; she wants to look nice, but not as if she's trying hard, and—

"Mari," Javier calls from the front door, and he just *sounds* as if he's smirking. "There's some chick here asking for you."

Oh, my God! I took too long!

Maritza nearly trips on her sprint out of the kitchen and catches the thin heel of her sandal on the shag rug under the table. She yanks her foot free and clatters into the living room, about as far from her intended cool, dignified entrance as it was possible to get. "Hi," she gasps out, resisting the urge to spread her hand over her racing heart.

Sarita's eyes widen slightly. "You okay?"

"Fine, I'm fine." She smiles, reaching out a hand for Sarita's and trying not to breathe heavily all over the place. "Just really happy to see you."

Behind her, Javier clears his throat. "So, you were going to do introductions and not just stand around being rude, right?"

Maritza manages to keep her smile from hardening in place until she cranes her neck around to look up at her brother. "Go help Mom," she grits out between her teeth.

"Sure, sure." Javi, as usual, is impervious to the insistent fury she's trying her damnedest to radiate in his direction. "I have to tell her how impolite you're being. Were you raised in a barn?"

He's out of her reach before she can do more than start to swing her arm, and he bounds into the kitchen. Maritza drops her face into the palm of her free hand and whimpers.

"Hey. It's okay." Sarita tugs on the hand she still holds, and when Maritza chances a look at her, she's got a smile on her face. "I get it. I have a brother too, remember? Don't worry about it." She plants a gentle kiss on Maritza's lips that works its usual magic in steadying her knees and calming her heart. When Sarita pulls back, her lips are curved in a sweet smile. "You look great. I'm happy to see you, too." Sarita glances around. "Oh, this is such a cute house. What's that awesome smell?"

"Do you mean the bamboo diffuser thing over there in the corner with the lemongrass oil, or the dinner smell?" Maritza asks as she tugs Sarita to the sofa and pulls her coat off.

"I always love lemongrass, but yeah, I'm talking about dinner." Sarita lets out a delicious laugh as Maritza drags her down onto the sofa. "I am loving the smell. And I am loving how you look tonight."

The palm of her hand skims over Maritza's belly as she makes the statement, and her voice drops to a husky timbre. Her eyes are dark and hooded. Her sweet smile is distinctly less sweet as she goes for another kiss, one that lingers, a little exploratory, a lot hot. Maritza's lips part to let out a sigh.

"Ahem."

When she tilts her head back, Maritza can just see over the arm of the sofa where her mother stands hipshot with arms crossed over her chest. A wooden spoon clutched in one of Susana's slender hands looks less like a cooking accessory and more like the threat it used to represent when Maritza was a child. "I assume this lovely young woman is Sarita?"

Sarita scrambles to her feet. A blush stretches down her neck as she holds out her hand. "Mrs. Quiñones. Hello."

"Mmm. Hello." Susana lifts an eyebrow and lets her gaze skim over Sarita. "You can call me Susana. Pleasure to meet you. You look very nice."

Sarita fingers the silver bangles on her wrist, tugging them out from under the long sleeve of her soft, deep-plum top. "Thank you."

"Come help me in the kitchen." It's not a request. Susana turns on her heel and marches into the kitchen. Maritza scrambles up from the sofa, making sure her mother isn't looking when she clasps Sarita's hand again and kisses her cheek.

"You do look nice. Thank you for coming."

"Any chance to see you." Sarita squeezes her hand and walks into the kitchen, pulling Maritza behind her. "What's for dinner?"

Susana looks up from the pot on the stove as the two women walk in. "*Pollo guisado*," she says, giving the contents of the pot a good stir. "You like chicken stew?"

"I like whatever smells great in there," Sarita replies with a grin, and Maritza can pinpoint the moment when her mother forgives them for the spectacle in the living room. She tries to keep her sigh of relief inaudible.

But Javi's sharp elbow to her ribs knocks the gust of breath out of her. "You going to introduce me now?" he asks around a mouthful of the rice he snuck as he was putting the bowl on the table.

"Gross, Javi, and I'm supposed to be the one raised in a barn?" She returns his jab with one of her own. "You didn't introduce yourself at the door?"

"She asked for you; I called you over," he says with a shrug. "I figured at some point you'd remember your manners."

"You're one to talk." Maritza flips her hair back over her shoulder and walks over to where Susana and Sarita have their heads together over the pot of chicken. "Sarita. You didn't officially meet my brother. This is Javier." She jerks a thumb over her shoulder. She doesn't have to look to know that Javi is grinning around another mouthful of food. "Forgive him, he's deranged."

Not bothering to acknowledge Maritza's crack, Javi does at least swallow the food in his mouth before walking over with an extended hand. "Call me Javi. Mari says you're in the philosophy program at UDub, right? It's a big campus, but I think I've seen you around, maybe."

"Well, I'm there more than anywhere else besides the bakery, so I guess it's possible. You look familiar, too." Sarita grins up at Javier as she shakes his hand. "You look... tall. But just about everyone does to me."

"Yeah, I'm not that tall, and anyway tall is a little less distinctive than your hair is," Javi points out with a chuckle. "You're like Mari: the higher the hair, the closer to actual human height."

"I will kill you," Maritza states and ignores her mother's chiding *tsk*. "Actually kill you. Maybe while you sleep, but maybe I'll let you see it coming."

But Sarita is laughing. "His short jokes are better than Devesh's. I don't mind. He can live."

"Thank you, Sarita. I appreciate your generosity and your sense of humor." With a nod, and clearly pleased with himself, Javier steps over to the table and pulls out a chair. "Come on. Sit next to me for dinner. You can sit next to Maritza any time."

As she passes, Sarita grabs Maritza's hand for another quick squeeze and plants a kiss on her cheek. "This is great. Thank you for the invitation. Your family is fantastic."

Her cheeks are still burning from Javi's ribbing, but as she watches Sarita sit down next to her brother, the warmth of relief pools in Maritza's stomach, relaxing her shoulders and stopping the pesky tremble in her knees. Maybe this won't be a disaster after all.

Behind her, Susana makes a tiny *hmph* that might be approval, and her fingers curl around Maritza's upper arm. "I like her, *mija*. So far so good. Much better than the last one. Too bad you can't dance with *her*, hmm?"

Maritza laughs, and hopes it doesn't sound as weak as it feels. "To say the least."

SARITA'S CHEST IS TIGHT, AS IF SHE'S BEEN HOLDING HER BREATH all evening. Out on the porch as she waits for Maritza, she sucks in a good lungful of the cool night air and forces it all out in a whoosh.

Better.

The door opens and floods the porch with the warm light from the living room. As Sarita turns and squints into the glow, Maritza steps out with her tote bag and a big duffel slung over her shoulder. "Ready?"

"When you are." Sarita tugs on the strap of the duffel. "All this for one night?"

"Morning rehearsal. You wouldn't believe how many pairs of shoes are in this thing." Maritza flashes a grin before she pulls the door shut behind her and zips up her jacket. "Okay, it's only three pairs, plus towels, two changes of clothes, et cetera, et cetera. The life of a dancer does not involve traveling lightly."

"I can see that." She thinks about being polite and offering to take Maritza's bag for her, but Maritza swings it around as though it's stuffed with feathers, and Sarita is not at all sure she could pull that off. She settles for trotting down the porch steps to pop open the trunk of her car, sweeping the lid up with a flourish. "Go ahead and toss it in here; give yourself a break."

Maritza tosses the bag on top of a stack of textbooks and closes the trunk. "Do you have books *everywhere*?"

"Pretty much." Sarita circles the car and opens the passenger door. "Hazard of the trade. Being an academic isn't without its baggage. Although I was supposed to take those back to the campus bookstore last year and haven't gotten around to it."

"Woman, do not leave that money on the table. I know Javi doesn't get full value back on his books when he sells them, but dollars are dollars. We can swing by the bookstore in the morning before you drop me off at the studio. I'll help you carry them." Maritza grins as she drops into the car. "Buy you a coffee, too."

"Hmm, tempting." Sarita grins back and starts the car. "Listen, thank you for dinner tonight. Seriously. That was great. Your family is great."

A chuckle. "Even Javi?"

"Oh, come on, especially Javi; he's hilarious." In fact, he'd kept her in stitches all through dinner with cracks about everything from the weather to physics, and he'd told stories about his and Maritza's childhood that had Susana reaching across the table to give him a good smack on the arm. "You won the sibling lottery there."

Maritza twists in the seat to face Sarita and tugs her hair out from under the seatbelt. "Didn't you win it too? Halfway at least."

"Halfway." Sarita sighs. Shanti had sent a text message earlier in the day while Sarita decorated an order of baby shower cupcakes. A picture message, actually. An old framed photo of Sarita, Anjali and Devesh at Disneyland with their skinny child arms flung around each other as they posed with huge grins in front of Sleeping Beauty's castle. Sarita could only guess that her mother had come across it while she was cleaning out the closets or the attic. She shakes her head, shakes off the memory and focuses on the road. "Trust me. You won it. I haven't been to a family dinner that peaceful since I don't know when. So thank you again. I liked your mom and your brother."

"They liked you too. Mom liked you right away." It's dark, and Maritza's head bows and her hair tumbles down to hide her face, but a sidelong glance lets Sarita catch a glimpse of the bashful little smile she's come to just about love to see. "She definitely wants me to bring you back sometime."

Sarita steers the car onto the highway. "I'd love to come back, for sure. I'm not saying especially for your mom's cooking, but it helps a *lot*."

"And that will take you from like to love in a hurry." Amusement warms Maritza's voice. "And I know for a fact that when your parents leave, she'll probably invite you over for dinner every week just to make sure you're getting fed."

"Parents never do believe you can feed yourself."

"Not really." Maritza pulls her knees up onto the car seat and wraps her arms around them. "Mom makes dinner for an army of Javi's friends once a week at least, unless she's called in for extra shifts at the hospital. And even then she leaves like, a big pot of soup in the fridge for Javi to heat up. No one goes hungry on Susana Quiñones' watch, not even for a minute."

Sarita laughs softly. "Just like my mom. She makes me bring leftovers to Craig and Alex all the time. She's probably going to worry more about them getting fed than me when she and my dad leave, now that they're both self-employed and in debt."

"Tell her my mom is *happy* to take over. She's never met them, but I can promise you that's the most likely outcome." Maritza grins. "Speaking of Craig. That was real at dinner? You might become the manager there? How are you feeling about that?"

Flipping the car's blinker, Sarita stalls by pretending to concentrate on moving across the all-but-empty lanes of the highway. It's not a long stall, of course, it can't be, but it gives her a precious second or two to think about her answer. "Still a little surprised by it. Not about Theo asking Craig to buy in; that's probably the least surprising thing. He's been there for so long and he works so hard, he deserves to be a part-owner."

"So the surprise is that they offered you a potential management job," Maritza guesses, nodding. "Haven't you been working there for a long time yourself, though? You're probably due as much as Craig is."

Sarita thinks of and discards a dozen self-deprecating responses in a handful of seconds. "I don't know about that," she finally says. "I don't know if I'm due any more than Natasha. She's been there about as long as I have, and she works as hard as I do. Harder, maybe, what with her whole single mom thing."

"You're a full-time grad student," Maritza points out—nearly literally as one slender finger taps at Sarita's shoulder. She moves her hand to tuck a strand of Sarita's hair behind her ear, a gesture that stalls Sarita's heart in her chest for a full second. "I would say you work at least as hard as Tash. You both basically have two full-time jobs."

Maritza continues to trace her finger along Sarita's jaw, up to the outer edge of her ear, back down her neck. It makes it hard for Sarita to concentrate on driving, let alone on their conversation. She manages to catch her breath and wills the shivers under her skin to pause. "That's another thing. Being the main decorator is already a lot to do, plus I'm still trying to fight my way into the doctoral program at school, remember." The familiar butterflies take flight in her stomach as Maritza starts flat-out playing with her hair. "I don't even know if I want to take on management responsibility. Right now I don't take my work home. As manager, I'd have to take at least some. Craig does."

"So say no." Maritza's voice is a whiskey-and-cigarettes purr, her fingers nimble as they twist through Sarita's curls. As far as Sarita can tell without taking her eyes off the road to look, Maritza is utterly oblivious to the gentle devastation her casual gestures are wreaking on Sarita. It's torture, but Sarita doesn't want it to stop.

She tightens her fingers on the steering wheel. "I probably should, but at the same time I don't want to dismiss it out of hand. I can't say the extra money wouldn't be welcome." The laugh she lets out is a little wobbly, probably due to Maritza allowing the back of her fingers to trace along the soft skin at the crook of Sarita's elbow. "But I don't know. I can't decide. I'm not a good decider. I don't know what I want to do; I'm not like you."

The fingers disappear, and it's such a disappointment. "Like me?" Maritza asks.

"Well, yeah, I mean, you know what you want to do. You dance; you've always danced; you've basically always known you wanted to dance. I don't have that." She wants Maritza to touch her again, but then again, her mental clarity is returning, little by little, and that is useful because she wants to find a way out of this conversation.

"Oh, right. Got it." Maritza withdraws into her seat and curls up to toy with her own hair. "But I didn't have to choose between two things; that makes the difference. I saw dancers and I wanted to dance for a living. Do you want to decorate cakes and manage a bakery for a living? I'm guessing not, since you majored in philosophy."

"No, but on the other hand, if I get into the doctoral program and then graduate with my PhD..." Sarita can't help the wry twist in her voice. "Well. Careers in academia are neither numerous nor well-paying. So I might be grateful to have a bakery management gig to go with the very expensive piece of sheepskin I'm trying to get my hands on. I really love philosophy, but I also love to eat. And I appreciate living in a place with a roof and doors and all that."

"Ah ha. I can see where that would be useful," Maritza says with a sage nod. "Says the girl who has to pay for her own dance shoes and sews her own costumes. A pizzeria paycheck only goes so far."

"I wish I could see you dance." It comes out of nowhere before Sarita stops to think, a wistful thread of a sentence that she hopes in the next instant that Maritza doesn't hear. *What a hell of a clumsy way to change a subject!*

So much for wishful thinking. "You do?"

"I didn't mean to just blurt it out like that but, yeah." Her entire face is heating up as if she's stuck her head in one of the bakery ovens. "Sorry. It just *came out*."

"You saw me dance at Alex's party," Maritza says and punctuates the statement with a light little laugh. "We danced together, even."

"Yeah but... I want to watch you." It sounds almost dirty, as if she's confessing to some fantasy, and Sarita's face burns hotter. Okay. She *is* confessing to a fantasy.

A thoughtful silence falls over the car like a blanket; there's no sound besides their breathing and the car engine. After a minute or two, Sarita's about ready to turn on the radio, if she can only remember what station she left it on. Probably NPR. Not ideal.

Maritza points up the highway. "Go two more exits past your turnoff."

Sarita risks a quick sidelong glance. "Where are we going?" she asks, as if she doesn't know. Her heart doubles its pace in her chest, and the butterflies are in full-blown riot.

Maritza's face is serene, but her eyes twinkle just before she kisses Sarita's cheek. "I've got a key to the studio and a hot lady friend who needs a distraction and wants to see me dance. I hope now's a good a time as any?"

THE ONLY ILLUMINATION IN THE STUDIO AS THEY TIPTOE IN COMES from dim security lights, soft golden light spilling down in streaks on the polished wooden floors. Maritza tosses down her bag and rushes to catch the alarm that's beeping faster and faster behind the reception desk. "Two seconds," she says, flashing a grin over her shoulder even as she flips down the alarm cover and punches in a code. "And... done. We are now officially not trespassers."

"Are you sure they're going to be okay with us being here?" Sarita shoves her hands into her jacket pockets and curls her fingers into fists against the silky linings. She can all but hear the thump of her heart now and she's half nerves from being somewhere she probably shouldn't and half excitement at the prospect of getting to see Maritza dance. "You won't get into trouble?"

"I'm the only dancer with a key and the alarm code." Maritza swings back around the reception desk. With a deft bend and scoop, she's got her bag back over her shoulder, and in another smooth motion her arm is linked through Sarita's, and they're sailing through the door to the first dance studio. "Fred trusts me."

Sarita blinks. "Just you? He doesn't trust your partner?"

"*I* barely trust my partner." The bag is down on the floor again with a clunk, followed closely by Maritza's purple coat. "I hope you don't mind if we don't turn the main lights on. I kind of like it like this. It sets a mood."

And that makes Sarita's mouth go dry, and then the butterflies start their abdominal dance again. "You... you want to set a mood?"

"I'm not going to pass up the opportunity when it presents itself." Maritza winks and drops to the floor, patting a spot right next to her. "Come on, get comfy while I put on my shoes."

The wood floor looks battered, but it's shiny with wax and seems immaculately clean, so Sarita wriggles out of her own jacket and spreads it out to put a cushion between her butt and the glossy wood. Settling into her improvised nest, she watches Maritza with interest as the bulky green canvas dance bag is unzipped and a pair of spindly looking sandals is extracted from its overstuffed depths. Sarita stares at the shoes. "You're not going to dance in those, are you?"

She gets an impish grin in reply. "That's kind of the idea, hon."

"But they look…" Insubstantial, unsupportive—she could break an ankle at the first good turn. "… fragile?"

"Also the idea. But trust me, babe. These shoes are built to take the beating I give them. They're harder on me than I am on them." Maritza fits her feet into the shoes and has them buckled up almost before Sarita can blink. She's on her feet in one fluid motion, bending over her purse to pull out her iPhone before she glides to the stereo system in the corner. The deceptively slender heels sound a series of substantial clicks as Maritza walks, and when Sarita lets her gaze travel up from the shoes, she notices that walking on them seems to be doing some amazing things for Maritza's already fairly spectacular ass.

Well, sign me up for that fan club.

In the next instant, Sarita is shaken out of her bordering-on-the-lecherous thoughts by a sudden boom of synthesizer and brass horns emanating from the stereo speakers. And then—

—then she is utterly captivated by Maritza.

The music is dance pop, not what Sarita would associate with ballroom dancing, but Maritza's movements are unmistakably ballroom, maybe not strictly so, but Sarita definitely recognizes them from the nights she's been stuck watching *Dancing with the Stars* with her mother. Sandaled feet twist and turn on the polished wood, the heels that Sarita was so worried about barely touch down—all of Maritza's movement seems to come from the balls of her feet and the tips of her red-pedicured toes flowing up through her legs to her hips. Sarita's gaze pauses there, locked on the back and forth shimmy, on the muscles of Maritza's thighs against the snug fabric of her blue jeans.

"Eyes up here." The order is delivered with a throaty laugh, and Sarita jerks her eyes up to see Maritza's broad, bright smile beamed right at her. There are mirrors on every wall of the studio, reflecting Maritza's good humor and her hypnotic movements in all directions. Maritza tosses her hair and points a finger at Sarita, turning her hand palm up to shift the gesture into a beckoning crook of her finger. "And get over here, pretty lady."

Sarita almost chokes on her own laughter. "Oh no. I do not dance. Remember the party?"

"I remember you were drunk, and I was drunk, and nobody was at their best, but we were having a lot of fun, so get your ass *over* here." Both hands now extended, she starts to sashay over to where Sarita is frozen. "Don't make me come pull you up. You'd be amazed at what I can do backward and in high heels. I don't think you want to test it."

"I wanted to watch you," Sarita protests as she curls up into a tighter ball on her jacket. "We came here so I could see *you* dance. This isn't fair."

"You're watching me now." But Maritza relents and she never lets up on her movement. Her feet flash back and forth and her hands run up the back of her neck to give her hair a playful toss. "You have until the end of this song."

"To the end of the next," Sarita bargains, tucking her hands under her chin while she bats her eyelashes in as innocent a manner as she can manage. "Please?"

Maritza rolls her eyes, but it's a good-natured eye-roll. "Well, how can I resist that face? Fine. This song, and the next one, and then you get up, and I show you how to dance when we're both sober."

Sarita nods. "Deal."

Maritza throws herself fully into the dance, shimmying and whirling her way around the studio in mirrored quadruplicate and then some. The light winks from her sandals and from the thin silver chain looped around her neck. Twinkles of light spark all around her as she twists and moves. Her hair takes on a life of its own, becoming as much a part of the dance as Maritza's feet as the chestnut waves toss and tumble around her heart-shaped face.

She's melting into the music, her face is alight with joy and Sarita can't take her eyes from her. *Amazing. She's amazing.* She's more than Sarita had even attempted to imagine; every move is precise yet liquid and her stage presence is magnetic.

And her smile, of course, is the cherry on the ice cream sundae, gorgeous and sincere and capable of making an entire room of people fall in love with her. Since Sarita is all alone, the force of it just about lays her out flat and sets every nerve ending on fire.

Forgetting the deal, Sarita gets to her feet, trying to ignore the fact that her movements are so much less graceful and sensual than Maritza's, and she steps over to where Maritza faces the mirror with her eyes closed, her arms up over her head and her hands clasped as she slowly shimmies in place. Opening one eye, Maritza spots Sarita's advance and offers a lopsided grin that makes Sarita's heart take off into space.

"You win," Sarita whispers as she slides her hands along Maritza's waist and gathers the hem of Maritza's shirt until she can glide her palms right against Maritza's smooth brown skin. "I want to dance with you now."

Maritza turns in Sarita's hands to curl her fingers down into the waistband of Sarita's jeans and uses the grip to pull their bodies close together. "Good," she purrs, taking Sarita's earlobe between her teeth for a quick nip. "This next song was for you anyway."

Goosebumps ripple across Sarita's skin as Maritza turns her around and pulls her back in, snug and intimate. Music pulses in heavy, thick beats around them, and Maritza guides their bodies into a sultry sway with one arm wrapped around Sarita's waist. Her free hand slides along the underside of Sarita's arm to nudge it upward until Sarita lifts her arm and bends it back to tangle her fingers in Maritza's hair. She tilts her head back and closes her eyes; her last glimpse is a hazy picture of the two of them reflected in the studio mirrors as Maritza lowers her head to press her lips to the curve of Sarita's neck.

The bottom of Sarita's stomach drops when Maritza's hand squirms into her jeans, past the barrier of her panties, to rest at the juncture of Sarita's thighs with palm and fingers cupped around the soft nest of Sarita's pubic hair and the warm mound there. She starts with a whimper and then melts into a moan as Maritza's middle finger crooks, gently working between the folds of soft skin to nestle, just for a moment, before she shifts her hand up so that the pad of her finger rests over Sarita's clit.

Torment builds in Sarita's chest as Maritza's finger lies still, a feather-light touch on the most sensitive part of her. She wants to rock her hips forward, to move, to relieve the tension, but Maritza's other arm tightens around her waist. One word then, on a teasing thread of a whisper.

"Patience..."

Sarita has to let out her breath, a formless shuddering sigh, as Maritza trails the tip of her tongue along Sarita's neck. Taut nerves make her tremble; her legs want to give out beneath her, to tumble the two of them to the floor so she can try to repay Maritza for this wonderful torture.

The fingertip moves then, the slightest of slips. Maritza's finger is soft, sliding over Sarita's clit with just a little bit of friction, delicious friction and warmth and wet—

"You're so tense," Maritza says, her laughter a light tease. The hand that's not down Sarita's jeans has slipped up under Sarita's sweater to lie against her skin where Maritza's thumb traces the same spot over and over. "Let me fix that for you."

She pulls her hands away and Sarita tries not to pout as she opens her eyes, tries not to feel bereft. She lets Maritza guide her to where they've left her bag and their jackets and lets her lower them to the floor. Her sweater is tugged away and rolled up to make a pillow, and she grins when Maritza sees that she didn't wear a bra.

"You are *gorgeous*," Maritza breathes, just before she takes one of Sarita's nipples between her teeth. The tip of her tongue flicks across the nipple to make it tighten and send ripples of excitement all through Sarita, ripples that pulse from her middle to every nerve ending.

She tugs at Maritza's top. "Off," she says as she gathers fabric under her fingers and pulls. "Please."

"Greedy." But it's said with a chuckle and a soft, fond smile as Maritza sits back. Her sweater is tossed aside, followed swiftly by her pale ivory bra. She kisses Sarita. "Got to get the rest of you naked."

"Boots," Sarita gasps as Maritza unbuttons her jeans and starts to pull them down.

"I got it, honey." With a pair of zips and thumps the boots are gone, and Maritza takes care of the rest of what little Sarita is wearing without ceremony; she wriggles jeans and panties down Sarita's legs and throws them to join the rest of their clothing. She stops, then, kneeling between Sarita's thighs and staring down with a smile that manages to disarm the self-consciousness Sarita feels at being observed naked and sprawled out on the floor of a dance studio.

Maritza touches Sarita's stomach for one burning second before she snatches her hand back. "You're just so gorgeous," she says as her hands dart out now to trail down Sarita's thighs; her fingers curve to grip and pull so that Sarita's knees are up. "I can't decide..."

But she must, because in the next instant Maritza's lying on her stomach, and Sarita gasps at the first touch of tongue against her clit.

She'd forgotten how good it feels to go bare, tongue on skin, warm and wet and slippery-soft. Maritza's lips close with gentleness around her clit, alternating soft sucks with flicks of tongue, little teasing touches sparking need up Sarita's spine. It's a need that builds as Maritza pulls back with a happy sigh. "Love this," she says, and then she dips back down and this time, there's no more teasing.

The drawback of being on a wooden floor when someone's going down on you, Sarita realizes quickly, is that there are no sheets or blankets to grab when your climax starts to build. She can only gasp, breath catching in her throat, while Maritza works her over, working one middle finger and then another into Sarita with her hand palm up as her fingertips move in the soft wet warmth until Sarita's breath is not catching, no, it comes out in long, long gasps, one after another.

"Don't stop, oh, no, don't stop," she rasps, grabbing at Maritza's head, her fingers getting tangled in the long, dark waves of Maritza's hair. Sarita's hips lift off the floor, and Maritza's tongue, that gentle, relentless, caressing tongue, keeps up its work, tongue-tip stroking over clit, and Maritza's fingers move inside of Sarita; they shift and thrust in rhythm, a rhythm that builds steadily now, and Sarita reaches, she lifts, up, up, almost, so close, oh God—

She comes hard, sucking in one large, sharp gasp of air that comes right back out in a noisy cry that bounces off the studio walls. Her feet flex, her fingers tighten, her entire body is tense for a hard, amazing second before it all drains away and leaves her a limp puddle on the studio floor.

Soft terry cloth drifts over her just as she starts to feel chilly; Sarita lifts her head to see a huge purple towel draped over her torso. "From the bag of wonders," Maritza says as she curls up against Sarita. "Don't you love dating a dancer? We're so handy."

"Not my primary point of attraction to you," Sarita manages to get out, and she's rewarded with a rich, happy giggle. "But yeah, I am appreciating it right now."

"Gimme a corner, it's just big enough for two if we share." Maritza wriggles closer to get farther under the towel and tucks her head into Sarita's neck. "Mmm. That was fun. Never did it here before."

"Wow, I get to be a first something? Nice." But something occurs to her, and Sarita gives a quick glance around the studio. "Uh, wait. Does Fred do cameras?"

"I disabled them with the alarm," Maritza assures her. Her next happy giggle is a pleasant tickle at Sarita's neck. "I didn't *know* you were going to seduce me, but I thought, you know, just in case."

"I'm sorry, me seduce you? Oh, no. I am not the one who danced—"

"You *asked* me to dance, and then you *interrupted* me."

"Shut up," Sarita says, and her laugh rattles up from her belly. "Shut up and kiss me, and get your damn jeans off. I'll remind you of what me seducing you is like..."

Chapter Ten

ON FRED'S COUNT OF THREE, MARITZA WHIRLS AWAY FROM Nicky and spins out three twirls across the studio floor before she stops and tosses her hair back with a wink and a smile that feels more like a grimace. It must look like one, too, because Nicky answers it with a roll of his eyes.

"Try harder," he snaps as he comes down from a high kick with a half-twist back and then forward again before he pulls her into the next part of their Argentine tango. "It's fucking unprofessional that you can't fake a great stage smile. You never could; it always costs us points."

She doesn't answer, concentrating instead on her next steps. *You're the one that costs us points*, she thinks with no little resentment. *You showboat like you're on TV, you mug like an idiot for the judges. They're not dumb, they know what you're doing.* Their Presentation scores in recent months had suffered, and if her failure to convince the judges that she was unconditionally happy to dance with this walking ego trip was part of that, it was not and never had been a very large part, of that she was convinced. And Fred agreed with her.

Maritza lets Nicky guide her down, one knee bent and the other stretched elegantly back, her toes pointed, and this time, since she's facing herself in the mirror, her smile is without fault. Not that it truly mattered. Presentation wouldn't matter for *Dance Nation*, not the way it did in competition. The judging panels from preliminaries on up were looking for dancers with great technique, who stood out with personality and that intangible *something* that looked as if it would translate well to television.

She knows she has great technique and personality. She's not sure about the *something*. But she hopes. If either of them has it, anyway, it's her. Nicky's got technique and technique alone.

Oh, be fair. He's pretty, too.

But mostly, Nicky's advantage is technique. Very, very good technique. The sigh that bubbles up from her stomach, Maritza stifles before it can emerge. That technique makes her look good, she has to admit. For all of Nicky's faults as a person, he makes her look very good. That and her own assets are what will get them through preliminary audition rounds and to the main audition stage. *I need him*, she reminds herself, and with effort she can ignore the knot of despair that forms in her stomach every time she chants the mantra: *I need him. Five more weeks.*

Who's counting the days? Not her. Certainly not. She's absolutely not going to cross another day off her bedroom wall calendar in sparkly gold pen when she gets home, no sir. And she's certainly not about to run her third pen dry doing so. Heavens no.

"And... break." Fred claps and bends down to pick up a pair of water bottles. "Okay, you two. That Argentine is looking really, really good. I don't know if I can choose between that and your samba right now."

"I thought we decided on the samba." Nicky snatches a bottle from Fred's hand without so much as a *thanks* and twists off the cap, glaring at them before he takes a long swig. He swallows and snorts. "The samba gets people's attention. We have to catch the eye right off the bat; a tango just doesn't have the juice, even an Argentine."

"And you're not the only dancer that thinks that," Fred replies, and if his calm is forced, Maritza can't tell. It's impressive. "Samba, cha-cha, jive—everyone wants to pull out the big guns. You stand out if you go against the grain. They'll have seen dozens of sambas by the time they get to Seattle, and God knows how many that day alone." When Nicky rolls his eyes, Fred takes a step forward and snaps his fingers in Nicky's face. "Hey! You listen to me, kid. I'm following all the whispers, rumors and flat-out facts I can find and I am not doing it for fun. Every dance teacher in a four-state radius plus British Columbia wants to get their best dancers on that show. They haven't held auditions in the Pacific Northwest in years. Everyone sees this as an opportunity."

Nicky crouches by his bag and rummages through it for a towel. He glares up at Fred as he fishes out blue terry cloth and wipes his face. "Yeah, Fred, I *know*. And that's *why* we're doing our samba. We've got the best one in the region. It stands out *against* everyone else. We're *better*."

Maritza tilts her head. Nice of him to include her for once.

Her movement catches Nicky's eye. "You agree with me, don't you?" he demands. "You know our samba is unbeatable. We have to stand out, Mari." His voice is almost a plea, but she knows him too well to believe it's at all sincere, even if he did actually deign to call her by name. He just wants his way.

The hell of it is, she doesn't entirely disagree with him. Their samba *is* incredible; it does stand out in competition. Even with their abysmal Presentation scores, it's one of the best dances they do and always has been. It's bright, it's flashy, it's sexy, and technically it's the most complicated number in their repertoire.

But Fred has a point. Even if their samba is great, it will be one of hundreds. There's no telling where their number will fall on audition day, and she can't count on luck to go early in all of the rounds. She doesn't want to be just another spinning, whirling blur of sequins.

Their samba is indeed one of their best dances—but point for point, as much as Nicky has always considered it boring, their Argentine tango is better. They'll start off at an advantage just because it's not a samba or jive, but then the routine itself is tight as hell, low-key sexy with a slow burn and it shows off their lines and control as nothing else ever could. It truly is a showcase of technique and, yes, personality. It's also the one number that takes advantage of their mutual animosity, which lends a necessary tension to their movements and calls up a simmering chemistry to bubble between them.

She really, really would prefer that they do the Argentine tango.

"Well?" Nicky asks, still keeping up the façade of sincerity.

Maritza lets her sigh escape, blowing the air out to make wisps of her hair dance around her face. "Nicky, when we do the Argentine in exhibition, it's always a massive hit—"

The veneer drops, and Nicky's face twists in thunderous rage. "Fuck you both." Scrambling to his feet, he snatches up his bag and stomps out of the studio. His furious flounce is somewhat ruined by the fact that the door can't be slammed thanks to its air-control mechanism, but he makes up for it by snapping at a flock of eight-year-old tap students.

Fred winces. "I'm going to have to apologize to all of their mothers. Did I hear him drop another f-bomb at those kids?"

"Probably." Maritza drops to the floor to unbuckle her shoes. "I guess we're through for the day." Just as well. She really does love the Argentine, but it is *murder* on her feet and lower back. And she's got a shift at Trabucco's to work tonight to boot—no rest for the wicked.

Fred's gaze is sympathetic as she rubs her aching feet. "At least you're done a couple of hours earlier than you thought. You can grab a shower and go hang out somewhere before you have to work. Refuel, rest if you can."

"I could go to the bakery." Sarita had hit the ground running after their little romp in the studio last week; she's been in charge of the bakery all this week as part of her management audition-test-thing. Her days start extra early and run extra late, and she's been so tired she can barely do more than text Maritza for a few minutes every night. Dates have been totally out. "Get a few minutes to see my girl."

"I haven't met this woman, but I like her," Fred says with a grin and an authoritative nod. "She's great."

"You like her because she's not Nicky, but that's all right." She takes the arm Fred proffers and uses it to pull herself up. "I like her because she's not Nicky, too. Among other things."

"She makes you happy." It's a simple, direct statement. "I'm going to like anyone who makes you happy, Maritza. You've been part of my studio for five years now. You're family. It's important to me that my family members are happy."

That makes her raise an eyebrow. "Even Nicky?"

"Every family has an obnoxious cousin with noisy, terribly wrong opinions. They still have to invite him to Thanksgiving," Fred says, dry as a bone. "Go on. Go get your shower. I'll see you... Monday?"

"Monday," she confirms.

"Great. Okay, forgive me, I see a gaggle of angry mothers waiting for me in the lobby." Fred sighs and rolls his eyes heavenward. "God grant me strength. I may murder Nicky before you two get to audition."

"You can't do that; you're my backup partner. If you kill Nicky, you go to jail and then who will I dance with?" Maritza stands on her tiptoes to kiss Fred's cheek. "See you later, Fred. Good luck."

It takes her time to struggle through the crowd of parents who have gathered around the door of Studio 1, time and effort that taxes her already sore muscles. She chalks up another annoyed point against Nicky and adds a second for good measure when one of the women accidentally steps on her foot. It takes much longer than she would have liked to burst through the door into Fred's office, and she nearly brains not one, but two tiny tap dancers with her bag on the way.

"Damn it, Nicky. Even when you're not here you're a pain in my ass," she grumbles as she strips off her sweaty T-shirt.

"How sweet. I say the same thing about you. Soulmates!"

Maritza clutches her shirt to her chest and whirls around at the unexpected and wholly unpleasant sound of her partner's voice. Nicky's in the back corner of the office, tucked into the shadow cast by Fred's bookshelf of trophies. He pushes himself off the wall and steps forward with a nasty grin on his face. "Well, hi there. I just hid in the corner to surprise you, but thanks for the extra bonus of letting me see you topless. It's been too long, Mari."

She thanks God that he spoke up before she got her sports bra off. "Get out, Nicky. God. And fuck you while you're at it."

"Is that an offer? It *is* my lucky day." His face still fixed in that awful grin, Nicky reaches forward to run a finger under the halter strap of her bra, not flinching when she slaps his hand away. "Touchy much?"

Maritza swallows hard and clutches her shirt more tightly. "Get out, get *out*." She'd shove him out the door herself if she felt like chucking her thin layer of sweaty cotton protection aside to free up her hands. The urge to not let him get another glimpse of her scantily-clad breasts far outweighs that urge, though, much to her fury.

Nicky doesn't leave, but he does at least take a step back. His grin is all gone and his expression is almost one of boredom. "I don't want to. We need to talk."

"No, I need to shower, and you need to leave," she snaps. "There's nothing to talk about."

"Actually, there is." He resumes his nonchalant leaning on the wall, crossing his legs at the ankle while he pretends to examine his fingernails. "I wanted to tell you that we're going to do the samba at the *Dance Nation* auditions."

If Maritza could roll her eyes any harder, she would have a fantastic view of the back of her skull. "Seriously? You corner me in Fred's office like the creep you are and you want to talk about our audition number? Could you please go take a nap in traffic now?"

Nicky's bag is at his feet. Without taking his eyes from her, he crouches to search through the zipper pocket on the front. Whatever he pulls out, he cups in his hand and hides from her as he gets back to his feet. "We're doing the samba," he says again, and there's no boredom or amusement or anything but cold contempt in his blue eyes now, and ice water goes down Maritza's spine as she realizes it.

She tries to think about what might be at hand to use as a weapon if she needs it. Fred's nameplate on his desk is brass and wood. It's pretty solid; she could swing that at Nicky's head if he got close. There's a paperweight too and a cup full of pens. Not much else. Nicky's got the advantage, since he's right next to an entire six-foot-tall shelving unit stuffed full of big, shiny, pointy trophies.

But he doesn't seem interested in attacking her. He does throw whatever he's got in his hand at her, but it's not a blunt object. It bounces from her hand, which is still holding her shirt tight to her chest, and falls to the floor with a gentle plop. Maritza frowns down at it. It looks like cloth. "What's that?"

"Pick it up and find out." Nicky smirks. "Don't worry. It won't bite."

She doesn't take her eyes from him as she kneels and feels around on the carpet until she locates the soft little pile. She stands, chances a glance at the thing and frowns. "I don't know—"

But then it unfurls in her hand and she *does* know, she can see exactly what she's holding now. It's a small pair of gray cotton briefs, women's underwear. Women's underwear that she remembers quite vividly peeling down Sarita's legs just a week ago, peeling them off to toss them aside on the floor of Studio 1. *But we picked up all of our clothes. Didn't we?*

Clearly not. But Sarita hasn't said anything about her missing panties, so Maritza didn't know. And now somehow they'd ended up in Nicky's hands. Maritza curls her fingers around the soft fabric and glares at Nicky. "These aren't yours."

"No. They're a little small." He steps forward and, before Maritza can react, he's snatched the panties from her fingers and tucked them safely in his pocket. "So, a woman this time. Nice. I remember how you'd never let me bring another girl into the bedroom."

"Bisexuality isn't a party trick," she spits, furious at herself for ever telling him she swung both ways.

"Yeah, you made that clear. Boring." The nasty grin creeps back onto his face, and there goes the ice water again. "I don't care now. What I do care about is that I found these cute little panties in Studio 1, right out in plain sight by the door. You're lucky I beat Fred into the studio that morning. God knows what he would have thought if he found them."

Maritza's cheeks burn at the thought. Fred would have forgiven her, but not before making sure she knew how disappointed he was for the breach of his trust, and that would have been excruciating. Still, she'd rather face that than Nicky's unsettlingly satisfied smile now. "I don't feel lucky," she says and oh, she hates that her voice creaks when the words emerge.

"Yeah, okay. You're not. But I am!" He's grinning as though he's won the lottery, and his entire body is relaxed as he stands before her. "Because we're going to dance the samba."

"You keep saying that," she says, exasperated, and then it hits her. "Wait. Fucking... are you blackmailing me?"

"See, you're not stupid. Selfish, clumsy, slow and rude as hell, but not stupid. I always liked that about you, Mari." Nicky spins on his heel and backs up to lean on Fred's desk next to her. "Yes. I want to dance the samba at our audition, and you would prefer nobody knows you fucked your girlfriend on the studio floor." He holds a finger to his cheek and tilts his head in false thoughtfulness. "Gosh. I should tell the cleaning people to put extra disinfectant in the mop bucket."

She doesn't know if she should laugh or cry or punch him or yell for Fred or what. "You're blackmailing me. Over an *audition piece*. All the things in the world and *this* is what you pick."

"It's important to me." Nicky shrugs. "You don't have anything else that's as important to me as dancing the right number for *Dance Nation* so I get on the show and get the national exposure I deserve. So, yeah. I'm blackmailing you over what we're going to dance next month."

It's stupid. It is so entirely dumb, and yet she's just about ready to give in to the urge to cry. "Yeah, Nicky, I don't think I want to dance any dance with you anymore. I think I want to just call it quits, okay? We don't like each other. We haven't in a long time. I'll dance with Fred. You can find someone else too. Let's just—"

"No." He cuts her off and grabs her arms, turning her she can see his cold, cold eyes. "You don't get to back out, either. You're right, I don't like you. But I'm not an idiot. I know we dance better with each other than with anyone else, and I am not about to let you ruin my chances, Maritza. We're going to dance together, and we're doing the samba, and while I'm at it, you're also going to wear what I tell you to wear. I'm calling the shots."

"Tell Fred. Go ahead and tell him I brought someone here. I don't care." All that's important is getting out of this, getting away from Nicky for good. She hates the frustrated, frightened tears that roll hot down her cheeks now. "He'll forgive me; it doesn't matter. You don't have anything to hold over me. I'll tell him myself."

The look on Nicky's face is almost tender, almost sorrowful. Except for his eyes. "I'm beginning to regret giving you credit for having a brain. I wouldn't tell Fred, Maritza. I'd make sure the *parents* found out."

It's a punch to her gut. "What? You'd *what*?"

His calm is obscene as he explains. "All those little tap dancers out there. All the baby ballerinas that come here in the mornings, all the teenage ballroom dancers that look up to us, what would their mothers think if they found out one of the studio's star dancers was allowed free rein to come in and fuck whoever she wanted right on the studio floor their little butterballs roll around on?" His gaze is steady and cool as he gestures at the shelf of trophies. "What would they say if they knew half those trophies were won by Maritza Quiñones, Champion Slut?"

Maritza wants to believe that they wouldn't care, that there would just be salacious gossip for a couple of weeks, that she'd just have to endure whispers and stares for a while, and then it would blow over. But she knows better. Even here in Washington, the most liberal of parents would have a problem with the idea of one of the studio's adult dancers screwing around *in* the studio after hours. And she could never explain it was just once, that it was just for fun. Once would be bad enough in their minds—even if they believed her. Nobody wanted people to have sex in places where their kids played, especially not in places where they were *paying* for their kids to play.

The worst part is, it wouldn't hurt her. Not really. But the damage it would do to *Fred* was terrible, and Nicky knew it; that is what he's counting on. Parents would pull their kids out of the studio; God only knew how many would do it. The studio is barely solvent as it is, she knows from Fred's occasional mumbles. That's just how dance studios are. If enough parents pull their kids out...

The bottom drops out of Maritza's stomach. She can't do that to Fred. He loves his studio; he loves teaching people how to dance. Dance is all he's ever known. And Nicky knows full well Maritza would never do anything to hurt Fred. She'd never take a fraction of a chance.

He has her right where he wants her, stuck between the rock and the hard place of his choosing. And it's her own damn fault.

"Fine." She surrenders in one word, unable to even look at him for one more second. She turns away, feeling physically safe enough now to take her eyes from him. He wouldn't hurt her. Even if he was inclined to, he needed her healthy and whole too badly to chance any injury. Somewhere, there's irony in that she can't quite untangle.

Nicky kisses her on the cheek and smirks as she shudders away. "And there you go being smart again, Mari. Good. I'll see you tomorrow. Go ahead and shower now; you stink enough for three people."

Whistling a jaunty tune, he saunters out of the office as Maritza stands alone by Fred's desk with hot tears streaming down her cheeks.

Chapter Eleven

"ORGANIC OREGON BLUEBERRIES," SARITA CALLS OVER HER shoulder; clouds stream from her mouth with each word. It's all she can do to keep her teeth from chattering as she leans farther from the stepladder in the deep freezer to get a better look at Sucre Coeur's frozen berry stash. "Two ten-pound boxes. My plan is to have you make Craig's scones this week—those are always a bestseller—so write down another couple of boxes to order just to keep the stash going."

"Say please," Tash says, with the prim reproving tone of a mother.

"Please," Sarita says with a grin. She hops down from the ladder; her boots crunch on the icy freezer floor. "That's it, right?"

Tash scans the inventory list on her clipboard; her green eyes narrow as she checks things off. "Did you want to order more raspberries too? It's the same supplier as the blueberries."

Sarita places her hands on her lower back and stretches backward with a groan. "Ugh, I forgot. Um, yeah. Let's go ahead and get a couple of boxes of those. I didn't see any in the freezer, and you've got that raspberry cream wedding cupcake arrangement coming up during your management rotation."

"Don't remind me." Tash puts down her clipboard and flexes her fingers to get the kinks out as she follows Sarita from the freezer. "God, why did I have to get my rotation and the Hamilton-Bosch wedding at the same time? Why does Lindsey Hamilton want that weird cupcake tower and cake layer hybrid sculpture whatever it is? Why is her entire wedding circus-themed?"

Sarita bites back her laugh. "What's that last question have to do with her cake choices?"

"Nothing, I just think it's weird. How are you going to decorate the cupcakes to fit the theme, though?" Tash rumples her red hair and frowns.

"We'll arrange the cupcake tower in a shape like a circus tent. You'll bake the cupcakes in striped cups, plus the top cake layer and some extra layers so I can sculpt a tent-top out of cake and frost it to match." Sarita can't help her grin of pride. It took significant gentle coercion to get the bride to commit to a vision for her cake in their consultation. And then once agreed-upon, Sarita had to figure out how to *build* the damn thing so she could decorate it. If she can pull this off, it'll be the best cake she's built yet. "The groom's cake is a double layer, graduated tiers of chocolate with ganache, and I'll decorate the top of it with circus rings and sugar animals."

"That's what I don't like about the circus. All those poor animals. A wedding that celebrates that is in poor taste." Tash's pretty face twists into a scowl, and she snorts with contempt. "Do you think the groom is going to dress as a ringmaster?"

Sarita laughs. "I don't think they're going that far. Just the cake and the decorations. And this might make you feel better." She casts a smile at Tash as they walk through the kitchen. "Poppy Lawrence called me to get the dimensions of the cakes so she can plan her catering arrangements around them and she told me they're doing a completely vegetarian menu *and* asking for donations to a charity for rescued circus animals instead of gifts."

Tash pauses mid-step. "Okay. That's pretty cool."

"I thought so." Twisting her neck to work out the kinks, Sarita hitches herself up to drape over the counter by the cash register. "What else do we need to do today while it's quiet?"

"You're the boss—this week, anyway. You tell me." Tash peers over to inspect the contents of the display case. "I'll tell you we're sold out of the St. Patty's sugar cookies, though. And the Dirty Girl Scout cupcakes, and the Signatures cookies with the Bailey's." She leans on the case top and props her chin on her hand. A lock of red hair works its way out of her paper cap. "Everyone's Irish in March."

Sarita chews on her bottom lip. "The cupcakes should be special. We don't want to do too many of them too often, or we lose the scarcity appeal before St. Patrick's Day. Besides, it's the afternoon. People are going to go out and get drinks in a few hours; who needs an alcoholic cupcake then? Let's do another couple big batches of both kinds of cookies, though. People will stop in on their way home from work and pick up a dozen at a shot."

"Good call." Tash bobs her head in a quick nod. "You know, Sarita, you've been really good at managing this week. I'm nervous as hell about it being my turn soon, but you've been nothing but cool. I don't know how you do it."

"I just want to do a good job for Craig's sake." Still flat across the counter top, Sarita manages a shrug and drums her boot-toes against the cabinet. "I'm not saying it's not terrifying being in charge without Craig, because it completely is. But he's my friend and my boss. So I don't want to wreck his brand-new baby, you know?"

Tash is thoughtful. "That does make a whole lot of really good sense."

"I feel good about calling him every night to let him know we didn't burn the place down." She wriggles backward to plant her feet on the ground and stands upright. A glance around the otherwise unoccupied bakery satisfies her—all the bright clean surfaces, the scent of the cinnamon-apple air freshener Theodora prefers, the display case showing clear evidence it's been a good sales day, as if the cash register wasn't even better evidence. She squirms in pleasure at how well she'd planned today's treats. That deserves a reward. "Hey, Tash. Before we get started on the cookies, can you go grab a couple of coffees for us? My treat."

"I'll do anything if you're paying." Tash sticks out her tongue and winks. "Yeah, no problem. I'm still freezing right down to the middle of me. I could so use something warm to drink."

Sarita pulls her purse from the cabinet and hands over a twenty and Tash's jean jacket. "Don't forget to get Cliff to give you some of that Sugar in the Raw stuff."

"No problem." Tash shrugs into her jacket, then pauses as Sarita groans and yanks her buzzing phone from her pocket. "Ooh. Mom again?"

"She wants me to come over this week and clean out my old bedroom." She presses the lock button to dismiss the call and quiet the buzzing. "I'm not ignoring her, but I'm also *not* not ignoring her. Her timing is the worst. It's *March*. She can freak out at me when they actually sell the house."

"She probably wants to get it in showing condition," Tash points out as she slides her own phone into her jacket pocket.

That just makes Sarita roll her eyes. "I haven't lived in that bedroom in five years, and it's not like I was a messy teenager to start with. Seriously, I have a paper to write, classes to go to and a bakery to run. Never mind seeing Maritza. Or not, as it happens." A tiny headache starts to bloom at her temples. "Ahh. Caffeine. Now. Please. I'm starting to feel it."

"I'm on it. Anything else?" Tash pulls a hat over her sloppy ponytail.

"Nah. Just the biggest coffee Cliff'll give you. Wanna order pizza or go get teriyaki for lunch when you get back?" They hadn't eaten before they started on the inventory—a mistake Sarita intends never to repeat again. A handful of day-old chocolate chip cookies was in no way a reasonable substitute for a full meal.

Tash sweeps her up into a huge hug. "Yes, pizza, please, and thank you," she whispers in exaggerated gratitude. "My stomach is about to climb out and go foraging."

"Okay, that's a gross image, and you can go now." Sarita laughs and waves Tash out the door. "Out, ugh, go. I need caffeine to erase what you've done."

"You love me," Tash calls, blowing a raspberry as she lets the bakery door crash shut behind her and set the brass jingle bells in noisy motion. Sarita shakes her head, still chuckling as she ducks back into the counter cabinet to withdraw her Spinoza text and notebook. She's been taking every available minute she's awake this busy week to cram in more reading and note-taking time. Too often she's found herself asleep sitting on her couch with a crick in her neck, bent over her book and laptop, but she's on a roll with good old Baruch lately; her paper is coming along, and she can't stop now.

She's buried deep in the text within seconds, nodding at the familiar words and picking out new, expanded meanings. Her pen scratches, the only sound in the bakery apart from a few creaks and cranks from the equipment in the kitchen. *For peace is not mere absence of war, but is a virtue that springs from force of character...*

The bang and jangle of the bakery door nearly gives Sarita a heart attack and yanks her right out of her studious absorption. She flails and sends everything in her hands flying: notebook, textbook and pen all thump and clatter to the floor. Even her paper cap flutters off at the violent jerk of her head and falls to the floor with a whisper. The bakery door clangs closed again with another brassy jangle of its bells, and it's Maritza, hair in disarray, eyes red and fingers clutched tight around the strap of her bag. "Sorry," she whispers, the one word cracking at the end right before she bursts into tears.

"Oh, my God, Mari." Sarita scrambles from around the counter. Tears soak her uniform T-shirt quickly, almost before she can get

Maritza's head down on her shoulder. "Mari, what is it? What's going on? Are you hurt?"

Maritza's hair tickles Sarita's neck as she shakes her head. "No," she creaks out as her shoulders heave. "No, I... no, it..." Her sobs double in force, shaking her entire body and Sarita's along with it. All Sarita can make out now is what sounds like *puñeta, puñeta,* over and over again.

Sarita gently steers Maritza to the tiny table by the milk and soda machine and eases her into a chair with a silent thanks to God that the bakery is empty. "Sweetie, can I get you some tissue? My bag is right under the counter. Let me get you something so you can blow your nose, okay?"

She takes the wordless wail and Maritza's faceplant into her own palms as a yes and disentangles herself, then steps back over her discarded stuff to get to her purse and fish out the two mini-packs of Kleenex there. With luck, two packs will be enough. But by the look of Maritza, Sarita would have been better off if she had a box of the stuff. "Here," she whispers as she extends her hand with the open packet. "Come on, honey, breathe, okay? Breathe with me, nice and slow, shhh..."

With effort, Maritza lifts her head and takes in a deep breath, nodding and rocking back and forth as she lets it out and inhales again. Sarita dabs at Mari's tear-ravaged face with one tissue after another. "Shh... it's okay. You're here now, okay? It's okay, you're safe..." The words are meaningless next to Mari's clear distress—even *distress* is too mild for what's in front of her now, for Mari is sucking in breaths, her body is shaking, the tears are still streaming down her face. Sarita tosses the tissue packet aside and takes Maritza's face into her hands, brushing her thumbs over tear-stained cheeks. "Shh, please, keep it up, breathe with me. Okay? In on one... hold it..."

Gradually the shaking ebbs, and Maritza sits up straight. She wraps an arm around her own waist as she pulls back and shakes her hair from her face. "Jesus Christ," she says, the words emerging as if they had to be pushed. She grabs a tissue and wipes at her nose with a grimace. "Ugh, gross."

"It's okay." It's lame, it's not enough, obviously nothing is okay, but Sarita doesn't know what else to say. She lets her hands drop to Maritza's knees and rubs her palms on the denim. "You want to talk about it?"

Maritza's mouth twists. "No... yes..." A sigh bursts from her. "Nicky."

Of course. Sarita scowls. "Can I meet him?" she asks, and her hand flexes in and out of a fist. "I really want to meet him. Apparently he deserves to be punched in the face. I can make that happen."

"He does, but no." Maritza tosses aside a wad of tissue and hugs herself tightly with her head bowed and hair tumbled all around to conceal her face. "It's not... he didn't..." Her head droops farther. "It's nothing. He was just an extra-massive fucking asshole today at rehearsal."

"Is that why you're here now?" Sarita fishes her phone from her back pocket. "You don't have to be at work for another hour and a half. I thought you were going to go straight there."

"Yeah, we called rehearsal early, and I came over here." At once, Maritza jerks her head up with a look of horror on her face as she grabs at the neck of her T-shirt to sniff at her skin. "Oh, shit! I didn't shower. I forgot, I was going to and then I just put on my work clothes and came here. Oh God, I am so gross."

"Don't worry about it, in two hours you're going to smell like tomatoes and oregano anyway. Nobody is going to notice." Sarita pushes Maritza's hair back. "What did Nicky do? Has he ever made you this upset before?"

"No, it's, it just..." Maritza's gaze darts around the bakery, touching on the counter, the kitchen, the display case, and never quite settling down to look at Sarita. "It was a hard rehearsal, and he just exploded bigger than he usually does. It's not..." She swallows, and finally looks at Sarita with a smile. "It's not a big deal."

Sarita's eyes pop. "You came in here in tears, you looked like you must have been crying on the whole bus ride here, and it's not a big deal?"

"I'm PMSing." The smile disappears, and Maritza's eyes go hard and dark. "It was just a really sucky day all around."

Sarita doesn't believe it for a hot second, but clearly Maritza doesn't want to go into it. Fine, they can drop it for now. She tugs Maritza's arms free so she can clasp their hands together. "I still say he deserves a punch. Or I could kick him in the balls. Hmm?"

Maritza lets out a hiccupping giggle. "You'd have to catch him off guard. Maybe in a dark alley on a rainy night."

"Paranoid much? I guess I would be too if I knew I was a fucking jerk." Her knees are starting to ache from crouching. She shifts up and into the other chair. "Do you need anything? Milk and cookies? Because let me tell you how you came to the right place for that."

Another giggle. "Strawberry milk and a chocolate muffin?"

"I can also do that." Sarita gives her a gentle kiss and swipes her thumb over a lingering tear. "Be right back. Keep breathing."

She nudges her book and things out of the way on this pass through the space between the counter and the display case. There will be plenty of time to pick them up when Maritza goes; no need to make her feel worse than she already does, not that Sarita is sure that's even possible. She's never seen anyone this upset. Definitely this is a testicle-kicking offense. It wasn't as if she and Nicky would ever be on civil terms, she already knew that, but he's officially on her permanent shit list now. Her mouth sets in a grim line. *I bet he wears his hair in a man-bun.*

With a flourish and a smile that belie her anger, she sets the last chocolate-chocolate chip muffin on the table in front of Maritza. "Here you go and..." She grabs a bottle of strawberry milk from the cooler. "There. All set. Eat up."

Maritza's mouth turns up in a wan smile, and she takes nibbles out of the top of the muffin. "Thank you," she mumbles around a chocolate chip.

Sarita sits down again and tugs her chair close so she can rub a reassuring hand on Mari's knee. "Anytime, babe."

"No, really. Thank you." Maritza and pushes the muffin aside in favor of the milk. She takes a long drink before speaking again. "Thank you for making me feel better. Like, Mom would have freaked out, and Grace would have made me tell her everything that happened. But you just wanted to make me feel better. I really appreciate that."

"It seemed like the most important thing." The image of Maritza's face when she came through the door will probably haunt Sarita for a while. Curious as hell she might be, but it's easy to prioritize feelings over facts when someone you care about is that worked up. "I can't really fix whatever happened, I'm sure."

"Noooo." Maritza shakes her head as she draws the word out. "Not really."

"And you looked awful, and it turns out I can't stand you being upset. So there you go." She scoots her chair over some more so she can wrap her arms around Maritza and rest her head on her shoulder. "You do feel at least kind of better?"

"The chocolate and the hug are definitely a big help." Maritza takes another bite of muffin, washing it down with more milk. "You're the best."

"Mmm, I'm pretty up there, yeah." Sarita smiles and kisses Maritza's shoulder. "You sure you're going to be okay to go to work, though? Is Grace going to be there?"

"She is, but between this muffin and the bus ride, I'm pretty sure I can pull myself together enough so that she won't suspect anything's wrong." Maritza tilts her head to rest against Sarita's. "She might wonder about me being all sweaty and stinky though."

Sarita snorts. "You really don't stink. But you can always tell her Nicky kept you late. I am sure she would believe that."

"If I told her Nicky set an animal shelter on fire, she'd believe it." Maritza's shoulders heave, then drop. "He's never made a good impression on anyone who's ever met him. That's why I'm trying to spare you the experience."

"Spare me? Or spare him?" Sarita raises an eyebrow. "Do you have to keep dancing with him? There's got to be dancers out there who have whatever skill he has but they're nicer people. You deserve that, don't you think?"

Maritza squirms, and her hair drops to curtain her face. "It's not that simple. It's not a good time. We have a lot going on." There's something left unspoken, some tension in the air Sarita can't quite put her finger on. But Maritza hurries on and cuts off any questions Sarita might have been able to muster. "It would feel like everything Mom and Javi sacrificed was for nothing if I dropped him now. Trust me, if I could dump him with a clear conscience, I absolutely would. First chance I get." The words are bitter as unsweetened chocolate, astringent as vinegar.

Sarita opens her mouth; she doesn't know what she'll ask but she has to know *something*—

The bakery door bangs open, and the brass bells collide with the tile wall in a discordant crash. "Sorry, Sarita," Tash is a breathless whirlwind as she races through the door, coffee caddy in one hand, the other frantically trying to remove her jacket. "Cliff and I got to talking about his old band and..." She draws up short, eyes wide as she spots Maritza. "Mari, hey. I'm sorry, I didn't know you were coming, I would have gotten you a coffee."

But Maritza gets to her feet, shooting back the last of her strawberry milk. "It's okay, Tash. Thanks anyway. This wasn't really a planned trip; there was no way for you to know." She wraps the last of her chocolate muffin and stuffs it into her jacket pocket.

With a smile, she bends down to give Sarita a sweet, small kiss. "Thank you again, babe. Seriously. I feel a million times better."

"You're sure you're okay?" Her preference would be to keep Maritza with her until they closed the bakery, then whisk her back to the apartment for cuddles, movies and pizza until she was sure everything really was fine. "I wish I could do more. Maybe you don't have to go to work?"

Maritza straightens up, then hesitates with her fingers stroking absently through Sarita's hair as she seems to consider. "Saturdays are too busy; there's no one to fill in on the cook line. And you did enough, I promise." There's a sureness behind her smile this time, and it reaches her eyes. "You did more than enough. I'm okay, Sarita. Honest. Okay enough." She tugs Sarita up for another kiss. "Call you when I'm off work?"

"Yes, please." The sensation of words left unsaid, of distant resolution, still hangs like a cloud, but what can Sarita do about it? She walks Maritza to the bakery door. "Have fun at work."

Maritza's answer is another twinkling smile, a swift kiss farewell, and she's gone, jogging toward the Metro stop. Sarita stands at the bakery door and frowns after her, unable to forget the look she saw on Maritza's face just thirty minutes ago.

"Something up?" Tash appears at her elbow, holding out the big paper cup of coffee. "Don't worry, Cliff gave me fresh ones before I left, since the first ones he gave me got cold while he talked. This one's still hot."

Sarita takes the cup without really paying attention. "Yeah, thanks."

A nudge. "Something up?" Tash repeats, leaning over Sarita's head to peer out the door. "All quiet on the Western front?"

The sip of coffee that Sarita takes is tasteless on her tongue. "I don't know. Maybe. Something."

"I'm sure that all made sense in your head." Tash takes a noisy slurp of her coffee. "Try again?"

Tossing her hair back, Sarita levels a glance over her shoulder. "Tash," she says, and lifts an eyebrow. "If I had to murder a guy, would you help me hide the body?"

Tash doesn't miss a beat. "What are friends for?"

Chapter Twelve

I'D MAKE SURE THE PARENTS FOUND OUT

Parents

Parents

Parents

As Nicky's slimy laughter echoes through Maritza's dream, she jerks awake and sits up with a wail that she strangles off before it can gather too much steam and wake Javier in his bedroom. She can't stop the tears, though, can't stop the sob that she buries in a hastily-grabbed pillow.

Stretching out in a long puddle of dark fur, Coco uncurls from her spot at the end of Maritza's bed. She yawns and follows this up with a chirrup of something that sounds like concern and pads over the quilt to shove her head insistently under Maritza's arm. The rest of her soon follows, until Coco is a warm, purring bundle squeezed between Maritza's belly and the pillow that muffles Maritza's sobs.

Just another night, same as all the other ones in the last week since Nicky dropped his bombshell on her: nightmares, tears, no solutions. She'd love nothing more than to have Sarita's arms to fall into for comfort, but then she'd have to explain everything, and she can't bring herself to do that. It feels too dirty to think about, let alone try to speak aloud. It crawls along her skin every day; it doesn't come off in the shower.

She's tried.

Coco stands up in Maritza's lap and presses her front paws into Maritza's breasts. Her small, soft head butts up under Maritza's chin, working the same magic it does every night and making Maritza chuckle, just a little, just a tiny thread of a laugh. "Hi, Coco."

A trill, a chirrup, and Coco pulls back to stare at Maritza. Her eyes glow green in the moonlight that streams in through Maritza's blinds. "Pretty girl," Maritza coos, setting the pillow aside so that she can give the cat a brisk massage, rubbing Coco's ears and back and earning a king's ransom in purrs, squeaks and tiny meows of happiness. "Who's a pretty girl, yes, you're pretty, you're my pretty girl."

If cats can't hug, they make up for it by not being able to ask troublesome questions either. Maritza will take that; she will take every tiny bright spot she can get right now.

She closes her eyes and picks Coco up to press an ear to the warm body and listen to the gentle rumble of her purrs. It's not until Susana's slight weight dips the end of the bed that Maritza's eyes fly open and she gasps, making Coco bounce down and away, off the bed and out the open bedroom door to go bother Javi as he snores like a freight train next door. "Mama! You're home!"

"And you're awake. I heard you moving around in here when I was about to go to bed." Susana shifts and scoots until she's sitting up next to Maritza and leans around to set a glass on the bedside table. "It's three a.m., *mija*. You can't sleep?"

Maritza dips her head and allows her hair to fall around her face as she lifts a shoulder in what she hopes is a casual shrug. "Just a nightmare."

But Susana tucks Maritza's hair back and lifts her chin so that their eyes meet. "Every night this week?" Her eyes are dark, opaque in the dimness of the room, but steady. "I've heard you. I let it pass for a few days but it's not going away, is it?" She pulls Maritza's head down onto her shoulder. "What's wrong?"

Her mother's sympathy threatens to undo her in a way Sarita's had not been able to—the magic, of course, of mothers. "Nothing, Mama. It's nothing. I'm just stressed out, that's all."

Susana is not fooled for a second. "Mmhm. You work too hard. But you always work too hard and you still sleep like a baby. So." She sits back a bit and the dark of the room does nothing to hide the expectant, skeptical look on her face. "Tell the truth, Mari."

"I..." *Oh, no way. Absolutely no way.* Part of her wants to, a part of her that is still ten years old and fully believes that her mother can fix anything. That part wants her to fall into her mother's arms and sob out every sordid piece of Nicky's blackmail scheme, to tell her mother just how out of hand Nicky has gotten since their breakup, to let Susana comfort her and then to somehow solve the entire thing. She is tired and upset, and the idea of putting it all into her mother's hands is so appealing.

Her fingers curl against her chest, over her aching heart. She's not ten anymore, and Susana can't solve this problem—even if Maritza could get past the shame of explaining it to her. Not that she's ashamed of Sarita; she's not ashamed that she's had sex, and never has been. She is, after all, an adult.

But there's something about Nicky knowing it, something about him using it against her that fills Maritza with shame, and, no matter how ridiculous it is, she can't get past it. All she wants to do, all that it seems right to do, is ride all of this out and put it behind her, nightmares and all. If she can just get through the audition, it will all be fine.

So she puts on her best smile and beams it at her mother right before she kisses Susana's temple. "Mama, it's fine. Really. I mean, I really am stressed out, the audition's only a month away now. It's so big, you know? This is national television; that's a new level for us." She takes Susana's hand when her mother seems unconvinced. "Nicky *is* being a bigger jerk than usual, but you know I'm just with him until we get to the auditions. And then, even if we don't make it, I'll never dance with him again."

"You *will* make it. I did not pack up and move this family across the country for you not to." Susana draws back her shoulders and sits up, and there's pride in every line of her body. "You have worked too hard not to, *mija*. The *blanquito*..." She wobbles her hand noncommittally. "I don't know about him. He dances all right. But you're better, hmm? You know you are; you passed him up years ago."

"I know we're good together," Maritza says and she hates that even now she can't help but be anything but fair to her slimy, blackmailing, asshole partner. "And if I have to put up with a few nightmares for the next month, whatever, I'm okay, Mama."

Susana's mouth twists again—her skepticism is practically a third person in the room—but she relents. "If you say so. You are an adult. But." She leans over to the night table and picks up the glass. "You still need your sleep. I brought you some *horchata*. Ah, and..." She rummages in the pocket of her jeans and pulls out a blister packet of pills. "The sleepy Nyquil stuff, without the cold medicine. Just for tonight, eh? Nurse's orders."

The sweet, cool sesame milk rolls over Maritza's tongue, sending waves of comfort through her body as it has done her entire life. "Ah, Mama. Thank you for this. I didn't even know I needed it, it's perfect."

"Well, sometimes you don't know; that's what mothers are for." Susana slides from the bed and drops the pill packet on the night table where the glass had been. "Take the medicine; get a good rest at least one night."

Maritza smiles. "Okay, Mama. I will." She watches as Susana crosses the room, grateful for the millionth time since they moved here that she didn't come alone, more grateful now than ever. "Thank you, Mama. I love you."

Susana turns, a lovely smile on her face. "Of course, baby. Anything. I love you, too."

She leaves the room and somehow, even though her problem isn't anywhere near solved, Maritza feels as if her mother has taken the nightmares with her, at least for tonight.

"OH, GOD, THIS IS SUCH A NIGHTMARE."

Sitting up, Sarita tugs her phone from her jeans pocket and declines the incoming call—her mother's fifth of the day, in addition to the flurry of text messages she'd sent before Sarita had even had her morning caffeine—before she dumps the damn thing into her purse and flops back down into her supine position on her brother's carpet. "Can't she take a hint?"

"Have you met our mother?" Devesh chortles from his position above her on his couch before he drops a decorative beige cushion over her face. "No, she can't take a hint, Reeti. Ma doesn't even know what a hint is."

Sunil leans over his husband's lap and catches the cushion in mid-flight when Sarita hurls it back upward. "I'm honestly surprised she hasn't come to your place to drag you out by your ear."

"Why do you think I came to yours for our Big Gay Brunch? If she finds a minute between attic cleaning and yard sale planning, it's going to occur to her to try that." Sarita laces her fingers over her stomach and wriggles her toes, settling herself comfortably into the plush pile of the carpet. "Although honestly, the crepes alone were worth the trip; good job, Sunil."

Over by the fireplace in Devesh and Sunil's living room, there's a snort from Craig as he plays tug-of-war with Fitz. When Sarita rolls her head to the side, he's making a mock-offended face. "And here I thought you came for the chance to lay eyes on my smiling face. Thanks a lot, Sarita."

"Well, I heard you were bringing your dog too, and you know I don't pass up the chance for a Fitz encounter." She rolls over onto her stomach and fishes a squeaky toy from a nearby basket, one of a dozen baskets scattered around the living room for the ever-changing herd of Yorkies that Devesh and Sunil breed and raise. After a squeeze, the toy lets out a high-pitched squeak that catches Fitz's attention and makes his little ears perk up. Sarita grins at Craig and squeezes the toy again. This time Fitz abandons the tug toy in Craig's hand in favor of a joyful yap and romp across the living room to sink his teeth into the rubber rabbit. "Yay, I got a puppy, I win."

"He'll be back. He knows who cooks his food." Alex reclines near Craig and runs a brush through the long, silky fur of the Grande Dame of the house, Fitz's mother Bella. Bella is wholly uninterested, accustomed as she is to such royal treatment. Alex tweaks the pink bow between her fuzzy ears. "Okay, is it up to me, then? Am I really going to be the one who points out that this is a Big Gay Brunch and the lesbian didn't bring her girlfriend or whatever she is?"

"Hey! No one said this was a couples' brunch," Sarita protests, sitting up.

Sunil makes a thinking noise. "It was sort of implied. Assumed, at least."

"I just really wanted to hang out with Maritza. I haven't seen her for a while," Alex adds.

"Oh, you know her? I wanted to actually *meet her.*" Devesh nudges Sarita with his foot. "You scared of letting family meet this chick? Not fair, Reeti. I'm harmless. Well, Sunil is harmless, and he keeps me in check. Why not bring the girl? How come Alex gets to meet her and not me?"

"Alex introduced me to her, remember?" Sarita swats Devesh's foot away and scoots over so he can't reach her again. "He met her before I did. And no, I'm not afraid, jerk." She fishes a soft toy from the basket and throws it at her brother, rolling her eyes when Sunil intercepts it yet again. "She's busy. I did ask."

Alex sits up and digs into the basket closest to him to pull out a bag of treat biscuits that immediately gets the attention of both Bella and Fitz. "Dancing?"

"It is a day of the week that ends in Y." She spreads her hands out and shrugs. "Girl's gotta do what a girl's gotta do. I can't fault her for practicing her toes off. At least she knows what she wants to do and how to get it, right?"

"Yes, but I made *crepes*," Sunil says.

"I brought the chocolate cherry almond muffins especially for her," Craig points out.

Alex flaps toward his satchel with the hand that's not feeding biscuits to Yorkies. "I've got the glossy action prints from her last competition. I was going to give them to her."

Sarita cranes her head to look back at her brother, who clasps his hands under his chin and bats his eyes. "I just had all the hope in the world in my heart."

"You call that black lump of coal a heart?" She barks out a laugh. "Come on, did anyone actually just want to see me?"

The men look around, exchanging glances and shrugs. "Sure," Craig says, "but we also wanted to see you with your lady friend."

Sarita looks at all of them in turn. "Okay," she says at last. "One, I wish I *had* gone to clean house with Ma after all and two, now I have to wonder if you all don't need to just start settling down and acquiring babies, because I do not need four gay dads, not at my age, and not when one of them is my brother."

The room is quiet as a tomb, apart from the sound of small dogs crunching down on dog biscuits with a ferocity out of proportion with their size. Alex is the first to speak up. "We've talked about it, but Fitz and the businesses are our babies right now. We just don't have the money—or any idea which way we'd want to go about it."

"Oh." Sarita blinks. She had not seen that one coming. "Okay, I was kidding, but, cool. For the record, I do think you and Craig would be awesome parents."

Behind her, on the couch, Sunil and Devesh shift around, and when Sarita can practically hear them thinking *you, no you* at each other, she turns to see them holding hands and beaming at each other in the goofy way they did the day they got married. "Well," Devesh begins, his eyes still on his husband, "do you think *we'd* make good parents?"

This time the silence includes the dogs, who, in apparent reaction to the shock that fills the room, are looking at their humans, ears up. Sarita rubs behind her own ears, not sure she heard or understood Devesh correctly. "Say what?"

"That's why there aren't any puppies right now. We're not breeding Bella." Sunil tears his eyes away from Devesh and smiles at the shocked faces of friends and family. "We didn't want to be raising and selling puppies while trying to adopt and raise a baby."

Alex gasps out a laugh, and Craig's face erupts into a huge grin. "Fantastic. This is really fantastic, you two. How much longer had you been planning to keep this a secret?"

"Well, the mother we've selected is about four months along, so we really weren't going to be able to hide it anymore. You were going to notice the diaper stockpile and the baby bathtub and everything else eventually." Devesh is practically bouncing in his seat, he's so happy. "Plus the baby shower in three months was going to be a dead giveaway."

"Dibs on taking your first baby pictures," Alex volunteers.

"Yeah, like we'd go to anyone else." Devesh throws back his head and lets a big belly laugh rip. "Like we were going to let anyone else do the baby shower cake besides the two of you, too." He points to Sarita and Craig. "We want one of those horrible-looking baby butt diaper cakes. I insist. Red velvet, too."

"You have a really sick sense of humor, Dev, you do know that?" But Craig is laughing, too. "I love it. Absolutely we will make your awful cake for you. Congratulations."

Alex sits up straight and scoots closer to the couch with Craig close behind. "Okay, so tell us all about this kid, your process, everything."

Sunil starts to speak first, hands and face animated and bright. "Well, we started thinking about it last year…"

Devesh slips off the sofa and curls up next to Sarita. "Hey."

"Hey." She inhales deeply and shakes her head. "Wow, Devesh. Damn. I mean. Wow."

"I love the wisdom of the grad student. It just really gets me here." He spreads his hand over his heart and grins before he nudges her with his elbow. "Okay, so tell me how you really feel. The five minutes of silence is not like you, and I'm finding it really unnerving."

Sarita crisscrosses her legs and props an elbow on one knee so she can bite at her index knuckle. "Ma is going to be amazingly excited and then she's going to kill you for telling me and Craig and Alex first."

"Goes without saying. Couldn't be helped. And you're the one who opened the door with the four gay dads crack, so don't think I won't make sure she knows that." He nudges her again. "But that's Ma. Tell me what *you're* thinking."

She puffs out a breath and sends the little wisps of hair around her face flying. "I'm kind of in shock still. But you know I think it's awesome. My inability to handle surprises is not a reflection on how amazing a pair of dads you and Sunil are going to be." Imagining that future makes an uncontrollable smile spread across her face. "I can't believe you two have been planning this for an entire year and not a peep."

"To be perfectly fair and honest, we were going to talk about it at that last family dinner, but Ma and Dad had their way bigger announcement to make." Devesh's smile vanishes then. "I hope they'll still be stateside when the baby is born. Talk about things you didn't see coming…"

"Oh, God, of course Ma will stay at least; she'll insist on it even if she has to live in a hotel or on my couch, whatever. You know she's going to want to be around to help you two, if only to tell you everything you're doing wrong." Now it's her turn to nudge Devesh, giggling and leaning her head on his shoulder. "You might not be able to get rid of her; maybe she'll move in with you."

Devesh pretends to look afraid. "Okay, maybe we shouldn't tell her. We'll just keep it a secret until he goes to college, but you have to help distract her."

"It's a boy?" She kneels, grabs Devesh's arm and bounces up and down with excitement. "Another boy! Someone for Ramendra to pick on in a few years."

"Hey, no one is picking on anyone," Devesh protests.

"Yeah, you weren't the baby of the family long enough to remember getting picked on. Yes, he's going to get picked on; whatever, it's the lot of the youngest." She sits back on her heels and she's so happy she could burst. "I'll get to teach him how to deal with it, that'll be me, the Coping Auntie. Oh, man, this is so great."

Devesh's smile returns. "I'm so glad you're happy about it."

"You didn't really think there was a chance I wouldn't be?" She scoffs. "Right. Sure. Because I hate babies and I hate being an Auntie, yes, it's all terrible." She punches him gently on the arm. "I still need to adjust, but trust me, Dev. I am really, really happy for you and Sunil."

He grabs her in a hug. "I am really, really glad to hear that, Reeti. Thank you." In a swift motion, he's up onto his knees and adjusting his grip to put her in a headlock. His knuckles grind against her scalp as she flails and struggles. "Did you ever come up with a coping mechanism for this?"

"A punch to your balls was usually the quickest fix," she howls, prying at his arm. Fortunately the threat to his testicles makes Devesh let her go in a hurry, and she sits back with a scowl. "Jackass."

"And you love me anyway," he says, his grin unrepentant.

Sunil clears his throat. "So… anyway. Sarita, your purse is buzzing, I think your mom is trying to call you again."

She scrambles to her feet. "Oh no, wait, no…" A quick dip in her purse produces her phone, and she groans at the screen. "No, it's not Ma, it's my alarm. I have to go. I scheduled myself to be at the University library fifteen minutes ago. Shit, guys. I'm sorry."

Craig looks up. "More work on the paper?"

"Always work on the paper. My life is frosting and research." She snatches up her bag and goes around the room to give hugs to all the guys. "See you all next month. I'll try to bring Mari."

She manages to get to her car and even to start driving before she lets loose with the big, body-size sigh she's been holding back since Sunil made the announcement. "Shit."

Now more than ever the weight of not knowing what the hell she's doing is heavy on her shoulders. *Babies. Businesses. Dance careers. Everyone has something, and all I do is write papers and study weird concepts of life and religion. What can I do with that?* She's asked herself that question ever since she settled on philosophy as a major, but never before has it felt so unanswerable. The puzzle of her life seems further away from forming a recognizable picture than it ever has.

I like it. Isn't it all that matters, that I like what I do, that I love it? I should do it for as long as I can if I like it, right? That's what had gotten her into grad school, what had pushed her to decide on going for a PhD. But today it rings hollow, mocks her lack of direction and throws everyone else's clear life choices back in her face in answer. It hurts. It shakes her to her core.

But it doesn't give her any clear idea of what to do about it. *What do I have?*

"Frosting and research," she grumbles with no little bitterness and stomps on the gas.

Chapter Thirteen

"OKAY, YOU CAN HAVE..." AS SHE'S WALKING INTO THE LIVING room, Sarita inspects the labels of the ice cream cartons in her hands. "Peanut Butter Cookie Chunk or Coffee Toffee Twist."

From her perch on the sofa, wrapped in a fleecy blanket, Maritza perks up. "Oh, yeah. Give Mama the Coffee Toffee Twist, mmm."

Sarita chuckles. "Gimme a kiss first." She plops down next to Maritza with both containers held out of the way as she puckers her mouth. "Kiss, kiss, kiss. Come on, I feel silly."

"You look silly. I need to take it in a little longer." Maritza sits back and grins at the sight of this ridiculous and adorable woman, arms extended, head tilted up, lips pursed in a comical fashion. As she waits, the pucker gives way to a half-smile, narrowed eyes twinkle and at last Sarita collapses in a heap of giggles into Maritza's lap.

"You left me hanging." The words are muffled by a mouthful of fleecy blanket.

"I'm sorry, it was too funny." Maritza wriggles so she can smack a noisy kiss into the soft nest of Sarita's hair. She brushes curls away until she can catch a glimpse of fine golden-skinned cheekbone and jawline to trace her fingers along. "Forgive me?"

One big dark eye opens up. "Maybe."

"Well, while you think about it, maybe you can sit up?" Maritza wriggles again. "My thighs are getting really cold all of a sudden."

"The ice cream!" Sarita hands over the Coffee Toffee Twist and a spoon. "Gah. Sorry about that."

"You're forgiven," Maritza says, and this time when Sarita makes her silly pucker-up face, Maritza doesn't leave her hanging. The playful peck she starts with quickly dissolves into sweet slowness, into soft lips and the gentle brush of noses against cheeks curved into smiles that make the kissing more difficult, but no less sweet and joyous. As the kiss goes on, Maritza can't help her little sighs and hums of contentment, tiny happy noises that make Sarita giggle more, and that makes Maritza giggle back, and soon they're laughing altogether with their heads tucked into the curves of each other's necks.

"Ah! Cold. Cold hand, cold hand." Sarita jerks back abruptly, and puts her forgotten ice cream on the coffee table. "Sorry. My fingers went numb."

"Poor baby. I'll warm them up for you." Maritza's own ice cream had been quite sensibly set aside before she got the kissing started. She picks it up now, using her other hand to tug the fuzzy blanket out from under Sarita and hold it up. "Get under here, I wanna eat ice cream and snuggle."

"I am on board." Sarita scoots close until they're hip to hip under the blanket with their legs entwined and stacked like Lincoln Logs. "God bless Tash and Craig for giving me the rest of the week off. Pajamas and Netflix on a Thursday is the best kind of date. We need to do this more often."

"We'd need the time to do it." And time is swiftly ticking away from them, not that Sarita knows it. Maritza ducks her head as a rush of anxiety makes her stomach churn. She opens her mouth and she has every intention of telling Sarita about the *Dance Nation* auditions that are just over a week away now, confessing what it might mean and trying to figure out what they can do, but what comes out is, "But may I compliment you on your truly sexy nightwear choice? Not every girl has the confidence to wear a giant holey T-shirt in front of the person she's sleeping with."

Damn it.

Oblivious to Maritza's frustration, Sarita looks down at her faded green T-shirt and plucks at the fraying collar. "Hey. This is a classic piece of Seattle history. Have some respect."

Maritza licks her ice cream spoon clean and lifts an eyebrow. "I can actually see your nipple, just the one, right through the fabric there." She points with her spoon.

"My nipples are not something you've complained about once in the last two months." Sarita responds with an arched eyebrow of her own as she gets her ice cream. "Also, you, a grown woman, are wearing yoga pants covered in ballet-dancing penguins, which are very cute, but I also think leave you with not a whole lot of pajama-judging ground to stand on."

She somehow manages to make eating a spoonful of peanut butter cookie ice cream look smug. Maritza is duly impressed. "All right. I give. No more judging."

Sarita nods. "No more judging. Only cuddles and movies." She picks up the remote. "What do we want? Fluff? Stupid explosions? Dwarves and dragons?" With a press of a button, she's skimming through the various movie options.

"Nothing with long-distance relationships," Maritza blurts.

The television screen, busily scrolling through options, stands still as Sarita lifts her thumb from the remote and tilts her head with her eyebrow once again arched. "That's a kind of specific request."

"I have bad associations with them." And it is not, technically, even a lie.

"Fair enough." The scroll resumes. "*Center Stage* is always a classic."

That does cheer Maritza. "The chick who plays Jody, first time I realized I liked boys *and* girls. I was fifteen and it was on cable one night when we were in New York. The thing at the end when Cooper spins her out of her tutu into that little red dress?" She pretends to fan herself. "Oh, mama."

Sarita throws back her head and lets out a full-throated laugh. "Ha! Eva did it for me. Oh, God, I know smoking is bad for you, but when she stubbed out her cigarette with her toe shoe, I fell in love." She rests her head on Maritza's shoulder and starts the movie. "Listen, don't take up smoking, but if you happened to, like, dress up in a leotard and wear toe shoes one day, I'm just saying I think it would do things for me."

I wonder if I can figure out in a hurry how to walk in toe shoes? It'd be a nice goodbye thing. In one fell swoop, Maritza is bummed out again, and not even the fleeting mental image of Sarita in a tiny red ballet dress is lifting her spirits.

I should tell her. Just get it over with. I like you. I'm leaving. It's not you; it's my career.

It's depressing. And besides, it doesn't even brush up against the whole blackmail thing, but then Maritza is sure she's going to take the humiliation of *that* to her grave. No one can solve that problem. That can only be ridden out and put behind her. She hates it, but she'd rather die than admit to anyone in the world that Nicky's got Fred's livelihood and her own career clutched in his hands for a fucking *dance routine*.

It's the first time in her life she's felt hung up about sex at all, and it annoys the shit out of her, and having her hands tied—over such a stupid thing, too—is the most frustrating experience she can recall in her life, let alone in five years of dancing with Nicky.

She shovels a too-large bite of ice cream into her mouth and tries to hold back the involuntary full-body shudder when the frozen treat hits her soft palate. *I should have suggested cookies. Oreos are better for angry eating. They don't cause brain freeze.* She blinks in a vain effort to clear the sting from her eyes.

Sarita lifts her head. "Are those tears in your eyes? We're like maybe five minutes into the movie! You're a soft touch."

Maritza swallows the ice cream and does manage not to shudder. "I'm just so happy that Jody gets into the academy; it gets me."

"You're cute." Two little words, loaded with affection, and now it's not the ice cream that's making Maritza's eyeballs puddle up. *Why can't I just talk to her? I'm not a teenager; this is so stupid.*

She tilts her head to nestle against Sarita's, and of course she knows why, and it's awful and selfish, and she judges herself harder for this than she does for the Nicky thing. She doesn't want to talk to Sarita like a grownup because she doesn't want to risk losing out on a single second of time like this. She doesn't want to risk Sarita walking out, and then they never kiss again, they never have nights like this again, she never sees Sarita's eyes sparkle with excitement as she describes a cake she's working on, they never joke, they never fuck, they never watch stupid movies, they never cook together, none of it ever again before she leaves town, and certainly not at all afterward.

She wants to hoard as many precious sparks of time like tonight as she can, wants to live in this brightly lit bubble of affection and companionship. She can't bring herself to burst it early. Every time she tries, the words hang in her throat.

Sarita nudges her. "You're making noises."

"I am?" Maritza sets her ice cream aside, using the movement to wipe the back of her hand over the tear streaks on her face in what she hopes is a surreptitious manner. "Sorry. I just love this movie."

A hand on her arm pulls her back to face Sarita, whose mouth is pulled into a skeptical frown. "You always cry over dancers sassing teachers?"

"What can I say, it's kind of my life?" It's a feeble joke, and they both know it. With no need to hide now, she rubs at the tear streaks again and offers a thin smile that doesn't fool Sarita for a second.

"Yeah, I've been able to hear you thinking since you got here. I didn't want to pry, but hey, you want to talk about whatever it is?" Sarita pauses the movie and twists to sit on the couch facing Maritza. "You're upset all the time lately. That's not a condemnation, I swear. I just want to help if I can."

"You do help. Being around you is a help." She's always found that if she starts with the absolute truth, it helps her launch into embroidering the truth as she goes. "It's just Nicky, he's hard on me lately, and Fred can't get him to stop."

Once again, not entirely a lie.

She hates how good she's getting at this.

The mention of Nicky makes Sarita's mouth tighten into a line. "I know we've only been dating for a couple of months and you've been with him for years, but Mari, he sounds *awful*. Why do you put up with it? He can't be that good a dancer."

"We… have obligations." Again, not a lie.

A lie of omission is still a lie. The chiding voice in her head always sounds like her mother, a disappointed version of Susana that makes her insides crawl with guilt.

She shakes it off. "We have obligations," she says again. "Competitions it's too late to back out of. But this is my last season with him, honestly." She uses the heel of her hand to scrub at a few more wayward tears. "I can't take much more."

Nothing has ever been more true than that.

Sarita gathers Maritza's hands in hers, forming a ball that she rests her chin on. "I want you to know," she says, eyes still and voice solemn, "that Tash and I have discussed this, and we are fully prepared to, um, go all *Fried Green Tomatoes* on him."

Maritza can't help her frown. "I don't get it."

"You've never seen…? Never mind." Sarita shakes her head. "Another movie for another time. And we wouldn't *really* cook him into barbecue, we wouldn't know how—"

Maritza's eyebrows shoot up and threaten to take off into space. "Barbecue?"

"—but we *do* have access to an industrial oven, a deep freezer and many, *many* sharp or pointy implements of destruction." The merry light that dances in Sarita's eyes is a stark contradiction to the mayhem she just implied. "All you have to do is say the word."

Tears are forgotten in favor of helpless laughter at Sarita's outlandish suggestion. It takes Maritza ages to compose herself so that she can assume a demeanor of mock sternness. "Sarita, you cannot murder my dance partner and bake him into a pie."

"No, he's probably too big for *one* pie—" Sarita shrieks in laughter as Maritza hits her with a pillow. "Okay, okay, no Nicky pie. I'm too cute for prison anyway."

"Damn right you are." Maritza casts the fuzzy blanket aside and crawls over to straddle Sarita's lap. "And life is too short to go to jail for Nicky anyway." She twists a curl of Sarita's hair around her finger and sighs. "It's not much longer. I can stick it out, if you can put up with me being all weepy and shit."

Sarita is clearly unhappy. "Well, yeah, but I don't like that you *are* all weepy and shit. I don't like him being gross to you and I wish you didn't feel like you *had* to put up with it."

And Maritza wishes that he didn't have a way to turn their relationship into something awful, something that could wreck people's lives. "*No me digas,*" she mutters, sucking her bottom lip between her teeth.

"Huh?" Sarita rears back, puzzled.

"Sorry. I mean, no kidding." Maritza pushes her hands through her hair and closes her eyes while she takes deep, calming breaths. When the requisite steadiness has been reached, she opens her eyes and manages a smile. "Okay. I'm sorry. Why don't we just turn the movie back on? Hmm? We'll get back to the cuddles and the pretty girls and their pretty costumes and the pretty dancing?"

"Okay." Sarita reaches for Maritza's ice cream. "Our ice creams are melting, though. Let me put these back in the freezer." With a quick kiss, she's on her feet, picks up her own sweating cardboard container and sashays into the kitchen. "We can have cookies instead. I think I've got some Oreos in a cabinet somewhere."

"Aren't you just a total keeper," Maritza says, and if she smiles hard enough, maybe she'll stop feeling as if she stabbed herself right in the heart with that one.

WAKEFULNESS MOVES SLOWLY AND DRAGS A RELUCTANT SARITA down a slow-moving river. Everything is warm, and some things are heavy, and her nose itches.

No. Tickles.

She manages to get one eye open. Friday sunlight streams through her blinds and gleams from dark, gold-streaked brown hair. Her nose is buried in it, hence the itches. Tickles.

The heaviness is where Mari's arm and leg are wrapped around and flung over Sarita; the warmth is from being entwined for who knows how many hours. At some point they evidently kicked the blankets off into a pile of flowery fabric along with her ridiculous pajama pants, so it's just the two of them, a stack of pillows and Mr. Poffles, Sarita's ancient stuffed bunny.

She slides a hand under her pillow. Yep. There's Mr. Poffles, safe and sound in all his raggedy glory.

As slow as she can, trying not to jostle Mari awake, Sarita squirms until she can roll over onto her back with Maritza's arm still wound around her waist. She flings her own arm over her head and lets out a big sigh. "Ugh."

Frosting and research.

Devesh's baby news still has her out of sorts nearly a week later. She's turning and turning her life over in her head like sneakers in a washing machine, and that mental load is just about as noisy and unbalanced. *What do I have? What?*

Her plan last night had been to talk it over with Maritza, but in the end she just didn't know how to bring it up. *Two months is too soon to talk to a more-or-less-girlfriend about existential crises, right? Maybe?* She's not a frequent-relationship person; she doesn't remember what milestones are important when.

She tilts her head so that it rests on Maritza's and conjures up the images of all the relationships she knows about. Craig and Alex, for starters. No. Bad example. They didn't even know each other's middle names until they'd been about eight months into seeing each other, and they had not been using the "boyfriends" word then either. They didn't have milestones so much as stumbling blocks.

Devesh and Sunil? *Eh.* They'd known each other since junior high school. Sunil had just about been part of the family. Sarita had actually labored under the mistaken impression that Sunil was a cousin of theirs for a long time, which made the day her ten-year-old self had stumbled on the two of them making out pretty awkward. So no, that wouldn't work either. They skipped right past milestones.

"Derail," she mumbles aloud, shaking her head to snap herself out of it.

Next to her, Maritza stirs and her mouth opens wide in an adorable yawn as she moves into a lazy stretch. "'S morning," she says through the yawn, ending it in a sweet, sleepy smile as she blinks at Sarita. "G'morning."

"Hi there." Ugh. She doesn't want to weigh this relationship down with her own baggage. Not this early. No. Cute, sleepy, tousle-haired sort-of girlfriends are not for bumming out with personal issues. They are for kissing. So, Sarita does exactly that, holding Maritza's face gently in her hands as she presses a slow kiss to those happy, smiling lips. "Morning to you, too," she says, pulling back for a nose rub and laughing low when Maritza giggles.

Yeah. This will be just fine for now.

Maritza squirms and breathes out a happy sigh as Sarita resumes kissing her, letting her hands roam over Sarita's arms, bringing skimming fingers to Sarita's waist. "Oh, what a way to wake up! I love it."

Sarita lifts an eyebrow. "What, you're not going to negotiate for breakfast in bed?"

"Hmm." Maritza slings a leg over to straddle Sarita and tilts her head, looking thoughtful. "Do you have anything that is breakfast-suitable?"

"Do you like chocolate croissants?" Tash had baked too many yesterday, and Sarita is pretty sure anything with *chocolate* is something Maritza likes.

She is not wrong. "I love chocolate croissants, and if they're the ones Tash made yesterday, then I extra love them, and you are free to bring them to me." Maritza nods and rolls off Sarita. "I will accept that offer."

"Oh, you will?" Sarita hops off the bed before Maritza's smack at her butt can make contact. "Okay. I see how this is going. Mmhm. Yeah, I'll bring your chocolate croissants and then I'm going to tell you what you're going to do to get them."

Maritza reclines against the flowery pile of pillows, seeming quite pleased with herself, if her half-smirk is any indication. "I look forward to opening negotiations. We do have all morning to come to..." She slides a finger into her mouth and draws it back out slowly from between her full lips before giving it a slow, sensual lick. "...an agreement."

Sarita turns so that she's backing out of her bedroom. "And I'm sure you'll drive a hard bargain."

A toss of that mane of hair. "The hardest."

And that's as far as either of them can take it. Fragile control collapses into raucous giggles, and it's dumb and wonderful and, yeah, Sarita made the right decision, and as she wanders into her kitchen and gets milk and chocolate croissants from her fridge, she's feeling very good about her life choices.

So, of course, that's when the authoritarian knock sounds at the door.

Chapter Fourteen

"**D**ID I JUST HEAR A KNOCK?" MARITZA'S VOICE IS WIDE AWAKE now from the bedroom, wide awake and a little alarmed. "Is someone at the door?"

"Yeah." The knock sounds again, and Sarita tugs at the hem of her nightshirt, grateful that it goes almost to her knees, because she doesn't think whoever's on the other side of that door is going to wait patiently for her to get her bathrobe before they knock again. And sure enough, a sharp rat-a-tat-tat is drummed on the door even as she's walking toward it. "Stay in there," she calls back as she starts undoing the locks. "I'll be back in a... Ma?"

Shanti Sengupta is indeed on the other side of the door, in flesh and blood and with a gleam of maternal fury in her eyes that sends Sarita back a step or two. "You," Shanti begins, and Sarita has the feeling she'll be dispensing with endearments, "are to come with me. Right now, Sarita."

"I'm kind of underdressed..." It's the wrong thing to say, and she definitely shouldn't have let that nervous giggle slip out, because her mother's eyes narrow as she advances on Sarita, who has just run up against the cabinet island that divides her living room from her kitchen and is now out of back-away room. "I have company."

"I am sure your friend will understand that you must come with me, especially once she knows you have been ignoring me or putting me off for several weeks." Shanti comes to a stop a scant step from Sarita, so still that even the skirt of her sari doesn't so much as flutter. "I am out of patience. Go dress."

Sensing that she will be dragged out by her ear and in a Sonics T-shirt that has definitely seen better days if she fails to comply, Sarita retreats to her bedroom and closes the door behind her, leaning on it as she squeezes her eyes shut. "Well, shit."

"Did you really ignore your mom trying to get hold of you?" Sarita cracks an eye open to see that Maritza has gathered the blankets from the floor to clutch them to her chest as she stares in naked incredulity. "Seriously? Are you insane?"

Sarita twists the lock in the doorknob and stalks over to her closet to drag out some clothing. "Oh, come on! Like you've never put off answering your mother?"

"No! Because I don't have a death wish!" Sliding out of the bed, Maritza tosses the blankets aside and shakes her head. "Why the hell would you ignore your mom?"

"Because I know her, I know she's going to have something planned to make me talk to Anjali and I don't *want* to and I didn't know how else to get out of it besides ignoring her calls and hoping the issue would go away." She shimmies into a fresh pair of underwear, then yanks a pair of jeans from a hanger. "So, yeah, there's my big grown-up plan."

"I see that's working out really well for you." Maritza peers around the room. "Shit. My bag's out there."

Sarita wriggles into a Sucre Coeur T-shirt and pulls a hoodie over it. "Put your pajama pants back on."

"You want me to meet your mom in my pajamas?" Maritza's jaw drops.

"I want you to meet my mom wearing *pants*, and you won't fit into any of mine! Wait." Sarita digs around on a shelf. "Okay, here, yoga pants, those should fit. At least they're not covered in ballet-dancing penguins. Will they work?"

"I don't have a bra in here," Maritza points out as she tugs the pants on.

"Can't help you there. I'm an A-cup, and you are... blessed." Sarita pulls her hair up into a ponytail and throws a hair elastic over at Maritza. "We have to make do. I'm sorry."

She's surprised when Maritza steps over to her for a kiss, sweet and simple. "I forgive you for making me take the walk of shame in front of your mother," she says with a wink and a grin. "And for forcing me to ride the bus in pajamas and for the total breakfast fail."

Sarita drops her head into her hand. "Oh, that's a lot to forgive. Ugh."

"Yeah, well, you being adorable goes a long way." Another kiss. "Okay, let's go meet Mom like the adults we are, and then the next bus should be here soon."

"I'm sure she'd drop you off somewhere, maybe at the Java Stop or the studio," Sarita offers as they head for the door.

"I'd have to be willing to sit in a car with more tension than a room full of bungee cords. No, thank you. Hello, Mrs. Sengupta!" Maritza's got the bedroom door open and she sails out, head high, silly pajama pants tucked under one arm, the other extended for a handshake. "I'm so glad to meet you. Sarita's told me so much about her family, I feel like I know you already."

It's a show of confident charm even an angry Shanti is susceptible to, and she visibly relaxes and her face lights up in a smile. "Hello, good morning." She takes the extended hand. "It's a pleasure to meet you...?" Her voice rises with the question.

"Maritza. Maritza Quiñones." In a smooth series of movements, Maritza shakes Shanti's hand, then glides past her to gather up her bag and jacket. "I don't mean to be in a hurry; I've just got a bus to catch."

Shanti's anger gives full way to distress. "A bus? Oh, no. Where do you need to go? We can drop you off. Please. It's bad enough I'm running you off thanks to my daughter's bad behavior."

"No, I'm in the wrong direction; it's fine. I take the bus all the time." She buttons on her jacket, slings the bag over her shoulder and smiles her best and brightest smile. It's a performance of charm so good that Sarita thinks she should be taking notes.

Shanti is clearly torn between the desire to be hospitable and her determination to get Sarita to Bellevue as soon as possible. She has a hand over her mouth as she watches Maritza wedge her feet into her flats. "We can at least help you," she finally says, apparently coming to the decision to compromise. "Sarita can carry your bag down for you."

Maritza chuckles. "Thank you, but I'm a dancer; there's a lot of gear in here. I've seen Sarita try to lift it, and it is very cute but not very productive." She plants a farewell kiss on Sarita's cheek. "Call me later?" She whispers, "if you survive."

"Thanks for the vote of confidence," Sarita grits back, but she can't help smiling. "Yes. I will call you later."

"Great. See you. Nice to meet you, Mrs. Sengupta." Maritza waves over her shoulder and blows a kiss to Sarita before she disappears out the door.

Shanti gazes thoughtfully as Maritza vanishes. "Nice girl. Dancer? What kind?"

"Ballroom." Sarita shoves her hands into her jeans pockets. "Professional."

"You should get us seats for the next time she performs. I'd like to see that." And then the interest falls away, and she turns to Sarita, and, oh, shit, the anger is back. "Now. You get down to the car. You have thirty minutes to explain to me exactly why you have been ignoring me and then you have a lot of house to help me clean."

All of a sudden, cleaning is very appealing. Sarita can only hope she survives the car ride in order to get to it.

"PLEASE," FRED SAYS AS HE PINCHES THE BRIDGE OF HIS NOSE. "Please stop trying to kill each other."

Maritza glares up at Nicky from where she's in a heap on the floor, clutching the knee she fell on. She's afraid to peel her hands away, afraid to see... not *if* it's bruising, but how badly, how fast it's swelling, whether she's feeling a trickle of blood from a cut or just imagining it. "If I were trying, Nicky would *be dead*," she grits out between clenched teeth. "I can show you, as soon as I can stand up."

Nicky stands, arms crossed and hipshot, as he checks himself out in the mirror and looks utterly bored. "It's your own fault, Speedy Gonzalez. Why do I have to keep reminding you how to follow the right tempo—" He's cut off in a gurgling shriek as Maritza lunges up from the floor, heedless of the pain in her right knee, and grabs him by the throat. Fred's there right away to pry away her fingers and haul her off Nicky.

"Break time," he yells, dragging Maritza to a chair. "Let me look at that knee. Nicky, go get my first aid kit. I'm afraid to leave the two of you alone together."

"But my th—" Nicky whines as he examines at his neck in the mirror.

"*Now*, Nicholas." Fred kneels in front of Maritza and tugs her fingers apart. She's clutching her knee again; the momentary adrenaline rush from her leap to strangle Nicky is already wearing off. It hurts, it really, *really* hurts, and she doesn't want to let go of it because maybe if she does it will just fall off or something.

She rolled her eyes at him, at some nasty whispered jackass comment he made, and he spun her out too quickly, deliberately tilting her off balance as he did so. Down she went on her right knee, all of her weight on it, and starbursts of pain went off behind her eyes. She swore in the moment that it had to be broken; there was no way it wasn't.

"It's not broken," Fred tells her, holding her hands away so she can't snap them back to grab it again. "You can bend and move it.

It can't feel good, I know, but Mari, it's not broken. You have a cut and it is definitely going to bruise, but we can take care of most of that." He brings her hands together and clasps them inside of his. "Mari, please. I can't let you dance with him any longer."

It's nothing she didn't think in the screaming instant when she hit the floor, and Maritza knows he means well, but she can't, she *can't*. Just looking at him, looking around at the studio he's poured his life into, she can't risk it. She can't take even a tiny chance on ruining this place that has become her second home. "It's the last few days, Fred," she gets out as she blinks back tears of pain and frustration. "He won't do this to me on stage. I don't trust him, but I do trust in his ego."

Fred pushes a hand through his hair. "I'd be an irresponsible teacher. I *have* been an irresponsible teacher. I should have insisted you two break off this partnership when you two broke up your romance."

"Fred." Though her first impulse is to agree with him, she pushes that aside and cradles his distressed face in her hands. "Nicky and I are adults. We have been this entire time. You can't force us to do anything, you know that." With a hard swallow, she finally takes a look at her knee. "Yuck."

Nicky returns and, with a sneer, tosses the first aid kit down by her chair. "What's the matter, Princess? You never used to faint at the sight of blood."

"Shut up, Nicky," she and Fred snap in unison. Maritza looks more closely at her throbbing knee. "This is manageable; you're right, Fred. But I need to clean it up and get an ice pack on it for a while."

"Then let's get started. This is going to sting." He pours a capful of hydrogen peroxide over the bleeding cut in her knee and apologizes when she hisses. "Sorry. I want to make sure it's clean." He pours on another capful, and then covers the wound with a clean washcloth.

"Nicky, go practice your solo. We're going to be a while. Don't give me that look. This is your fault."

Nicky stomps off to the back corner of the studio to exchange the CD with their samba music for his solo piece and arranges himself in front of the mirror. Fred lifts the washcloth from Maritza's knee. "It's stopped bleeding. Let's get some of antibiotic and a bandage on it, okay? Take two of these." He tosses Maritza a bottle of ibuprofen.

"Thanks." She swallows the pills dry and watches Nicky as he spins and twirls. He really is a beautiful dancer. It's a shame she forgets that whenever he opens his mouth to talk.

Part of her remembers when Nicky was sweet and excited about a partnership with her. He sought her out. He begged her to come to Seattle. He believed they would bring out the best dancing in each other and he was right—for a while.

New tears threaten to spill as Maritza remembers. "We used to be good for each other," she whispers, and her heart aches for those lost days, for days when she looked forward to going to rehearsal with Nicky, instead of counting down the minutes and hours until she'd never have to dance with him again. "I used to think I loved him."

Fred looks up from where he's applying antibiotic to the cut on her knee. "I know," he says, the sorrow in his eyes almost a match for what's in her heart. "And it's not your fault, Mari. It's not your fault he resents you for growing into a better dancer. It's not your fault he cheated on you, and you broke up with him for it. It's not your fault you're not a compliant little doll." He carefully pastes a sticky bandage over the cut. "It's not my fault either, but I still think I should have done more."

"You've done plenty, Fred," she says and means it. "You've gotten us this far. Just get us through a few more hours. I can handle it."

A selfish little voice wishes she didn't think she *had* to handle it, but she ignores it and beams a smile at Fred. "Okay. So, how about that cold pack?"

Chapter Fifteen

THREE HOURS AFTER BEING HAULED OUT TO BELLEVUE BY HER mother, Sarita is sweaty, tired and hungry. She's cleared out her old bedroom closet; every last scrap of clothing and every last outgrown shoe is packed neatly into plastic bags or boxes and out in the garage. She's made good headway on the rest of the bedroom, too—four boxes of books and CDs are now stacked by the front door by the household shoe rack, ready for Sarita to take to the used bookstore.

That, as far as she is concerned, has earned her a break and lunch, especially since she was hustled out of her apartment this morning without her breakfast. Really, for all of that, she probably deserves a pony and a trip to Disneyland.

She will settle for a bottle of apple juice and a sandwich—magnanimous of her, really.

In the kitchen, she revises her list to add back Disneyland and the pony, plus a small fortune and a large estate anywhere but here, because fuck, there's Anjali. Sometime while Sarita was upstairs blaring Beyoncé and cleaning out her closet, her sister had managed to sneak into the house. "Oh, damn it," Sarita groans. "You. Where's Ma?"

"Out. Ugh, I didn't know you were here." Anjali, dressed for running in a pink tank top and snug pants, grimaces as she reaches into the fridge to get a bottle of water. She does not offer

Sarita anything to drink before she stands upright and nudges the refrigerator closed with one pink-socked foot. "I hope you're leaving soon."

"Whenever Ma wants to take me back to my place, I'll go." Her wells of patience have only slightly refilled since her last encounter with her sister. It takes considerable effort for Sarita to keep her voice calm as she crosses into the kitchen to pluck a pear from the fruit bowl on the counter. "I just came by to clean out my closet."

"Why? So you can go back into it? Let's hope." Her smile saccharine, Anjali leans against the kitchen doorjamb. Sarita has to turn her back on her to keep her face calm and smooth.

Right. She's hungry. That's why she's here. Sarita concentrates on the act of washing and slicing the pear. She pops a slice into her mouth and ignores her growling stomach's insistence that she wolf the whole thing down. Better to chew slowly, methodically, and to count each grind of her teeth so that she can try to retain some semblance of control. After thirty chews, she swallows. "It's Friday. Shouldn't you be in the office?"

"I took the week off to help Ma with the house. You know, like you and Devesh didn't." Sarita hears her crack open her water bottle and take a long swallow. "She told me to come by and grab some clothes for the girls. Yours, I assume."

"Ma didn't ask me to take any time off, and I'm sure she didn't ask you either, so you can stop with the perfect child act," Sarita snaps back, with more heat than she intended. She bites into another slice of pear, more savagely. Her free hand is curled around the rim of the kitchen sink and clutching it white-knuckled. "The clothes are in the garage. There are plenty of things that should fit both girls, even some saris and other things they can grow into. They're all clean. You might need to air them out; they were stored for a while."

She waits for her sister to say something about disinfectant, or about gay being contagious so no thanks for the clothes, but Anjali doesn't offer anything more than a snort before she walks out of the kitchen toward the garage. Sarita waits for the door to close before she peels her fingers free of the sink and turns around. Wobbly knees mean she has to lean against the sink to regain her composure.

"Food," she says aloud. That will give her something to do. Within a few minutes, she has a sandwich assembled, peanut butter on whole wheat with thin slices of the pear layered in. She takes it and a glass of apple juice upstairs to survey her bedroom and figure out what to do next.

There's one more shelf of books to clear out. A quick check shows her that she's run out of boxes. Sarita closes her eyes and sighs. That means going downstairs to get some from the garage. If she's lucky, Anjali has loaded her SUV with the bags of clothing and gone, but she doesn't think she *is* that lucky; she hasn't heard a vehicle pull out. Then again, she didn't hear her mother leave, either.

Sarita pokes her head from the bedroom door and listens for any sign of life: a door slam, or sweep of Anjali's sock feet over carpet or, Sarita's favorite option, a departing vehicle. She grips her sandwich in one hand and the doorjamb with the other and leans farther out into the hallway.

Silence.

If Anjali is gone, she might come back, and Sarita has had about all she can stand of her sister today. It takes her a split second to decide to run down the stairs full-tilt toward the garage. She can get down there, get the boxes and be back upstairs in a jiffy, safely tucked away behind her bedroom door.

What she doesn't anticipate is Anjali not only returning, but coming back through the front door. Sarita is going too fast to stop at the bottom of the stairs. In a flurry of shrieks, hair and peanut butter sandwich, the two women collide and fall to the carpet in the first-floor hallway, screaming and kicking to get away from each other.

"What is *wrong* with you?" Anjali howls as she peels half of Sarita's sandwich from her hair. "Idiot! You never think before you do anything!"

"Shut up, Anjali! Why did you come back through the front door, anyway?" Sarita rolls aside and grabs her nose. Thanks to her sister's thick skull, she has a nosebleed. She scrambles to her feet and goes to the downstairs bathroom to press a wad of tissue to it. "Damn it! That hurts!"

Anjali limps after her. "You deserve it for being stupid! Look at me, I'm a mess! My ankle's sprained! There's peanut butter in my hair!"

"I am *bleeding*," Sarita points out, tilting her head back.

Anjali glares at her. Then, with a roll of her eyes, she stomps off to rattle around in the kitchen. She's back in a short time with a handful of ice cubes wrapped in a dishtowel. "Put this on your nose," she orders as she shoves the bundle into the hand Sarita isn't using to stanch her nosebleed. "Go on."

Sarita rolls her eyes to look at her sister and the ice cube bundle held limp at her side. "Say what?"

"Put it. On. Your nose. Did your brain fall out when we hit the ground or something?" Anjali snatches away the tissue and lifts Sarita's ice-pack hand to her nose. "My eight-year-old follows directions better than you do. My *toddler* does."

"Well, excuse me if I'm not used to you doing anything remotely nice for me." Sarita secures her grip on the ice and swats Anjali's hand. "It takes a minute to sink in."

Anjali stares at her with conflict gleaming in her eyes. "I don't like you. That doesn't mean I want to see you hurt."

Sarita opens her mouth, but has no idea how to take that or what to say in response. Before she can make a decision, Anjali draws back her shoulders and limps out of the bathroom at as fast a clip as she can manage. Sarita blinks in confusion and follows her, with the improvised cold pack still pressed to her nose.

In the living room, Anjali stands by the fireplace with a silver-framed photo in her hands. From the gap in the array of photos on the mantel, Sarita deduces that it's the largest one from Anjali's wedding day, the one with her in her red sari, her gold jewelry and garlands of flowers. Anjali's grip on the frame is white-knuckled, as if her life depends on it. She breathes deep and casts a glance over her shoulder at Sarita.

"You have no idea," she begins, and then stops. With care, she sets the photo back in its place on the mantel. She stands with her back to Sarita and balls her hands into fists. "I didn't realize it until right now. You have never figured it out, never thought about what you cost me, never asked."

The non sequitur sets Sarita back a step. "I what?"

"All these years, it's been over a decade, and you *never asked.*" Anjali's shoulders shake, and her words come from between gritted teeth. "I just said I don't like you, and even now you *don't ask.*"

The snort Sarita can't help hurts her nose, and it takes her a second to gather herself and push past the pain. "Um, homophobia is a pretty clear thing. I don't really need a deep explanation for your prejudice and hatred."

Anjali casts another quick glare over her shoulder. "All that education and you're still dense as a box of rocks. Sit down, Sarita."

"I can listen to you standing up," Sarita shoots back.

"Sit down and lean forward, stop tilting your head back." Anjali hobbles across the living room and is all over exasperation as she leads Sarita to a chair. "You don't know anything about nosebleeds, apparently. Someone has to fill you in."

Sarita wrenches her arm from her sister's grip and sits under her own power. "Okay, stop being thoughtful; it's too weird." She wants to run for the bus stop, and to hell with cleaning the rest of her room. "What's up with you? Did you hit your head when we went down?"

Anjali huffs an indignant breath through her nose. "I can be concerned about you. I'm not heartless."

That earns Anjali Sarita's very best eye roll. "Right. I'd actually believe that if you hadn't spent the last decade giving me and Devesh shit because you decided you hate *the gays* for no reason. You're still a terrible sister, and I'd really like it if you just left me alone, okay, Anjali? Thanks for the nosebleed tips, but get lost."

"*I'm* the terrible sister." Anjali's laugh is bitter. She glances down at her hands and starts to pick at the cuticle on her thumb. "Right. Me. Because you're totally clean, you didn't ruin my wedding plans."

Sarita sits back to rub at her forehead, where a headache is beginning to spread. "What are you talking about? I behaved exactly as instructed for your wedding. I wore what you told me to wear, I didn't bring a girl as my date and I helped with the decorations and cleanup. In fact, I did absolutely every stupid, tiny thing you asked, even though you were a raging bitch to me my entire senior year, I remind you."

"Not my wedding. My wedding *plans*," Anjali spits. "To Vikesh."

Sarita's understanding is still about as clear as mud. "Vikesh? That guy you dumped when he transferred to Brown? You didn't have wedding plans with him."

But... the thing is, there's something in the back of her mind now; something vague and dark and buried from her sophomore year begins to unfurl: the sound of Anjali in tears, images of their parents whispering together, tense and wary. And Devesh, Devesh always there, never leaving her side, always taking her to the movies with him and Sunil, or the three of them going out to dinner or going ice skating or anything, anything at all to keep her out of the house, as though he was standing between her and something big, something bad.

It hadn't seemed that way at the time, but now...

Sarita takes a deep breath. "Anjali. You're going to have to explain what this has to do with why you hate me. I really thought you just,

I don't know, joined the Young Republicans in college or something, and that's why I lost you."

It had happened almost overnight. One day Anjali had gently teased Sarita about her tomboyish clothing, had offered to help with makeup and hair and her nails. And then the next: anger, tears, horrible insults and no explanations. She went from sister to enemy in the blink of an eye, and Sarita never knew why. And she never knew how to ask.

"One gay sibling was questionable enough for Vikesh's family," Anjali says, facing away, the words squeezed out and soft. "Two? No way. That wasn't a family they wanted their precious son marrying into." She whirls, face creased with anger and pain. "You had to come out. You couldn't stay in the closet one more year; you had to be selfish. You never *think*; you never have. You never consider what effect your actions might have on anyone besides yourself!" Her fingers curl into fists, and her breaths are harsh, ragged and rasp like sandpaper. "Everything is about you. And everyone defended you. My life is in ruins, and they defend you, protect you."

All Sarita can do is stare up at her sister, the makeshift ice pack forgotten at her side as she tries to make sense of it at all. "I didn't... Anjali, I never—"

"No. You never. Never thought, never knew, never asked, never apologized, you never did *anything*." Anjali's angry pacing is tempered by her injured ankle. "You ruined everything."

Of the hundreds of horrible things Anjali has said to her over the years, this is the one that stings most, to Sarita's surprise. Every homophobic slur, every sneering insult, pales next to this entirely unfair accusation. Sarita's grip tightens around the ice pack; the fingers of her other hand curl into her palm and the nails bite into the skin. "No, you know what, I didn't do shit."

Anjali lifts her chin and glares down her nose. "You—"

"No. I didn't." The more she thinks about it, the more she knows she's right, and she's not going to take Anjali's crap for another minute. All these years, and it's not simple homophobia? Or it is, but it isn't *Anji's* homophobia. It's a relief to know that Anji doesn't actually hate her because she's gay, she just hates that Sarita came out.

"I did *nothing*, Anji. Yeah, I came out, okay. Sure. It felt right; I wanted to do it." Sarita struggles to her feet and holds up a hand to forestall Anji's attempts to object. "But Vikesh's family's reaction to that is *not* my fault, not even a little bit." She shakes her head, amazed to feel pity for her sister for the first time in a very long time. "I didn't know you two were planning to get married. I'm sorry his family were absolute assholes about it."

Anjali stands still. She keeps a steady gaze on Sarita and her hands are still in fists, but she's stopped trying to say anything. She is quiet, watchful and wary. It makes Sarita comfortable enough to take another step forward. "Their choices, their decisions, that's not on me, and I won't let you put it on me anymore, Anjali. I hate to say it but..." She clutches the ice pack to her chest. "Anji, you and Vikesh were adults, legal actual adults. He could have stood up to them. He could have fought for you, right?"

It's the kindest way she can think of to say, *if he'd really loved you, he would have married you anyway, no matter what they said.* There's enough pain between them already; she has no inclination to add to it.

Anjali still isn't speaking, but her eyes are wet with tears. Sarita steps forward again. "I always wondered why you married Bimal so fast," she murmurs. Things are starting to add up; there's so much she understands now. "You didn't date anyone for so long after Vikesh left, and then Bimal came along, and it seemed like it happened right away. And now I get it; you weren't taking any chances."

A tear spills, and Anji wipes it away with a sniffle. "No. I love my husband. I have always loved him, I married him because I loved him so much, and I love our children, and..." She tilts her head back and wipes at fresh tears with her thumbs. "It just *hurt*, Sarita, it hurt *so much* and Vikesh never apologized. He never even called me. He just *left* and you were so *happy* and free, and I lost everything and I just, I—" Anjali drops her head into her hands and sobs, her broken heart beating in every gasp.

The pain echoes through Sarita, the hurt of all the years lost to anger and insults and sniping. Sorrow holds its hand and walks with it—but forgiveness, that's a few steps behind. Still, she can unbend enough to touch Anjali with kindness for the first time in a decade. It's not a hug—there's too much between them for hugs, too much to wade through, too much Sarita doesn't know she'll ever be able to forgive—but she strokes a hand over her sister's hair as Anjali cries, spilling years of repressed pain into her palms.

The sobs are a fierce storm, huge breaking waves that ease and ebb slowly until at last Anjali lifts her head to look at Sarita with eyes that are bloodshot, but somehow clear and light, with no edge of anger. It might be too much to expect to see regret or sadness there, but as near as Sarita can see, the bitter hatred isn't there. Anjali swallows hard and opens her mouth. "Sarita, I—"

"No." Sarita steps back, snatching her hand away to hold it up between them, palm forward. "Uh-uh, no, Anjali. If you're about to apologize, don't." Her knees start to tremble, but she refuses to even appear to be ceding ground by taking a seat. "Not yet. I can't... I can't accept any apology from you, not yet."

Anjali's mouth snaps into a tight line as she takes a sharp breath. "Fine," she says, her eyes dark as she steps back and crosses her arms over her chest. "Okay."

Grant. Me. Strength. "You need to think a lot more deeply about what you're apologizing *for*," Sarita points out as she crosses her own arms. She swallows hard and lifts her chin. "You assigned everything Vikesh and his family did to me for *years*. You were vicious, Anjali. And I was a *teenager*. I don't know what I was supposed to do for you when nobody told me what was going on."

"You could have asked." Anjali lifts an eyebrow.

"By the time I realized there was something to ask about, I didn't want to talk to you anymore. And you were being so awful, I didn't really care. All I wanted by then was for you to stop. You didn't. You didn't tell me anything, you just piled on more and more horrible stuff and..." Her chest is tight. "I didn't do *anything* to deserve it. I'm sorry you got hurt, but none of it was ever, *ever* my fault, and I need for you to really understand that before you apologize."

Anjali draws herself up to stand straight and tall as she lifts the hem of her tank top and uses it to blot at her still-damp face. Sarita can't shake the sensation that she's stalling for time. Anjali pats at her cheeks and reddened eyes with care, wiping tear tracks away as slowly and softly as she can.

At last, with a nod, Anjali speaks again. "You have... a point. You have several points. And yes, you're right. I do need to think about that."

"I have a lot to think about too." Her throat is tight, and her knees are still weak. She looks around. "Listen, do you know where Ma went? I think I need to go home."

"She told me she was going to Mrs. Malakar's." Anjali shrugs, and her face shifts; hesitation grows in her eyes, and her next words come slowly, as if they're being pulled out. "I can, I mean, if you need, I could drive you home, or wherever. The kids are in school. Bimal won't be home till late because of his fracking case in Wenatchee, I've got time."

A simple ride home shouldn't be an epic occurrence. In any normal family it wouldn't be. Sarita shakes her head. "I appreciate it, but I need space, too. Thanks anyway."

Anjali nods and glances at the sports watch on her wrist. "There should be a bus along in a little while. Not long. If you walk fast you should be able to catch it."

It's as good a plan as any. Actually, it's all she's got. "Okay. That'll work." She thinks she should say more, find words, clear the air of unfinished business, but she racks her brain to no avail. All she can do is offer her sister a half-smile. "Thank you, Anjali."

Three tiny words. She puts all the sincerity she can into them. They're a start.

And Anjali's answering smile, if wobbly, is just as sincere. "You're welcome."

That, too, is a start. Sarita turns on her heel and goes into the kitchen to get her purse and leave.

Chapter Sixteen

Frederick Corbett is not a man who easily regrets.

Fifteen years of his life were devoted to professional ballroom dancing, in an era when costumes were elaborate and of questionable taste. He entered into that freely and of his own will and, even in the most electric-colored and boldly sequined ensembles, he was happy because he was doing what he loved most in the world, and that was more than enough.

When he retired from professional dance, the next logical step, in his mind, was to open a studio. It took a lot of money to start up and a lot of hard work. He had to find the building, then find clients. He had to offer classes other than ballroom to bring in money until people caught on that ballroom dancing was a fun way to pass the time while their little munchkins were in their ballet and tap classes. It was very hard work, and it is still hard work, but Fred is happy because he still gets to do what he loves most in the world and now he gets to share it with others, and that is fantastic.

Today, though... today, Fred regrets.

Fred regrets that he convinced Susana Quiñones to move to Seattle and bring her enormously gifted daughter to learn at his studio. He regrets that he listened to Nicky in the first place when Nicky pleaded for help to get Maritza to Seattle. He regrets not being more meddlesome when Maritza and Nicky fell jubilantly into bed together after a record high-scoring night at the Pacific

Northwestern Latin Ballroom Sectionals three years ago and he *definitely* regrets that he did not interfere outright after they broke up in September but kept accidentally having hate-hookups, usually fueled by pitchers of margaritas and an extremely noisy argument, into December.

And right now, he very much regrets that he didn't insist they find new partners when it became clear that Nicky wasn't taking the breakup well at all.

He watches his dancers as they practice their solos at opposite ends of the studio, carefully not looking at each other. Nicky has dropped Maritza again, not a hard drop, not one that would cause injury, but one that clearly conveyed the contempt he had for her. Fred called a halt to any further samba practice for the day. Mutual antipathy aside, there were no further improvements they could make before next week's auditions.

Fred rubs his forehead and tries to keep his sigh as quiet as possible. He doesn't really regret anything that brought Maritza here. She's good, better than good, and Nicky had been right to want to partner with her. When things were good between them, they were very, very good. And even now when things were terrible between them, they're still amazing. Fred can't regret working with this much talent.

Still. They hate each other, and even if the angry sparks between them fuel the chemistry of their dance, it's unsustainable. But Maritza, good God, she refuses to give up on Nicky for the *Dance Nation* audition. Fred does not understand it. Emotionally, mentally, Maritza can't trust Nicky. All the trust she has is in the basket of Nicky's inflated ego, and Fred doesn't particularly consider that to be a stable perch. And yet Maritza stubbornly refuses to yield and is going along with everything Nicky dictates for some reason.

Fred tried again an hour ago to convince her to drop Nicky, and that earned him a level glare and the coldest tone he's ever heard from her. "I've made my position clear, Fred," she said as she bandaged a fresh blister. "I'm dancing with Nicky. One last time. We're each other's best shot, and that's it. Please don't ask me again."

But when Fred watches her dance her salsa-flavored solo, when he sees her smile into the mirror and it's a real, genuine smile, the kind she never beams anymore when she has to dance with Nicky... when he sees that, he can't help but want to tear his hair out.

After hours in the studio, hours of fighting and sniping, Nicky and Maritza are both close to collapse; their steps blur, and their heads nod. Fred claps his hands. "Okay. I'm calling it for today." He lifts his hands to forestall their protests. "No. Come on, you two. You know your samba and your solos inside out. The most important thing for the rest of this week besides light rehearsal is to rest, to eat well and to go to bed early every night. Mari, you're off work most of this week, right?"

She nods as she shoves a sweaty clump of hair back from her face. "Yep. And I managed to get the car tonight, so I don't have to bus home... but, Fred, can I borrow your shower?" She rolls her eyes, but her smile is good-natured. "Javi hates it when I drive sweaty. He says he smells it for days. Obviously he's full of crap, but you know me, peacekeeper to the end."

And to your detriment, Fred doesn't say. He smiles. "Sure thing. Knock yourself out."

With another of her much-too-bright smiles, Maritza grabs her belongings and bounces out of the studio with more energy than anyone has the right to have after being thrown around and insulted all day. Fred does have to marvel at her resilience.

He does not, however, have to let today pass without a word to Nicky. Fred spins on his heel and stalks over to where Nicky is in a sulk as he packs his dance bag. "Nicholas."

Nicky looks up, blue eyes narrowed into icy slits. "Frederick," he says, his tone mocking. He gets to his feet and his movements are slow and deliberate. "How can I help you today?"

Since Fred's plan is to deliver a brief lecture on professionalism, he decides it would be a bad idea to grab Nicky by the throat and squeeze him against the mirrors. And he does have all those pesky memories of when Nicky *hadn't* been such an egotistical, hateful little shit. Fred can't just set them aside. So he confines himself to a casual slouch and shoves his hands into his jeans pockets. "Listen, Nicky. It would be great if, for the next few days, you weren't such an asshole to your partner."

Nicky rolls his eyes. "Oh, come on, Fred, accidents happen. Mari just needs to—"

"Mari, like you, needs to be able to trust the person she's dancing with. But more than that?" Fred raises an eyebrow. "The judges at every stage of *Dance Nation* know the difference between an accident and a dick move. You won't make it out of preliminaries if you behave the way you did today."

"Is that a threat?" Nicky tosses his head and, oh, sweet Jesus, Fred is tired of this pout thing Nicky has picked up over the last year.

"I don't see how it can be a threat if I am not one of the judges," Fred points out. He forces himself to remember that once upon a time, Nicky actually had half a brain in his head and didn't *need* logic spelled out to him, and oh, those halcyon days. "It's a warning, Nicky. I want what's best for you. After all these years as your teacher, I want to see you succeed. And I know you want to get onto this show, so I'm telling you to *behave*." To back Nicky against a wall is still probably not a good idea, so Fred settles for reaching forward to poke Nicky hard in the chest. "Dance your best; treat your partner like a human being and not a punching bag. You only have to dance with her a few more days. Make the best of it."

Fred can't be sure it actually sinks in, but Nicky draws back his shoulders and offers a stiff, polite nod. "All right, Fred. Okay."

"Okay. You better mean it." The alarm on the main studio entrance beeps, and Fred steps backward, pointing at Nicky as he goes to see who it is. "That should be the next tap class. Remember, behave, Nicholas."

But when he gets out to the lobby, it's not any of the studio's students. A slight woman with golden-brown skin, a sloppy pile of black curls and big, dark eyes that are teary and bloodshot stands by the desk, wary and uncertain, poised for flight. "Hi, excuse me, I... "

Fred stops in the doorway of Studio 1, not wanting to spook her. "Hi. Do you need a dance lesson, or were you looking for help?"

She takes a deep breath and smiles, but it's a shaky smile. "I was hoping to see Mari... Maritza. Maritza Quiñones?"

Behind him, Fred senses Nicky's looming presence. Fred flaps a hand to wave him off and shoots a scowl over his shoulder for good measure. "She's here; she's in the back cleaning up after rehearsal. Is there something I can help you with?"

But before the woman can speak, Nicky slithers past Fred with his hand extended and a smirky, unpleasant smile on his face. "Ah, you must be the girlfriend. I'm Nicky. The boyfriend. I'm sure she's mentioned me?"

Fury rushes through Fred, and his hands curl into fists. He doesn't get to take so much as a step forward, though, before the woman—Sarita, he now realizes she must be—draws herself up and somehow makes herself taller, more intimidating. "Oh, yes. Mari's mentioned you." Her tone makes it very clear that it wasn't at all favorable, and Fred has the pleasure of seeing Nicky's face flush with anger at the slight.

But an angry Nicky is a dangerous Nicky, so Fred does step forward, less concerned about the woman's flight now that she seems to have gathered a significant amount of admirable pluck in the face of Nicky as his usual charming self. He brushes Nicky aside before he can say another word. "*Ex*-boyfriend, Nicky, you're the *ex*. And I'm Fred, Maritza's teacher. You must be Sarita. It's a pleasure to meet you." He wraps an arm around Sarita's shoulders to draw her farther away from Nicky, who huffs out an annoyed breath and stomps off. "You're absolutely free to wait with me for Maritza. I hope she'll be out soon."

Sarita nods, looking much steadier than she did a few minutes ago, though she is twisting her fingers into white-knuckled knots. "I don't mind."

"You can sit here." He guides her behind the desk to the reception chair. "Can I get you anything? We've got a water cooler, or I can grab you something from the snack machine."

"No, thanks. I'm okay." To Fred's surprise, she looks over his shoulder and sticks her tongue out. He turns to see Nicky flipping Sarita the bird as he stomps from the studio. Sarita sits back and hoots with laughter and only gets louder when Fred turns to face her. "Sorry. Sorry! God, the look on your face." Her hooting dissolves into helpless giggles. "That wasn't mature of me. I've just... I have never heard a good thing about that guy from anyone."

"I'd probably be the only person in the world besides his mother who *could* tell you anything good about him." Fred offers her a wry smile. "I promise, I'm not trying to sell you on him, but there was a time when he actually wasn't so bad."

"Birth, I'm assuming." It's impossible not to respond to her grin with one of his own. Her smile is as infectious and bright as Maritza's; it's clear what drew the two women together.

"Listen," he says with a look back at his tightly shut office door. "Let me go see if I can hurry her along, okay? She always takes too long in the shower."

"She always smells great afterward, though," Sarita says with an absent expression on her face that quickly shifts to horror as her cheeks burn red. "Oh, no! I did not just say that."

Fred bows in a show of chivalry that's meant to conceal the fact he's about to lose his head with laughter. "I heard nothing," he tells her, though it's an effort not to choke on the words. "Be right back."

He walks down the hallway toward his office, and he hears the loud bass boom of techno dance pop reverberating off the walls long before he gets to the door. Even as he lifts his fist to bang on the thin plywood, he knows it's a hopeless endeavor. "Mari," he calls, knocking as hard as he can without making his knuckles ache. "Mari? Company."

The music doesn't break, and, even if he strains, he can't hear any footsteps. He knocks again. "Mari?"

One song shifts into another, just as loud, and his cause is a lost one, of course it is. It's a miracle that he hears the studio door beep over the cacophony. Surely this time it's the tap class.

But when he turns around, it's not. It's nobody, actually—the reception desk is vacant again, and Sarita is nowhere in sight. Fred frowns and pokes his head into Studio 1. "Sarita?"

Nothing.

Maybe she went out to get some air. He notices it's a little stuffy in the studio and adjusts the thermostat before he walks toward the main entrance to check on Sarita.

"Fred?" His office door opens, and Maritza steps out, wet hair piled up on her head and bag slung over her shoulder. "Was that you at the door? Sorry."

"No problem. Just wanted to let you know Sarita came here." He frowns. "I think."

Maritza walks into the lobby and looks around. "Adorable, about five feet tall, with two feet of that being an awesome head of hair?"

"That'd be the one." He beckons for her to follow him outside. "I think maybe she stepped out for some air. She looked stressed out when she got here."

"I wonder what's up. She's supposed to be with her mom today." Mari drops her bag and joins him to walk outside, but draws up short when they get the door open. Since Fred stopped short about a second ago, she runs into him and it takes her an instant to catch her breath before she says, "What the fuck?"

What the fuck, indeed. Fred has to wonder that himself as he sees Sarita, bristling with anger and apprehension as Nicky smirks at her, quite pleased with himself. Fred starts to step forward, but Maritza pushes past him in a dead sprint to put herself between Nicky and Sarita. "Fuck off, Nicky."

"Why?" The high, fluting tone in Nicky's voice is always the clearest tell that his innocence is a pretense. "Are you afraid I'll tell her something she doesn't know about you? Because too late for that."

Wind and traffic are the only sounds in the air as Maritza stares at Nicky in confusion. He, of course, continues to smirk down at her with his arms crossed over his chest. Maritza whirls to face Sarita, who also seems confused, but also small and pale and somehow, all of a sudden, sad. Maritza reaches out. "Sarita?"

But instead of letting Maritza take her hand, Sarita steps back and puts her own hand up between them. "Hang on. Sorry. I need a minute." Head bowed, she takes in several deep breaths as her small slender shoulders heave. "Wow."

Maritza drops her hand; her brow is creased and troubled. "Sarita..."

"You should have told her about the audition, Mari," Nicky drawls as he sidles back to where he'd left his bag near the studio door. "She didn't even know you were thinking of skipping town." He clucks in faux-sympathy. "Not like you to keep secrets, Mari. Oh, no, wait. Never mind. It totally is."

Maritza's face falls. Her heart breaks right in front of Fred's eyes, and she takes a step closer to Sarita. "What? I... no, no, Sarita, it's not like that; it wasn't a secret."

Nicky picks up his bag and starts to walk off, but Fred snags him by his jacket collar and hauls him back, with no concern as to whether or not Nicky can keep his balance on the rain-slick sidewalk. "Oh, no, Nicholas. You're not going anywhere. We need to have a little talk." He curls his fingers more tightly on the collar fold. "Ladies, if you need to talk, I can offer my office."

"No, I…" Sarita shakes her head and finally lifts it to look at Maritza; her sadness is a mirror of Maritza's. "Mari, I… I need to go."

"Please. I can explain." Maritza reaches out again, but Sarita backs away.

"I'll text you later. I promise. I just need some time to think, my day, it's…" Her laugh is short and bewildered, bitter as antiseptic. "Hell of a day. Hell of a day. I… later. Later, Mari."

She turns and walks in the direction of the bus stop three blocks down, leaving Maritza to stand still and quiet on the sidewalk with her hand still outstretched in entreaty. Slowly, as Sarita recedes into the distance, Maritza lets her hand fall, then her head bows and her shoulders droop, and she is dejection personified. Fred yanks involuntarily on Nicky's coat collar at the sight, and Nicky gurgles out a strangled yelp.

That snaps Fred back into action. "Inside, both of you." He spots the first tap class students at last, and he thanks all the gods he can think of when he sees their teacher Stephanie, catching a couple of students by their hands in an exuberant race. Stephanie can take care of the class, and that will leave him free to deal with this mess. Fred grabs Maritza's wrist and drags her toward the studio. He lets go of Nicky for only the second it takes him to get the door open and the three of them through it.

Nicky grumbles, and Maritza is silent as Fred marches them down the hallway and into his office, then shoves each of them toward the chairs in front of the desk. "Sit," he orders as he takes his own seat, and they do, although Nicky's contemptuous eye-roll and huff are in sharp contrast to Maritza's quiet, controlled sadness—so much so that Fred turns his attention to Nicky first. "Nicholas, you're no longer welcome at this studio."

Maritza's mouth falls open, and Nicky sits forward in his chair with his hands tight around the armrests. "You can't do that."

"I can, I do, and it's as of right now, by the way." Fred sits back. "Well, as soon as I'm done saying my piece, anyway. You will no longer represent the Corbett Studio in any way. I will no longer teach you. I'm done, Nicky."

Nicky leaps to his feet and starts to pace. "Are you an idiot?" he asks, whirling to point at the shelves of trophies on the back wall. "Seriously? After everything I've brought this studio? After ten years? There's no way."

Fred shrugs and he feels very good about this decision—free, in fact. The Nicky here now isn't the Nicky who came to him so many years ago, who was young and raw and talented and eager to become the best ballroom dancer he could. Fred tried for too long to remember that Nicky and to hang on to him. No more. "There's every way. I own this studio. I get to say who represents me. And that won't be you anymore." He looks at Maritza, sorry to put her through this. "Mari, I know this is last-minute. I know it's not what you wanted. I apologize."

But her shock has worn off and… is that glee on her face? She looks from Nicky to Fred for just a moment before she stands and grabs Nicky's bag from beside his chair. She has it unzipped in an instant and she goes through the contents lightning-fast. With a laugh of triumph, she shoves Nicky back with one hand and pulls out a crumpled wad of fabric with the other. "I can't believe you were stupid enough to carry these around." Before Fred can wonder for too long what *these* are, Maritza opens her hand and lets the fabric unfurl to reveal a tiny pair of women's underwear. Maritza laughs again. "Yeah. We're done, Nicky. We are totally and forever done, and now there's not a damn thing you can do about it."

The brush fire of embarrassment that lights up Fred's face might be intense enough to make him pass out. "Did I miss something?" he asks, not nearly as composed as he would have liked.

Maritza bites her lip, and there's contrition in her eyes as she turns to him. "Fred, I'm sorry. I brought Sarita here one night after hours and we…" The tomato red of her face has got to be a close match to his own. "Anyway. Nicky was blackmailing me about it. If it had gotten out it might have damaged the studio's reputation, and Fred, I couldn't... " She swallows hard. "I had to keep this place safe. I couldn't let anything happen to it. To you."

Clarity dawns on Fred, and the last weeks are all at once illuminated with a harsh brightness. "Oh, God. I should have realized. You've been too tolerant. I should have known... you should have told me."

"Does it matter now?" She turns back to Nicky and she is every inch a champion as she faces him. "No one will believe you now. You're just a bitter ex-student with no proof. News travels so fast in the dance community, don't you think?" She is relishing this, and Fred can't blame her. Her face is completely serene for the first time in weeks as she turns to look at him. "Fred, did you have anything else you wanted to say to Nicky?"

"I didn't, actually." Fred gets up and waves toward the door. "You can go now, Nicholas. Don't forget your bag." He waits a moment before waving again, more emphatically this time. "Go on. Out."

Nicky stands still, a dumbfounded expression on his face as he flexes his fingers into and out of fists. When he doesn't otherwise move, Maritza shoves his bag into his arms and gives him a good push. "Bye, Nicky."

Nicky stares at the two of them, face red with anger, but finally he slings his bag over his shoulder and stalks out the office door. Fred holds his breath until he finally hears the sharp beep of the front door alarm and lets it out in a rush. "Jesus. Thank God that's over."

Maritza is gazing out the office door with a small smile on her lips. "I'm free. Thank God," she echoes, before turning to face Fred with a guilty look. "Fred, I'm sorry about the Sarita thing. I should have told you."

"I'm not entirely pleased about it, but it's water under the bridge. Not a real concern now. Also? I don't want to think about it." He sits back down. "Right now, I have to worry about you. I just left you partnerless for the auditions."

Maritza rubs at the back of her neck. "Not really."

It takes a few seconds for what she's saying to sink in—a few seconds of her slow, amused smile and steady eyes. "Mari. No. No way. I'm just emergency backup."

"And it's an emergency." She leans across the desk; her smile is growing impossibly bigger and brighter. "Come on, Fred. You're all I got. My solo isn't going to cut it for these auditions; it's strictly for tiebreakers. It's got to be you up on that stage with me."

He rubs at his knee and grimaces at the slight ache of arthritis. "Mari, I mean. We never really thought it would come to this. My knee isn't going to be up to that samba."

"Then it's a good thing I really wanted to do the Argentine tango anyway, right? Solves that problem." She grabs him by the upper arms to drag him up and out of his chair. "Come on. We've got some rehearsing to do."

"You just showered. You have to be exhausted; you're supposed to go home and rest," he points out as she hauls him from the office and toward Studio 2.

"Desperate times, Frederick. Let's go." For one brief second she turns to face him, and her bright smile flags. "I've got a few hours to fill before I can explain everything to Sarita anyway, right? Might as well put them to good use."

Right then, Fred thinks that a better use of time might be finding a way to murder Nicky and hide the body, but before he can say so, Maritza's got the tango music on the stereo. "And one and two and..."

And they're off.

Chapter Seventeen

*I*N THIS, *SPINOZA IS NOT EXCESSIVELY OPTIMISTIC, BUT A REALIST. In fact, one could hypothesize that in his beliefs, Spinoza...*

Sarita's head bobs, droops and hangs for a moment before she jerks awake again; the sudden motion sets the untidy bun of her hair into ludicrous motion. When it yanks against her scalp, she grabs the knot and she groans.

According to her laptop clock, it's eleven o' clock at night. The question is, what *day* is it? Every night for the last week she's been holed up in her bedroom with her laptop, where she's alternated between watching action movies and working on her paper. Work, she always found, was the best way to distract herself from major problems. When work got boring, then watching things get blown up was the next best course of action. It's a philosophy that has served her well for many years, and after a week like the one she's had, if she devotes more of her limited energy to movies than to her paper, well, she thinks that's fairly understandable.

With a yawn, she rests the back of her hand against the tea mug on her nightstand. *Cold. And half-full, too, poor abandoned tea.* She swings her legs over the side of the bed and picks up the mug, determined to finish the section of her paper she's working on before she gives in to sleep. When her stomach growls, she figures dinner might be a pretty good idea as well, if somewhat late.

In the kitchen she pours out the cold tea and refills her kettle. With a flip of a switch, the water is set to heat, and she moves on to the pantry to see what she can find to soothe the beast of ravenous hunger that's suddenly rearing its head. Her choices all seem to be of the global pasta family: macaroni and cheese, spaghetti, or a Thai rice noodle bowl.

She bends farther into the pantry to look in its depths, and that's when her cell phone goes off behind her, buzzing against the island countertop like a short-lived but very angry swarm of hornets. The sound is a surprise in her quiet apartment, and she bonks her head against the top shelf of the pantry. Her hair absorbs most of the blow, but it's still a firm enough hit to send her backing out of the cupboard as she lets out a vicious curse and clutches at her head.

It's Maritza, she's sure. She knows that before she picks up the phone, and a pang of guilt seizes her heart. She promised texts later, and, well... later didn't happen. Ever. At the bakery her phone stayed resolutely in her purse and at home she plugged her phone in out here at night in order to ensure it. She told herself it was so she didn't get distracted while she was working, but yeah, she knew the truth.

She reads the message—rather, the list of messages—without unlocking the phone screen.

Please. It's been days, Sarita. Please.

I need to explain everything. I'm sorry.

Are you going to text me? Please?

If you want, you can come to the auditions tomorrow. They're at the Paramount.

I know it might be weird, but I wish you would come, I promise...

The last message is too long for the preview screen. Sarita slides to unlock and read it.

I know it might be weird but I wish you would come, I promise to tell you every thing after the audition, you can watch me dance and then you and I can go talk, no matter what happens.

Sarita sighs and sets the phone back down. No matter what happens? That means if Maritza gets on the show, of course. Of course she will; Sarita is sure of that even if she's only seen Mari dance once. Maritza has everything it takes to look incredible on television; of course they'll take her. And then she'll go to Los Angeles. For good. Nicky said as much.

"I can't imagine we'll come back here," he said. She can still see him as he flips his hair out of his face and glares down his nose at her. "I mean, even if we eventually get booted off the show, we've talked about staying in L.A. Getting on *Dance Nation* can give you visibility. We'd be stupid not to capitalize on that."

Just the memory of the words, of Nicky's gloating, slimy tone of voice squeezes Sarita's heart. Of course she knows perfectly well she can't fully believe a damn word Nicky says. No one likes Nicky, and after meeting him she certainly sees why. But still—there's enough truth to it; she can't see Maritza coming back to Seattle once she's spent time dancing in California. Maritza has always, always known what she wanted. Sarita would never fault her even a little bit for continuing to chase her dream as hard as she can, for seizing every opportunity no matter how small.

That doesn't mean this doesn't hurt, or that she's not going to miss Maritza. It's just that they barely had any time together, really... and Maritza had never said a thing, never warned her.

The phone buzzes again, and, with reluctance, she picks it up.
Sarita?

Sarita shakes her head, blinking tears away. She fumbles and tries to type as best she can.

I can't. Please, I know what I said but I'm still trying to sort a lot of stuff out, it's been kind of crazy.

An immediate buzz.

I can help you sort out my part. If you let me.

Sarita clutches the phone to her aching heart and squeezes her eyes closed. Only when she can breathe easily again does she respond.

I have to go finish working on my paper. I know you're going to dance great tomorrow. I'll be thinking of you.

The kettle is boiling, and suddenly, she's lost her appetite. Sarita sets the phone down for the last time so she can prepare her tea and flee with it to her bedroom, ignoring the last forlorn-sounding buzzes from the countertop.

MARITZA TOSSES HER PHONE DOWN ON HER NIGHTSTAND. IT doesn't matter if it breaks or not, as far as she's concerned. "Well. She won't talk to me."

She tries to be surreptitious when she brushes away the tear that trickles down her cheek, but she can't fool her mother. Susana wraps an arm around her shoulders. "*Mija*, don't worry. She didn't say she never wanted to talk to you again, did she? No. She said she still needed time."

"I just... it's been a week. I never got a chance to explain. And I don't even know what she was *doing* there! Ugh. I have so many questions." Maritza drops her face into her hands for a moment to muffle a shriek of frustration. "I just need to be able to talk to her."

Javier appears in the doorway with a glass of *horchata*. "You need to chill out and rest," he says as he hands her the drink. "You gotta get up mad-early tomorrow, and you were dead on your feet when you got home."

She thanks him with a smile and takes the glass. "I'm in bed. I'm chilling; I'm resting."

"You should have been asleep hours ago," Susana chides. "You have to line up at five in the morning; we have to pick up Grace on the way. You're not going to get a full night of sleep."

"But the sleep I get will be solid, believe me." She doesn't see how it couldn't. She was dancing with Fred until she dropped every day, and then, not able to face an excess of rest time when she tried to reach Sarita and ended up ignored over and over, she's picked up shifts at Trabucco's. The money never hurt, and Grace had been good about not prying into what was going on.

Susana reaches over to the nightstand and picks up Maritza's phone. She slides it into her pocket as she stands and waves off her daughter's protests. "I think I'll just confiscate this for the night, hmm? Don't worry. I'll come wake you up." She leans over to kiss Maritza's forehead. "Go to sleep. No more waiting for messages, just sleep and dream about how well you're going to do tomorrow."

Maritza watches as her mother glides from the room, serene and supremely unruffled. "She took my phone," she says to Javier and she can't help it. She pouts.

"It's almost midnight, you've been in bed for hours texting your girl and getting all kinds of stressed out. Mom had the right idea. It's not the way to spend the night before your big day." He taps the glass in her hand. "Drink up and go to sleep."

"But I need to explain." It comes out in a whine. It's not the most attractive moment of her life, but she *does* need to explain. She has no idea how they can work things out or even if Sarita will want to work things out, but she needs to try. "Oh, God, Javi. Her *face*, I still see it. And Nicky was awful."

"Nicky is always awful, Nicky will always *be* awful, and I'm glad you finally dumped him as a partner before any of us had to take drastic measures," Javier says, implacable. "Seriously, the number of hit lists that guy has to be on. But, whatever. You *can't* explain right now. So there's no use being stressed about it."

Maritza glares over the rim of her glass as she takes another long sip and finishes her drink. "You know logic has no control over emotions, right?" She hands the empty glass back to him.

"Yeah," Javier says as he gets up. "That's why Mom took your phone." He saunters over to the doorway and flips the light switch off, casting the room into moonlit darkness. "Sleep tight, Mari."

Coco slips through the door before Javier closes it and hops up on the bed to curl into a purring ball in the pool of moonlight at Maritza's feet. "Trying to set a good example, hmm?" she asks and gives a good scratch behind the cat's ears. Coco responds with a toothy yawn and then almost pointedly tucks her nose under a paw and closes her eyes tight.

Well. That's a hint Maritza can't ignore. She flops back onto her pillow pile and blinks up at the ceiling. In the dark, alone at last, everything hits her again, almost crushing her with the weight of tomorrow and how it won't be what she'd planned. "Nicky," she whispers, tears filling her eyes as she tries to filter through the confusion of relief and sadness the thought of her partner—former partner, now—brings up.

No. No, she's not going to do this. She won't cry for him anymore. The blackmailing stunt broke her heart, and the day he pulled it was the last day she intended to cry over him. No more. She's done. She's free.

But not without cost. She rolls over onto her side and sighs. "Sarita."

She knows Javi is right: There's nothing Maritza can do right now except trust that she'll get a chance to explain so they can work it out. She could wish that she knew what Nicky had said exactly, but she's fairly confident at least that Sarita was smart enough to see through Nicky's malice and faux-civility. That's something.

But why had she been there? Maritza racks her brain. *Did something happen with her mom? She said it was a bad day. Jesus, and I made it worse. I didn't mean to!* Mortification heats her face. *I didn't even ask her what was going on; I didn't think about her at all.*

She flops onto her stomach to stifle a groan of horrified frustration with a pillow while Coco yowls in protest and swats at her feet. "I am an asshole," she says. "Oh, my God."

And there's nothing she can do about it.

The bedroom door cracks open, and an affronted Coco makes a break for it. "Go to sleep, *mija*," Susana says, haloed by the hallway light. "Morning will come too soon."

True enough. As her mother closes the door, Maritza punches at her pillows to fluff them and snuggles under the blankets. If it hadn't taken her approximately five seconds to pass out once she finally allowed herself to close her eyes, she would have been pretty pleased about it.

"No," Sarita mumbles as she rolls away from the sound of the alarm and stuffs her head under the pillow. "Don't have to work today."

She does reach an arm back toward the night table to grab the phone and flip the alarm off, but she flaps and fumbles to no avail, succeeding only in dunking her fingers into yet another mug of cold tea. Yuck.

Sarita sits up and pushes her hair from her face. She is confused at the sight of her mostly empty nightstand, because she can still hear her phone alarm going off. Its piercing shriek fills the apartment from its perch in the...

Kitchen. It all comes back to Sarita in a flood, as it does every morning, and pushes her shoulders down with guilt and confusion and sadness. Maritza might be leaving. Anjali finally explained her decade-old grudge. Her parents really, really were going to leave the country. It's enough to start a headache throbbing behind her eyes. She glances out the window. *Is sunrise too early to start drinking?*

The alarm continues to squeal, and at last Sarita hauls herself out of bed to go shut it up and start the tea kettle. A look at the phone to see that the actual time is seven forty-five in the morning on Saturday makes her groan. "I'm supposed to be able to sleep in when I have a day off," she complains, choosing to ignore the fact that she's the one who forgot to turn the alarm off.

She's just sitting down on the sofa with her fresh tea when the phone starts to buzz again. "Not now, Mari," she groans. "Go dance, get your golden ticket out of here."

The phone lapses into silence, with one forlorn buzz when the call goes to voicemail. Sarita relaxes and sips her tea.

The buzzing begins anew. Sarita sets her tea mug aside and flops onto her stomach, burrowing under the end pillow. "Go away, it's too early," she groans as she clutches the pillow over her ears. "We can talk later. Maybe."

Silence, again. She pokes her head up. Again she hears the single buzz when the phone goes to voicemail and then nothing.

She's about to reach for her tea when the phone goes off for the third time, and this time she leaps over the back of the couch in a mad dash for the counter. She snatches the phone up and answers it without looking. "Don't you have an audition to be getting ready for?"

"We don't really go in for auditions in market analysis," Devesh says. "It's more of a merit-based kind of occupation."

Sarita slumps down on the countertop, rubbing at her eyes. "Devesh. Fuck."

"Sorry for the wake-up call. I waited as long as I could, but then I figured I'm up, I'm out on a walk with Bella, I want answers, here I am." Devesh whistles into the phone. "Sorry. I was trying to get Bella's attention. She's flirting with a Scottie."

This requires caffeine. Sarita wanders to the couch and picks up her tea. "Answers?"

"Yeah, I went to the house last week to box up some more stuff and I found Anjali in tears with peanut butter in her hair, half a sandwich stuck to the stair banister, Ma freaking out and a whole bunch of boxes of your old stuff by the front door." A laugh. "I drew a few conclusions, but I'm pretty sure you're the only person I can rely on to fill in the gaps with accuracy. Thought I'd give you a few days to cool off, first."

Cool off? Sarita's snort nearly sends tea up her nose. "Yeah. I have to fill in the holes? You helped to dig them, Devesh."

His silence speaks volumes, and seconds tick by. "Ah," he finally says, and his awkwardness is loud and clear. "Right."

"You could have told me why Anjali was being so terrible to us," Sarita says, and it is a hard, hard struggle to hold back her anger. "Not when I was a teenager, maybe, but later on when I grew up and I would have been able to understand what the hell happened."

The barks and howls of dog park denizens sound down the line. "Ma and Dad wanted to put it behind us," Devesh says at last. "They thought she'd get over it eventually. They were trying to protect you."

"They didn't really do either of us any favors. They let me think Anjali was just your garden-variety bigot; they let her think I didn't give a shit about her. And you helped!" She sets the tea down lest she squeeze the handle off the mug. "Ten years, Devesh? You don't think that's a long time to keep something like this from me? You saw how she treated both of us! You didn't think it was a good idea to maybe speak up?"

"I... underestimated her ability to hold a grudge. Clearly." He clears his throat. "I'm sorry, Sarita. It was incredibly dumb, I know. I hoped it would eventually go away. I hoped she would eventually chill out, and Ma and Dad were hell-bent on keeping it a secret. Bimal doesn't know either, unless Anjali told him."

That didn't seem likely. "I doubt it." She sticks the side of her thumb into her mouth and nibbles at the skin.

Devesh sighs. "You're probably right." He falls silent. "Look. I'm sorry, Reeti. I need to get back to the house with Bella. We'll talk later?"

A sharp bite of pain makes her jump. She'd pulled too hard on a hangnail. Sarita shakes her hand and holds back a whimper. "Yeah. I've got more work to do on my paper, but come by later, okay? You owe me a million hugs for this."

"I know, Reeti." Three small words, so heavy with apology. "Talk to you then."

"Bye." As soon as she clicks off, Sarita tosses the phone onto the sofa and scrambles for the kitchen sink to shove her thumb under a stream of cool water. "Ow. Ow, ow, ow, ow."

She's lonely, she's injured, she's hungry, she's upset about her sister all over again, and the woman she's dating is, right at this instant, doing her level best to leave town. "This sucks," she mutters, grabbing a dishcloth to wrap around her thumb. She stomps back to the couch and drops down with ill grace. "It really sucks."

What she wants is to be on this couch with Maritza, wrapped in a blanket while they watch a silly movie. Maybe she would have talked to Maritza about the entire situation with Anjali—or not. *We weren't at that kind of place, clearly. If we were, Mari would have told me about the audition, right? So, fine. Forget the heavy talk.* But Sarita would still have liked to have Mari with her right now, with her cheerful, soothing presence and sweet, sexy kisses and...

"Not going there." She hops up off the couch and starts to pace, squeezing her thumb as she talks her problems out to the thin air. "I do want to talk to someone, though. Can't talk to Tash; I promised to stay out of her hair. Can't talk to Craig, he..." She stops short. Why can't she talk to Craig? He's not at the bakery this weekend either; it's Tash's turn to run it unsupervised. "He's probably with Alex." Well, that's a given, he's always with Alex, but Alex was a pretty good help last time. He's conversant with her family drama and with Maritza. The more she thinks about it, the better Craig and Alex sound. Sweeping up her phone before she can change her mind, she hits the quick dial for Craig and waits.

"Hi, Craig Oliver here, I'm not available at the moment, but go on and leave a message; I'll call you back." The beep sounds shrilly in her ear as she clucks in annoyance.

"It's Sarita; call me back. Can we do dinner? I am having a really crappy day. Week. It all sucks. Call me?" She throws the phone on the couch and follows it a moment later with a huff. Lonely, injured, hungry, sad, upset—she is still every last one of these things. And no one is around to talk to about it.

Well, she knows the best remedy for this moment. "Hi. Yeah, I know it's early, but can I put in an order to be ready when you start delivery? God, thank you so much. Okay, shrimp lo mein and an order of dumplings, please? Sengupta, right. You have my address on file... ten a.m.? That's just fine."

Chapter Eighteen

"**M**om."

"No."

"Mom, come on."

"*Absolutamente no.*" Susana doesn't even look at Maritza as she denies, for the fifth time in as many minutes, Maritza's request for the return of her cell phone. She is an island of stillness and serenity in the absolute chaos that is the lobby of the Paramount Theater, with her smooth, untroubled brow and her hands folded neatly in her lap. It's aggravating. "I gave it back earlier and you spent an hour on it. You have two more performances today. You may have your phone back when you are done."

Fred looks up as he stretches, keeping himself limber and warm. "You're so close, Mari. Keep your focus."

Maritza slithers from her chair and onto the floor next to Fred and lets out a long, low whine. "But she might have called or texted, and I wouldn't know and I want to know and I've been so good all through all the preliminary rounds, and come on, pleease?"

Susana turns her head, and her level glare makes Maritza feel very like the teenager she knows she's acting like. "When you are done," she says with a slow nod and she returns her attention to the other dancers in the lobby.

Maritza flops down with a groan on the elaborately patterned carpet, swooshing her arms as if she's making snow angels. When

Javier teases her with a nudge of his toe, he earns an elbow to his instep for his troubles. Grace drops down next to her and makes a silly face, which at least sends Maritza into a flurry of giggles and distracts her.

A pair of shiny black shoes stops by her head. Maritza looks up and can't help her scowl when she realizes who it is. "Nicky. Ugh. Go away." She heard he made it through the first round. The producers must have been impressed with the moxie of a male ballroom dancer showing up to audition alone.

"I was going to say 'break a leg' but now I just hope you actually do break something," Nicky shoots back with a sneer. "It's been an entire week. You could try to be civil."

Maritza sits up. "You blackmailed me and tried to ruin my brand-new relationship. Civility is one of the last things I owe you."

Assuming an expression of patently false curiosity, Nicky cranes his neck to look around. "Oh, right. Where is the little lady, hmm? I would have thought she'd be here for you. No? Couldn't face you taking the first steps to ditch her?"

It's a punch to the gut that hollows her from the stomach out and steals all of her breath. Behind her, Grace sits up and puts a hand on Maritza's shoulder, but Maritza can see her other hand as it curls into a fist, and Maritza wants to do the same thing, wants to lurch to her feet and do something awful. Words, angry words, frustrated words, years of pent-up fury swirl in her head, just out of reach of being put into order so she can spit them into his smug, smirking face. *Hateful, hateful, hateful* is all she can think over and over as she stares up at Nicky, as she clutches at the V-neck of her maroon dance dress—right over her heart.

She doesn't have to say or do anything in the end; she doesn't get the chance. Nicky's words still ring in her ears as Javier leaps to his feet to give Nicky a shove that sends Nicky back several steps before he gathers himself and moves to shove Javier back. Fred's up, interposing himself between the two men, and then Susana has a hand on Javier's shoulder to pull him back. Other dancers come, too, some to watch and some to help, and a pair of security guards breaks up the scuffle for good. One guard takes Nicky away, but the other one stays to deliver a lecture and a warning before he follows them.

Fred crouches by Maritza and takes the hand curled over her heart while Grace scoots onto her knees to drape herself over Maritza in a hug. "You okay?" Grace asks with a gentle squeeze.

Maritza nods. All she can do is nod. Words are too much.

Fred understands; he has always understood when Maritza can't speak. He pats her hand. "We've got some time before we go in for the next round. You want me to send Javier for coffee? He could use the walk and the fresh air."

"Not coffee," Susana objects. "She doesn't need the jitters, especially now."

"So he gets decaf." Fred pulls out his wallet. "Javi, go ahead, get us some coffees, hmm? Decaf. Milk for me, two sugars."

"That will do for all of us," Susana says. "Keep things simple, hmm?"

Javier shrugs. "I can do that. Sure. Be good to get out. Anyone want a cookie or muffin or whatever while I'm out?" Nobody nods. "Okay. Coffee. Milk, two sugars, decaf. I'll be back."

"I'll go with him," Grace says. "He'll need the extra hands. Wait up!" Pushing through the crowd at the door, she chases after him.

On the floor, Maritza closes her eyes and lets Fred take her hand and she inhales deep, slow breaths. Millimeter by millimeter as she breathes, the tension melts from her neck, down her shoulders, through her chest and stomach and all the way down her legs to her toes. Slowly, very slowly, she rolls her neck as the muscles loosen up; then she drops her head and moves it in a careful circle. "What time is it?" she asks.

"Nine-forty-five," Fred says. "The next round starts lining up at ten. How are you feeling?"

Maritza opens her eyes at last and starts a series of exercises to flex and point her toes, stretching out the dull aches of round one. "Ready to kick Nicky's ass, to be honest."

It's the very *least* that she owes him.

She gets to her feet and bends straight over to press her palms to the carpet, which, of course, is when she hears it. "Maritza Quiñones?"

The very official-sounding voice belongs to a pair of perfectly pedicured feet in strappy black sandals, and Maritza peeks up through the end of her ponytail, up over two long, tanned legs, past a black leather skirt and red silk top to an absolutely gorgeous smiling face framed by impeccably styled chestnut waves—an intimidating sight and sound, to say the least. And it's one Maritza's seen on her television every week during every summer of the last several years. "Uh, yeah," she says, and then she realizes that the vision of beauty is accompanied by a grinning cameraman and that her own maroon-chiffon covered butt is waving in the air. She shoots up and her hands automatically move to cover her backside. "Me. I'm me. Maritza, I mean. Hi."

Smooth. Very smooth.

"Hi. Adrienne Hall. I'm the host of *Dance Nation*?" The vision that is one of the most popular television hosts in the country extends a graceful hand, tanned, moisturized and tipped with glossy red nails that match her top. Maritza accepts it for a shake as Adrienne beams at her and goes on. "I wondered if you had a few minutes before the next round. We've interviewed your former partner and, to be honest, I have to say, I *really* need to hear the rest of this story."

"I..." Her smile freezes, and all she can do is allow Adrienne to draw her forward, toward a pair of chairs tucked away across the lobby. A glance over her shoulder shows her mother and Fred rooted in place, looking like nothing so much as a pair of helpless, startled pigeons.

Adrienne guides her to sit down. "You did sign the waivers, right?" she asks as she settles into the opposite chair and smooths her skirt over her knees. "Do you have any questions before Danny here starts rolling?"

The giggle that comes from Maritza is nothing she's ever heard from herself. "Is it too early for a rum and Coke?"

"WE STRIVE TO FURTHER THE OCCURRENCE OF WHATEVER WE imagine will lead to Joy and to avert or destroy what we imagine is contrary to it, or will lead to Sadness," Sarita reads as she shovels her fourth pot sticker into her mouth, which makes it more difficult to snort in contempt without choking. She settles for throwing her chopsticks into the takeout box with more force than is strictly necessary. "Shut up, Baruch."

With her qualifying paper due by the end of the month, it's too late to switch her prospective doctorial focus to Descartes or Chomsky or Kant or *anyone* less irritatingly on the nose than Spinoza is being lately. "Aristotle. Thomas Aquinas. Yeah, why didn't I go with him? Oh, right." Picking up her chopsticks, she seizes a clump of shrimp lo mein. "Too Catholic."

Still, Aquinas might have been better than Spinoza's optimistic yet lecture-y it's-in-your-hands-except-for-when-it's-not brand of Deterministic philosophy. Another bunch of noodles follows the first into her mouth. "Physics. Chemistry. Comparative literature," she mumbles. "I could've studied anything else, but no. Thinking. I wanted to study thinking."

Her foot cramps, an alert that she's sat on it too long. Sarita uncurls and hoists herself from her desk chair for a trot into the kitchen and her fifth cup of tea for the day. She's made significant headway on her paper the last few days, fueled by caffeine that makes her heart race and the firm resolve to ignore her phone—a firm resolve made successful by the fact that the phone actually hasn't made a peep since she ordered Chinese at nearly nine a.m.

And that depresses her only *slightly*, but, apart from the food's arrival, it's meant an uninterrupted hour and a half of work, so, brownie points for her.

There *is* a message waiting on the phone when she picks it up, and her heart does a strange acrobatic twist when it's not from Maritza.

Hi. Sorry. Alex and I are covering auditions for this dance show for the Post. Are you here? We saw Maritza and her crew but they were hustling, no time to talk.

"Ouch, Craig," she mutters, but it's not Craig's fault, he doesn't know she didn't know.

No, at home, working on paper, dinner tonight?

Craig's reply is instantaneous.

Took you long enough. Hope the work is worth it. Your girl looks good. Alex is in the mood for Mexican tonight, you want to meet up at our place at seven and we'll do a taco bar?

She calculates how long she'll have been cooped up in the apartment by then. It's no contest.

Sounds great.

As soon as she tosses the phone down and turns toward the kettle, the phone rings. "I said tacos sound great."

"Do you even *look* at your phone screen before answering?" Devesh asks. "Hi. I wanted to give you some time to cool off so I could offer some conciliatory bagels. Or pancakes. Whatever, I'll take you anywhere you want to go."

"Disneyland might go a long way toward an appropriate apology," she snaps, more tartly than she intended. "I've already eaten."

"Dumplings and noodles do not fix all ills," Devesh replies, a little sing-song in his voice. "Neither do oversized mice. Can I interest you in a short weekend trip up to Vancouver instead?"

He could. "Really?" she asks as she flips through her tea caddy until she finds the decaf spice. Her skin is crawling; it's probably a good time to dial back the stimulants.

"Well, no. Sorry." Devesh sound contrite. "Babies are expensive, as it happens, even when they're not born yet. But I do want to apologize, make things up to you, *try* to explain without insulting your intelligence. And I just pulled up to your apartment building, so you have five minutes to decide where to go."

She looks down at her bare legs and ratty nightshirt and gasps. "Ass. I'm still in my pajamas."

"Then you better hurry." The line dies.

Sarita tilts her head up in a silent shriek toward the heavens because, ugh, yet again family members dragging her from her house with barely any time to comb her hair, let alone put on clothing. She is going to *move*; she is going to move to *Canada* and she is *not going to tell them*.

One cold water face wash, a pair of clean jeans and a UDub sweatshirt later, she's shoving her feet into Uggs and twisting her hair into a neat bun when her phone rings. "Devesh, you have to give me another two minutes. I might kill you if I don't get to brush my teeth."

"Sarita?"

She freezes with the phone wedged under her ear and her hands buried in her hair. The voice is familiar. "Javier?"

"Yeah, um, crap. Hi. I stole my sister's phone from my Mom, I, uh—"

The phone beeps. Sarita wraps a scrunchie around her bun and pulls the phone away so she can see it. This time it really is Devesh. "Javier, two seconds, okay? My brother's on the other line."

"I think your brother's here, actually." His voice gets distant. "Are you Devesh? I'm on the phone with Sarita."

There's an odd dual quality to his voice and to Devesh's puzzled response, and it takes Sarita a minute to realize that it's because she can also hear them right outside her apartment door. "Uh, yeah, I'm Devesh, and you are?"

Sarita yanks the door open before Javier can respond, catching him with his mouth agape. And it's not just Javier, either; Grace is behind him with a much too enthusiastic smile on her face. She's the first to regain the power of speech. "Hi," she says, with a wave. "For the record, I was opposed to this, but I wasn't the one with the keys to the car."

"Opposed to what, exactly?" Sarita looks at the three of them, not entirely thrilled about being ganged up on. "What's going on?"

Devesh clicks off his phone and shoves it into his pocket. "No idea. I was just here for breakfast, and no sane person opposes breakfast."

"Can we come in?" Javier doesn't wait for an answer, but rather gently pushes his way past Sarita, dragging an apologetic-looking Grace after him. He waves Devesh in before he closes the door and turns to Sarita. "Grace and I came to take you to Maritza."

Sarita steps to the door and opens it again. "And now you can go."

Grace lifts an eyebrow at Javier. "See? See what happens when you try to mess around with other people's business? You get escorted out. Told you."

Devesh, suddenly grinning in a way Sarita doesn't like, ambles to her couch and flops down. "This sounds like an interesting story I would really like to hear more about. Could the new players in the game please introduce themselves?"

"Grace Nguyen." Grace adjusts her jacket on her shoulders. "Maritza's friend. And this is her brother Javier, who likes to poke his nose in where he doesn't belong."

"And both of you can leave," Sarita says again as she pulls the door open wider and waves for them to get out. Her irritation level is off the charts. "I'm not interested. I like to do things in my own time, not that it's any of your business. So you can go back to Maritza and tell her this didn't work, and I'll call her later. Tomorrow, maybe."

Javier stands in her living room and doesn't budge an inch. "Are you kidding? Mari has no idea I'm here; she'd have killed me before

I left the theater. It was hard enough to get here as it is with Grace tagging along. I had to really work to convince her to come with me and not run back to tell Maritza."

"And how's all that effort paying off for you? Out, Javi." Sarita waves harder and looks to her brother for support. "Devesh. Help."

But Devesh ignores her. He leans forward with an elbow propped on his knee and his chin in his hand as he surveys the room. "I find it interesting that I'm meeting the Brother and the Bestie before I meet the actual Girlfriend. Trouble in paradise, Reeti? And here I thought you were just mad about the Anjali thing."

"I can be mad about entirely separate things that have no need to mingle." She is *definitely* being ganged up on. "*Everyone* can leave."

Devesh pats the couch and offers Javier a friendly nod. "Come on, tell me, brother to brother. What's up with our sisters?"

Javier lights up. "Okay, so my sister is a dancer and she's probably leaving town—"

"Oh, my God, this is not happening. It's not, it's just not." In the face of a hopeless cause, Sarita gives up and shuts the apartment door with a bang, then stalks over to Javier to jab a finger in his chest. "Your sister should have told me about her audition and her plans to leave town. Period. I shouldn't have had to find out from that odious jerk she dances with."

"Danced with," Grace informs the ceiling as she twirls a lock of her dark hair around her finger. "Not that I'm getting involved."

Devesh sits back. "Dance drama? I love dance drama. Tell me more."

"You're not helping! Could you try to be a big brother for once? Do you want to erase some of your karmic debt in this lifetime or what?" Sarita shoots a glare at her own brother before she addresses Maritza's again. "I don't care if it's present or past tense. And honestly, I am all for her doing whatever it takes to get where she wants to go as a dancer. I've seen her. She's good. I'm not mad about her leaving. I'm hurt..." Her throat closes up, and only a hard, painful swallow lets her speak again. "I'm hurt that she didn't tell me."

It makes her heart twist to remember Nicky's face and his sneer as he spoke, to think about the way Maritza pleaded with her hand outstretched as Sarita turned and walked away. "It's too much. I feel like I've been jerked around."

"Whoa. Whoa, whoa, whoa." Javier literally looms over Sarita with his face set in an angry frown. "Uh-uh. You can be mad at my sister, but you don't get to say she jerked you around. I don't know what Mari had going on in her head but I guarantee you she wasn't just messing with you. She's not like that."

Devesh is up and smoothly slides between Sarita and Javier. "Okay. Could you not hover and intimidate my sister? She gets to be hurt."

"I didn't say she didn't. I said don't accuse *my* sister of doing stuff she wouldn't do." Javier draws back his shoulders; his jaw is set as he looks up at Devesh. "And she'd know Mari isn't jerking anyone around and never would if she'd give Mari a chance to explain. We do that in my family, you know, we like to be fair."

Sarita slips back to stand by Grace and watch the two men posture and grimace at each other. "Odds of my living room getting out from this unscathed?"

"Pretty good, actually. Javier's a pacifist who's already having an existential crisis." Grace's mouth tilts in a half-smile. "He went toe to toe with Nicky this morning. Only pushes and shoves, but he got a lecture from security and it kind of freaked him out, so I don't think this is going to go further than sharp words. Unless..." She slides a sidelong glance at Sarita.

"Devesh? God, no. No. He's all talk; he takes spiders from the house and puts them in the garden." Sarita takes in a deep breath. "Look, Grace—"

"No, hang on." Grace lifts a hand. "I don't like that I'm involved in this; it took Javier thirty minutes to convince me that it was even remotely a good idea. Then we had to go to the bakery and get your address out of that Natasha girl, and I feel even more weird about that. But here we are. Sarita, Maritza wasn't jerking you around, I swear to God. I've been telling her for weeks that she had to tell you about this."

All Sarita can do is squeeze her eyes and mouth shut. Her hands clench into fists. "Then—"

"She didn't want you to dump her. She wanted all the time with you she could get. Honestly, she really thought she was going to be able to figure it out before now." Grace shrugs. "I don't claim to understand. It's not what I would have done, but I'm not her, et cetera and all that. But honestly. She really, really likes you, and she really, really wanted every moment to count and she didn't want to mess it up."

Grace's eyes are soft and sympathetic and utterly, completely sincere and clear to read. Sarita knows even after only two months with Maritza that Grace is telling the truth, that she is painting an honest picture of who Maritza is. Sarita has just tried to convince herself of something, anything, to make it all hurt less. "That's exactly like her."

"Isn't it just." Grace watches as Javier and Devesh break off their argument, staring at each other like a pair of angry bulls. "Sarita, will you come back to the Paramount with us? It's the most important day of Maritza's life, and I know she wants you to be there, even if you're mad at her."

This, too, is nothing more or less than the truth, and all of Sarita's anger drains away. The hurt is still there, but the desire to see Maritza overshadows it, makes it into something she can handle. And it *is* an important day, and Sarita realizes she would love nothing more than to be even a small part of what makes it wonderful for Maritza.

She nods. "Absolutely. But one thing. Can I please, *please* have two minutes to brush my teeth first?"

Chapter Nineteen

MARITZA IS A WALKING ACHE. SHE SHOVES THE DOOR OF Audition Room Two open and trudges out; her feet scream protests that go all the way up her calves. Behind her, Fred's in much the same shape; his walk is slow and careful as he favors his trick knee.

Susana waits for them. "Well?"

Yes, Maritza hurts, but it's all worth it. A smile spreads across her face. "We made it to the main stage rounds."

"¡*Mija!*" Susana flies forward to wrap her arms around Maritza and Fred in an exuberant hug. "Oh, I knew you could do it, I knew you would be just beautiful."

Fred's grinning his head off. "She was, too. I don't even have to do anything hardly; I'm a background prop. She blew them away, Susana. They said she was the best they'd seen so far this audition tour. And they were just in Salt Lake City, too. If she's better than anyone Buddy Schwimmer sent to those auditions, then she's a lock for callbacks." Exhausted as he is, Fred still manages to grab Maritza around the waist and swing her around. "You're amazing, Mari."

"Well, right now, I absolutely feel amazing for sure," she giggles. Fred sets her down. She smooths the rumpled front of her dress and looks around the lobby. All at once, her high spirits drop as she realizes Susana is alone. "They're not back?"

Susana's face falls. "I'm sorry, *corazon*. There's no sign of them."

"But they have to... it..." Maritza brushes past her mother to scan every face in the lobby, searching for Grace's high ponytail or Javier's leather jacket in a sea of sparkling hairdos and snug Spandex trousers. "How long does it take to get coffee? It has to have been an hour."

"Two hours. We had to wait our turn for a while, remember?" Fred shows her his watch.

"There are three coffee shops on the next block over. It can't take two hours to get coffee, not in *Seattle*." Maritza stands on her tiptoes and bounces up and down as she looks for her brother and best friend. "Where'd they go, frigging Siberia?"

"Javi had the car keys. Maybe they went out of the neighborhood. The shops around here are probably very crowded today." Susana puts her hands on Maritza's shoulders and gently forces her to stand still. "You need to rest your feet, *mija*."

She brushes her mother's hands off and bounces on the balls of her feet again. "I can't, Mama! I have to go right into the main theater and wait for them to call my number. I was supposed to go straight there." Maritza looks over her shoulder and spots one of the producers, a small, chipper blond woman named Carmen, headed her way with a big television smile on her face. "Oh, God, where are they, Mama?"

"Miss Quiñones?" Too late. Carmen is on top of them, pressing her fingers to her earpiece. "Found her. Hi, Maritza? I need you to come with me to the main theater, okay? The judges really want to keep things moving." She smiles, and it's a beautiful smile, but Maritza can see the steel behind it. She is under the distinct impression that if she doesn't go quietly, Carmen will take her by the ear. She steps back.

"Ah, Carmen, I'm looking for my brother, my friend, they went out for coffee..." Maritza cranes her neck, desperately seeking any glimpse of Javier and Grace. "They must have been caught up in a crowd."

"Oh, I'm sorry." To her credit, Carmen's apology and small, sorrowful smile do seem sincere, rather than a practiced put-on. "But we really need you and Mr. Corbett to gather in the theater with the other dancers. We're going to start with the main judges soon. You don't want to miss your chance."

Maritza bites her lip. "No, but..." She looks frantically at her mother and Fred. "What do I do?"

"We have to go, Mari. I'll be with you, and your mother will be there. It's okay." Fred steps in front of her and rubs her upper arms. "We'll make it. We'll get it done like we always do. Okay?"

Susana's fingers are tangled into a nervous knot. "Maybe I should stay out here and keep an eye out for them."

"Absolutely not. We can't let you do that, Mrs. Quiñones." Carmen's assertiveness, all out of proportion to her size, reminds Maritza of Sarita. That and the frustration of Javi and Grace not being there makes Maritza swipe carefully at a tear while Carmen hustles them toward the main doors. "We wouldn't have Maritza go on with nobody to cheer for her in the audience! We can keep an eye out for your friends and send them in with the next wave of auditioners. Do you have pictures?"

Another tear stings at Maritza's eye, and she pokes it away with a fingertip, trying not to smear her eyeliner. "Um. Yeah, actually. Mama, can I have my phone? I've got the photo we took outside the theater this morning. I can show Carmen that one."

"Of course." Susana lifts a strap of her brown leather purse from her shoulder and rummages inside. "Hm. I know I put it in here. Did I not zip it into the pocket?"

Fred reaches into his duffel bag and pulls out his phone. "Here, I'll call it."

But no beep or buzz comes from Susana's bag. She pokes on through the contents, pulling out her wallet and her hospital ID and a host of other objects that she passes to Fred, Carmen and

Maritza. "I know it's in here; it has to be. I took it from you and put it right in here."

"We really have to go," Carmen insists, as she hands a half-empty bag of honey-mustard pretzels back to Susana. "Can you describe them, maybe? Adrienne will be out here doing interviews; she and her crew can be on the lookout. Are there any identifying characteristics?"

Fred holds up his phone. "Never mind, I got a shot from this morning too. Here. Take a look." He hands his phone to Carmen, who looks at the photo and nods.

"Do you mind if I email this to one of Adrienne's crew so they know who to look for?" At Fred's nod, Carmen's fingers fly across the screen, and the photo message sends with a swooping noise. "Okay. There we go. Now I really have to insist we get in there. They're about to close the doors to this wave of dancers."

Susana pulls out a pack of tissues and hands it to Maritza. "Dry your eyes, *corazon*. We'll make the very best of this, and you'll dance like an angel whether or not they make it back. All right?"

It has to be. She has no choice. As she dabs at her eyes, Maritza lets Carmen take her arm and lead her into the bustling dim expanse of the main theater, and she tries not to hear the noisy thump of the door closing behind her as a knell of doom.

"Sarita." Javier's voice is still and controlled, an exquisite study in exaggerated patience. The flick of his hand at his right ear is less patient. "Stop hanging over my shoulder. I'm trying to drive."

"I'm helping; there's a spot right there." She dodges his hand to point at the last strip of space free on Stewart Street and tugs at his shirt sleeve. "Come on. You're driving a compact car, you can make it, it's bitty."

His frown is dubious. "Maybe."

Next to Sarita, Devesh laughs and shakes his head. "Javier, just park in that lot over there. I'll pay. Anything to get my sister from this car so she can walk off some of that nervous energy."

"Bless you," Javier whispers, again batting Sarita away from his shoulder. "Okay, seriously, sit back and buckle up. I don't know how we haven't gotten pulled over more than once already; this area is swarming with cops. Do you *want* to get a ticket?"

Sarita opens her mouth to protest, but only gets out an indignant shriek as Devesh grabs her and pulls her firmly into her seat. "Two minutes, Reeti," he says as he waggles a finger in her face. She resists the urge to bite. "Two minutes and we'll be parked and walking."

She sits back and crosses her arms over her chest. Sulking—it's not her best look, but whatever. "It already took almost an hour to get through all the traffic just to get here. It's going to be another ten-minute walk."

"Eight. Maybe seven if we really hustle. Do you jog?" Grace turns in the passenger seat to grin at Sarita. "Or maybe you want to start?"

"You should have dropped me off at the theater," Sarita grumbles.

Javier steers into a parking spot and shuts the car off. "Nope. Grace and I have the wristband passes to get back into the theater. You couldn't get in without us."

"You could have given me one of the passes," she points out.

Javier holds up his wrist. "You know these paper sticky things are like iron; there's no way to get it off in one piece. Besides, who wants to miss the fun?" He hops out and opens her door. "Not me. Come on, let's get a move on."

Sarita does not jog. Sarita's exercise is limited to walking around campus and the occasional half-hearted workout to an old Pilates DVD. By the time they end up at the Paramount—in eight minutes, as Grace had predicted—Sarita is sweaty, out of breath and contemplating revisions to her half-assed exercise routine.

Devesh pats her on the back as she grips her knees and tries to breathe like a normal human being while dancers and regular Seattleites swarm around them, in and from the theater. "I know a great couch-to-5K app," he says. "How do you feel about zombies?"

Before she can regain enough breath and strength to either take a swing at him or shoot back a witty retort, a familiar shout catches her attention. "Hey! You made it!" Craig's battered sneakers appear in her line of vision, and Sarita lifts her head to see both him and Alex grinning down at her. Craig waves toward the theater. "You're late; it's about time you got here. They've been sending dancers into the main auditorium, and Alex thinks he saw Mari going in."

"Are you covering the auditions for someone?" Devesh taps the notebook Craig's holding. "Both of you?"

"We do make a pretty useful team," Alex says with a smile as he holds up his camera. "One phone call and you get a freelance writer and a photographer. Good luck for the *Post* that I was home when they called Craig."

"Good luck for the *Post* that *I've* been home half of this month while I let Tash and Sarita run the bakery," Craig corrects, hitching the strap of his satchel more securely on his shoulder. "I've been bored out of my mind. We can use the extra funds, and I've quite missed writing. No time the last couple of months."

Sarita inhales and at last it's a good, deep breath, steady enough for her to let go of her knees and stand upright. "Okay, great small talk, but what's going on inside there? Are you sure you saw her, Alex?"

Alex gnaws at his bottom lip. "I'm *pretty* sure," he says as he ruffles a hand through his hair and makes it stand on end. "She wasn't with Nicky, so I'm not a hundred percent. But it looked like her, from the back."

Sarita's heart races. "Do you think they'll let us in? Maybe we can watch her dance?"

Craig exchanges looks with Alex. "We've got press credentials, so we might. Not sure about you, though," Craig says with a worried frown.

"Come with me." Javier grabs her by the wrist to lead her through the crowd of dancers still piled up outside of the theater. Some are still bouncing and stretching and waiting their turn to get in; some are crying as if their hearts are breaking. And through them all, Sarita looks and looks, straining but never seeing a familiar head of warm dark brown waves, never catching a glimpse of a bright smile and excited brown eyes. She hopes Alex is right, hopes he really saw Mari, hopes whoever is in charge will let them all in.

They snake through the dancers in a line, Javier to Sarita to Grace to Devesh to Craig to Alex, hand in hand and all craning their necks to look for Maritza. "She wouldn't be with Nicky, by the way," Javier calls back over his shoulder. "Big blow-up there. Fred let him go from the studio. She's with Fred today."

That makes Sarita jerk her head up, and she remembers Grace drawling "former partner" back at her apartment. "Seriously? Grace meant that?"

"You gotta hear them tell the story." Javier grins. "It's *awesome*. And I got in a kind of fight with Nicky earlier today. Also awesome. Basically, ding dong, the dick is dead. Can I get a woo-hoo?" He drops Sarita's wrist and holds up his hand for a high-five.

But she can only blink up at him and leave him hanging until Devesh leans over for the five. The worst part of that awful day was Nicky's insinuations about the time he and Maritza would have together, his gloating that, without her around, he might have a shot at getting back into her life. She'd never believed that, but she hadn't wanted him around Maritza at all, let alone around and making cracks when Maritza would be working hard and far from her family. It would have been extra stress Maritza didn't need.

He might still make it on the show, but if they both did, it wouldn't be as a team. There was a relief in that.

"Javier Quiñones?" The query startles Sarita, and she looks over to see an official-looking guy wearing heavy black glasses with tablet in hand and headset looped over his expertly tousled black hair. "That's you, right? You're the guy in this photo? And do I also have a Grace Nguyen?"

Grace takes a step forward. "Yeah, that's us. What photo? Who's asking?"

The guy gestures at his headset and raises an eyebrow. "Uh, me? I'm kind of, like, with the show?"

Grace is unmoved. "And this photo you're talking about?"

"Here." Show Guy holds up his tablet, and sure enough, there's a picture of Maritza, Fred, Javier and Grace all together in front of the theater, making faces and flashing thumbs up and peace signs at the camera. "Producers told us to look for you. Maritza's in the theater waiting to dance."

Alex snaps his fingers. "Knew I saw her."

A thrill rushes through Sarita to know for sure that Maritza is just behind the heavy wooden doors a few feet away. "Can we go in?" she asks, raising her hand to make sure Show Guy sees her.

He does and he frowns over his glasses. "Who are you?"

"She's with us," Grace says and grabs Sarita's other hand. "She's Maritza's girlfriend."

"Girlfriend?" Yet another unfamiliar voice utters the question, this time behind them, and when Sarita turns, her jaw drops: long legs, short skirt, gorgeous face, perfectly tailored red silk top and one graceful hand extended to shake Sarita's. "You're Maritza's girlfriend?"

Blinded by the brilliance of the woman's Hollywood smile, Sarita can do no more than allow herself a slow, single nod. "Basically? We hadn't really discussed it..." Awkward.

The smile widens, and its owner tosses back a mane of impeccable chestnut waves. "I'm Adrienne Hall, I host *Dance Nation*. We didn't know you were coming today."

"It wasn't planned," she whispers, suddenly conscious of a cameraman who hovers nearby; his video camera is an ominous, dark eye. "You're not filming me, are you?"

Adrienne slices a hand across her throat and glares at the cameraman. "No. You haven't signed a waiver." In a blink, her professional smile is back. "But I'd very much like it if you would sign one and talk to me. What a great story, the two of you, just met, clicked, now you're looking at a possible long-distance relationship. I'd love to interview you for the show."

The blood drains from Sarita's face; she feels it go, and dizziness overtakes her. "Me? On TV?"

"If you like." Adrienne just keeps smiling, that steady but somehow unnervingly perfect smile, and Sarita doesn't know what to do.

Javier steps forward and speaks up. "We were really hoping to watch the dancers, maybe sit with my sister."

"We can definitely try to manage that." Adrienne touches her ear, listening to a tinny voice. "They're between dancers. Jimmy here can slip Javier and Grace in and..." She looks at Craig and Alex, expectation on her face.

"Craig Oliver." Craig reaches his hand out to shake Adrienne's. "This is Alex Scheff, my partner. We're covering the auditions for the *Post-Intelligencer*."

"Local press, got it." She nods. "I can't let you in that far, I'm afraid."

"We'd rather wait with Sarita, if you're going to talk to her." Craig shifts his bag. "I'm also her boss at the Sucre Coeur bakery."

Sarita looks at them all. "I haven't decided if I'm going to talk to her. I really want to watch Mari dance."

Adrienne puts a hand on her shoulder. "It's Sarita, right? I'll do my best to get you in before she dances. If you hurry and sign the waiver, I'll just ask you a few quick questions. She's in the third audition group and they're near the end of the second. We could have time; maybe cutting it close, but it's possible."

"Why do you need my side of the story?" It bursts from Sarita, an explosion of the hurt and incredulity she's kept pent up since yesterday. "I'm not important. I'm just a student; all I do is go to school and decorate cakes. She's the one going places. She's the one..." *Leaving me behind* catches in her throat.

Adrienne looks at her for a long moment before she gestures to Jimmy. "Give me your tablet. Go get these folks into the auditorium." Jimmy hands over his tablet and vanishes with Javier and Grace—and Devesh, swept up with a shocked look on his face—before Sarita can do more than squawk in protest. Adrienne's practiced fingers fly over the tablet screen, poking and prodding in a series of beeps and clicks until she settles on something and turns the tablet to face Sarita. "Here's why," she says, face still, giving nothing away.

Sarita takes the tablet with trembling fingers and lets out a tiny gasp at the video already playing there. There's a small version of Adrienne on the screen, poised and seated with her legs crossed at the ankles and tucked behind the leg of her chair. Maritza, hair drawn to the side in a low ponytail, face made up with more makeup than Sarita's ever seen her wear, in a dress made out of floaty maroon chiffon, sits by her. Her hands are folded in her lap, but her left foot—crossed over the right in a mirror of Adrienne's pose—taps and jiggles, and her smile is bright but just as shaky. Sarita's heart goes out to the little Mari on the screen as she hits *pause*.

"We wanted to interview her because she didn't come with her partner—he danced alone, so we talked to him because that's unusual for ballroom, and that led us to her." Adrienne shakes her head. "I wasn't too awfully impressed with him. None of the other ballroom dancers we interviewed were either; apparently they're both well known in the community."

"They've won a lot of competitions," Alex says from over Sarita's shoulder.

"So we've heard. Didn't do a thing for his attitude, I see." Adrienne's laugh is dry. "I liked her, though. She's sweet. Go ahead, Sarita. Hit *play* again." When Sarita doesn't move, she taps the screen herself with one perfectly manicured finger.

Maritza jumps back to life, her head bobbing. "I was born in New York, in Brooklyn. And I've danced since I was a kid. My mama got me into it and she's supported me the whole way. She packed up and moved across the country with me and my younger brother a few years ago, all because I had met a potential dance partner online, and after a few meetings we decided we wanted to work together."

On the screen, Adrienne nods. "But that partner—Nicholas Alford, with whom you have in fact danced competitively for the last several years—is not here with you today."

Some of the sparkle falls away from Maritza's smile. "No." When she looks more closely, Sarita can see the faintest shimmer of tears in her eyes.

"Can you tell me more about that?" Adrienne asks, as she leans forward to hand Maritza a tissue.

Taking a deep breath, Maritza carefully dabs at her eyes before she nods and lets all the breath out in a long sigh. "Nicky and I dated for a while. But we, uh, we broke up last year." Another breath, her lips pursed into an O. "And he didn't take it well. And then I met someone, I met a woman I really, really like. And that was great."

"For you, I'm guessing," says Screen Adrienne, with a shrewd twinkle in her eye.

"Yeah, he didn't take that well either. He was blackmailing me—" Sarita hits pause there. "He what?"

"She's going to have to tell you that story, she didn't tell me." Adrienne taps *play* again.

"—and he was treating me not so great, and the last straw is when he met her. She came to the studio for some reason and he..." The tissue reappears. "He told her about this audition. I hadn't yet, because I didn't know how to say *I know we just met and I really like you but I might be leaving soon*, you know? And it upset her, she left, and Fred and I had just *had it* with Nicky, so... that was that. We were both done with him, and here I am, dancing with Fred. No partner, and no Sarita..."

"And I think that last one is what upsets you more," Adrienne says, and Maritza nods, reaching for a second tissue, which Adrienne produces.

"I really, really like her, and I really, really wish I'd been up-front with her, and I really, really wish she could be here with me today, because she's just great, and I really want this to work whether I get on the show or not," comes the slightly choked whisper.

Sarita hits *pause* again and hands the tablet back to Adrienne. "Damn it."

"She doesn't know you're here. Sarita, I know you want to watch her, but I'm going to think TV and tell you it would be amazing if you were out here waiting for her when she finishes." Adrienne passes the tablet to the cameraman and leads Sarita off to the side with a companionable arm over Sarita's shoulders. "If she could see you when she comes out the door, it could be a huge comfort to her if she doesn't make it to callbacks. Or if she does, it could be the cherry on the sundae, do you see what I mean?" Her eyes are bright blue, wide and hopeful. "I don't want to come off as mercenary, but really, it would be great TV."

Sarita narrows her eyes. "That is pretty mercenary, though."

"Well, it's my job." Adrienne beams. "No pressure."

Sarita closes her eyes and wills her spinning thoughts to settle. On the one hand, yes. She wants to see Mari dance. On the other, she needs some time to finalize what she'd say, how she'd apologize for being ridiculous, what they could do if Mari got on the show and left. She'd thought she had a vague idea, but then Maritza upped the stakes by putting her heart on national television. The occasion seems to call for something more than *vague*.

A warm hand cups her elbow and draws her aside. "Excuse us, Adrienne. I'm sure Sarita will have an answer for you in just a moment." Craig leads Sarita away toward of the few patches of space not taken up by stretching or spinning dancers. "Looked like you could use someone to help you sort things out."

"What's to sort out? I thought I was going to come here and apologize and now I have to possibly do it on *national television* and I don't even know, I just, holy shit." Hysterical giggles catch in her throat and cut her off as she coughs them out. "I'm going to be here working on my pointless doctorate for years and years and she's going to maybe go to L.A. for God knows how long, and all this might air on *national television.*"

Craig leans against a wall with his arms crossed over his chest. "It's not pointless. Your doctorate, I mean. Is it?"

"What?" Of all the things for him to focus on, that's what he picks? "No. I mean—what?"

"Well, it's not. You really want it, and that makes it not pointless."

Whatever. "Okay, fine, you're right; it's not pointless. You seem to be, though." She's doing a lot of glaring today. "Is this you being helpful?"

"Well, I hope so. I'm returning the favor, or trying to." He grins and taps her on the nose. "Tit for tat."

There is not much Sarita finds more irritating than unnecessarily cryptic remarks. "I don't follow."

"Last summer. A bridal shower with a God-awful, horrible and regrettable color scheme. You, me, the kitchen at the bakery and several dozen sugar cookies. Ringing a bell?" He waits, and when she can't summon up more than confused silence, he sighs. "You gave me some very helpful advice about Alex. Would you like me to return the favor?"

Oh. Sarita tugs at a stray curl and rubs at her head in a hopeless effort to dislodge memories of the occasion in question. "The pink and green sugar cookies?" she asks, hazarding a guess. "I vaguely remember. I've mostly blocked it out. Those colors were horrible. Besides, I've slept since then."

"Well, I can assure you that you were very helpful. I haven't forgotten a word. Let me see..." Craig taps a finger at his chin. "I seem to recall you saying that if you were looking for a girlfriend, you would want someone who looks at you the way your brother's husband looks at him. Right. Do you think you've got that?"

Sifting through memories of the last several weeks is both exhilarating and painful. But a warm sweetness courses through Sarita as she thinks about Maritza's face and her lovely sunshine smile, the one that goes all the way to her eyes and makes Sarita feel as if she's the only person in the world. "I think so."

"Do you think she'd be scared off by your sister?"

That one's easier. "Never in a million years; she wouldn't ever have been."

Craig nods. "And are you attracted to her? Is she someone you can talk to? Is, in fact, Maritza someone who just *does it* for you?"

She freezes mid-inhalation and bites her lip. "I have to work on the talking thing. I didn't want to saddle her with all my problems."

"I can only gather from the present situation that that one's a two-way problem, but you can resolve it if you both want to." He levels a long, steady stare on her, brown eyes dark and solemn. "But otherwise? You like her. You met a cute girl you like, who likes you back." A smile breaks the solemnity. "Plus, you've offered to make her breakfast at least once."

"Twice," she says automatically. "We keep getting interrupted."

"I stand corrected and very, very smug." He winks. "Sarita, for the love of God, you like the girl. You clearly think she's worth chasing, or you wouldn't *be* here right now. I'd bet my little dog you actually have some idea of something you can do if she leaves."

"Oh, sure. We could totally make the most of the time we have and then talk every day until I can finish my master's, and then I could apply to PhD programs in California?" Sarita snaps, sarcasm dripping from every word. "Sure, I could just do that, yeah."

Craig's face doesn't change. He just stands there with a calm smile, waiting for... for what? Sarita squirms, and breaks eye contact. "That would be crazy," she mutters.

"A little, yeah. Maybe." Craig shrugs. "Not *too* crazy, though. I mean, if you like her."

She scoffs. "No, not a little; it's really, really crazy. I was kidding."

Again with that steady smile, with that irritating calm. "Mm, were you really?"

"Yes!" Of course she was. It was just a thing that popped into her head, just a thing to say. It's completely insane to actually think about picking up and moving out of state for a woman she's only known for a couple of months, to go where she won't know anyone else, with no guarantee she'd get into any program.

But her stomach knots up. A PhD in philosophy *could* take ten years to complete. Obviously the goal is that it wouldn't, but even if she busts her ass it would take probably a minimum of five years. And she *wants* that doctorate. She still has no idea what to *do* with it, if she wants to teach or do research, but she *wants* it. She has always wanted it. *Of course it's not pointless.*

And she wants Maritza, too.

It resonates like a bell; deep down Sarita knows that if it were any other woman, she'd never consider it for a moment.

"It wouldn't be the worst thing in the world, to take a chance," Craig murmurs.

"We might not work out. I'd be stranded..." She trails off, unable to put any real conviction behind it. *A person can't really be* stranded *if it's California, right?* It would suck, for sure, if she moved all that way and they didn't make it, but she wouldn't be *stranded.*

Unable to believe she's considering an idea that had been absolutely marinated in sarcasm as she blurted it out, Sarita looks at her options. Five to ten more years here, doing the work she loves, but without Maritza. There is every possibility she could meet someone else...

...but that person wouldn't be Maritza. Her heart thumps that out like Morse code, and she hates the message. That person wouldn't be her.

She could go to California, and she thinks she could have a good shot at doing the work she loves there, *and* she would get Maritza. Maybe it would work out or maybe it wouldn't, but her heart very, very much is into the idea of trying. And her head? As much as she tries and tries to tell herself just how entirely crazy all of this is, it's half-hearted at best, and overwhelmed by thoughts of the two of them in some tiny apartment, on some sunny beach, under a sky that isn't perpetually gray.

She inhales. "It's not... it's not actually entirely crazy, is it?"

"I don't think so. Now, you've always accused me of being something of a hopeless romantic, so perhaps I'm biased." Craig's smile goes a bit lopsided, and he chucks her under the chin. "But come on, Sarita. She makes you happy, even now, even this soon. I'd miss you a lot if you went, but the alternative is seeing you so sad every day, when it's totally preventable. God, that's awful even to contemplate."

It is. It really, really is.

"I could... go. I could just... go." It should fill her with anxiety to even consider it, but there's only a rush of joy, a thrill of *this could work*. "I don't even know the deadlines for the schools, I didn't even look anywhere but UDub, but, I could go. There's no law saying I have to get all my degrees from one university."

Craig rocks back on his heels and sticks his hands into his pockets. "There's really not." Tilting his head, he raises an eyebrow. "So, are you going to do it?"

"I'm going to do it." It takes her breath away just to say it, but it also makes a huge smile spread across her face that she can't stop and wouldn't want to anyway. "I'm going to do it! I'm... I'm going to California!"

Craig grins. "So I should take you from the running for managing the bakery?"

She had completely managed to forget about that. Still, her answer is swift and sure. "Yeah, and is it okay if I give you a couple months advance notice of my resignation as your Head Decorator?"

He throws back his head in a belly laugh. "Hand it in to Tash, she'll be your direct boss now."

Sarita stands right up on her tiptoes to give Craig a kiss on the cheek that she hopes is full of all the gratitude she's feeling— gratitude that is quickly replaced with panic. "Crap, but what do I say when she comes out of the theater?"

"Oh, that? That's easy, keep that simple, say *I'm sorry* a lot and *I'm so happy for you*. No need to have a couple's therapy session on camera, good God." His eyes widen in mock horror. "It'd be all *cleanup on aisle five, messy feelings spill*; don't do that. Breathe."

She nods and sucks a deep breath into her belly. Her head is spinning with wonder and elation, worry and fear and the sensation of being right at the edge of a cliff. "This is crazy."

"A little. But I'd say you're due some crazy, Sarita. Have a moment, take it. Maybe just go with it and see what happens." He's got the biggest grin on his face, and those words, she does remember, she did say that to him.

The smile spreading across her face as she looks up at her friend and boss feels as if it could light up the city. "Simple as that, is it?"

He leans over and presses a kiss to her forehead. "If you let it."

Chapter Twenty

IT'S DARK IN THE AUDITORIUM. THE HOUSE LIGHTS ARE DOWN, heightening the sun-bright illumination of the stage. The footlights gleam across the polished wood of the stage floor, and a simple cobalt blue backdrop warms the stage without casting too much of the stage light out into the eyes of the audience.

Maritza can't take her eyes from it. *I'm going to dance up there. I'm going to perform in front of some of the most famous dancers and choreographers in the world.*

Some of the crankiest dancers and choreographers, too. Christopher Bjarnesen, former principal dancer with the Royal Danish Ballet, hasn't so much as cracked a smile or a tiny joke since Maritza and her much-diminished support team entered the auditorium. Lynette Anderson, 1999 World Ballroom Dance finalist and celebrity choreographer, has been extremely salty with the two pairs of ballroom dancers who have already graced the stage in the last forty-five minutes, pushing and needling like a harpy. Maritza's heart had gone out to one of the pairs, a brother-sister team of teenagers from one of the other studios in town. Mike Jacobs had had to physically remove his sobbing sister Carrie from the stage when Lynette was finished with them.

Fortunately, the third member of the judging panel, an Emmy-winning hip-hop choreographer, is in a far better mood than his colleagues. "Time for a fifteen-minute break," DeShawn Scott announces into his microphone. His lovely smile is a welcome change from the thunderous expressions of the other two judges. He tugs his Lakers cap down over his forehead and nods for the other judges to vacate the judging dais. "We'll be back, don't go anywhere."

Maritza likes him. He's new to the panel this season, and she appreciates his efforts to cheerfully balance the sour attitudes at the other end of the table. It eases some of the terror she's feeling about going in front of the panel. She sends a fervent wish into the universe that he'll be able to work some magic over the break, because right now she's scared shitless of Christopher and Lynette.

To her left, Fred squeezes her hand. "No worries," he whispers and gently bumps his head against hers. "You're going to be wonderful up there. Don't worry."

She can't help but fret. "They haven't let anyone into the auditorium since we got in here. Do you think Grace and Javi came back and they just can't get in? What if they never get in; they won't be here." Her foot jiggles with her nerves and sets the heel of her sandal clacking against the floor, earning glares from several dancers in the immediate vicinity. She uses her free hand to grab her knee and hold it down. "Why did you send them for coffee?"

"I didn't know Javier was going to take forever," Fred hisses. "And he needed to get away from the scene of the crime."

"What crime? All he did was push Nicky a little; Nicky totally deserved it. I should have kneecapped him." Which reminds her. Maritza sits up straight and cranes her head around to look at everyone in the dim auditorium. "I still don't see Nicky."

"Don't worry about Nicky. Worry about the judges. Or wait, don't worry at all because everything is going to be fine." Fred gives her hand another squeeze. "You've danced brilliantly all day. Just hang in there and do it one more time."

"Two if they send me to choreography." She settles back in her chair, but before she can lift her right thumb to her mouth to nibble at what little is left of the nail there, Susana grabs her hand.

"Calm," is all her mother says, the very embodiment of serenity, and now Maritza is pinned down. *Great.*

She closes her eyes, dismissing one by one the thoughts that try to pester her as she takes long, slow breaths. Nicky—gone. The judging panel—poof. The ebb and flow of conversational chatter around her is almost soothing, even punctuated as it is by the occasional shriek of nervous laughter.

Sarita's radio silence tries to come along and bother her, too, but with some effort, she manages to send it off. The time to deal with that will come. And if there's nothing to deal with... well. She will deal with that, too. She has no room right now to regret the action she was too scared to take.

The murmur in the auditorium heightens, and a burst of applause makes Maritza's eyes fly open. She sits up straight to see the judges as they return to the dais, waving and looking collectively much more cheerful than they had fifteen minutes ago. Relief washes through her as she snatches her hands free to join in the applause.

Christopher picks up his microphone from the stand on the table and spins his chair to face the clamoring audience. "Hello. Hi. Yes, if you could calm down, please." He waits, his smile steady as the dancers shout, chatter, mutter and eventually fall silent. "Thank you. Lynette and I would like to apologize for our rather..."

Lynette snatches up her microphone, tossing back her red hair with a huge grin. "Bad attitudes!" she hollers with her thick Texas drawl and waves her other hand over her head. "Sorry about that, Seattle. We'll get it together for the rest of the day, promise you that."

"And we'll be making some personal apologies as well." Christopher nods, and Maritza can see the contrition from her perch near the back of the theater. Her eyebrows go up. The producers must have given them an earful. There's always at least one episode a season that features epic judge meltdowns, but not in her memory had it ever been quite as awful as today. Still, it seems to have blown over for now, and that might mean good news for her. Maybe she can at least dance well enough to get through to choreography, and if not, well, at least now they don't look as if they'll tear her apart...

"Dancer 17152, you're up. Maritza Quiñones, please report to the stage." Christopher's smooth voice, with a hint of inquiry, bounces from the walls and ceiling of the auditorium. "Is there a Maritza Quiñones here?"

She's frozen in her seat; her hands are white-knuckled on the armrests. Dimly, from a million miles away, she hears Fred, he's up and tugging at her arm. "Mari. Come on. It's time."

Louder than Fred's voice is the pounding of her heart in her ears. Stares of the people around them, turning to look at her in a wave that ripples out across the rows, crawl across her skin like spiders, or maybe, given how cold they leave her, like an ice spider monster. Maritza stares up at Fred, and the usual butterflies in her stomach have vacated the premises and been replaced by frogs. "I can't," she croaks as she curls her fingers more tightly around the armrests. "Javi. Grace."

"It's too late now." Her mother's hands gently push her up from the safety of her chair. "You have to go, Mari. I'm here. Fred will be with you. It's all right, go on."

All inquiry is gone from Christopher's voice now as he speaks again, his voice hard around the edges. "Dancer 17152, report to the stage. You have thirty seconds."

"Oh, God," she whispers, but she's up and on her feet. Her mother pushes her inexorably forward; Fred uses both hands to grab hers and pull her from the row.

He smiles, the big, bright smile of encouragement he always gave her and Nicky right before they went out on the dance floor.

"This is it, Mari," he says. "This is what you've worked for. Let's go. Let's do this."

She stumbles from the row of chairs, remembering at the last moment that there are probably cameras on her. *They film everything.* Maritza straightens up and tosses her ponytail back over her shoulder. She forces herself to move with confidence, to pull in a deep breath and tug her hand out of Fred's grip. Her steps are sure as she strides ahead of him. *Chin up. Slow breaths. Big smile. Not too fake.*

By the time she mounts the steps to the stage, her knees are only a little weak. Maritza wipes her slightly sweaty palms on the back of her dress and steps to the front of the stage. "Maritza Quiñones," she says, pleased that her voice is steady.

The stage lights blind her for just a second. When that clears, she sees all three judges smiling at her from their dais. "Hi," DeShawn says; his broad smile reminds her of someone... *who? Oh, right, Sarita's friend. Craig.* She saw him outside talking to other dancers. He has a nice smile. DeShawn has a nice smile. Despite the reminder of Sarita, she finds herself relaxing in front of that smile and she nods as he goes on. "You look like a ballroom dancer."

"That's what I am." Her stage-self kicks in, and she spreads her hands out in presentation, offering him a responding smile. "Foxtrot, samba, waltz, jive, paso, you name it, I can do it. Salsa, too."

DeShawn sits back in his chair; his grin widens. "Nice. Can't wait."

"Me neither." Lynette leans forward, squinting at the stage. "But your partner there, he's not auditioning today. I know that face. Fred Corbett! How the hell are you?" She claps her hands over her mouth, eyes wide. "Oops. I'm not supposed to swear while they're filming. They're gonna have to bleep me."

Fred chuckles from his spot behind Maritza. "You haven't changed, Lynette. Nice to see you again."

"Look at you! Oh, I love seeing you." Lynette waves a hand at Maritza. "This girl here one of yours?"

"My best student," Fred says, and Maritza has to work not to burst into tears at the pride she can hear in his voice. "She's going to knock your socks off."

Lynette beams. "Good. Good, I'm in need of some sock-knocking."

Beside her, Christopher sits up and lifts his hand to cut Lynette off. "If you're ready, we'll just see what you've got, Ms. Quiñones."

She dips her head and takes a step back toward Fred. In the back of the auditorium, she sees a mere sliver of light that flashes for an instant as a handful of people are admitted. *Javi? Grace?* One of the figures appears to have Grace's long hair. She can only hope. "I'm ready."

Christopher nods back. "Cue the music," he calls, waving his raised hand.

In the instant before the thumping entrance of her music warps from the speakers, the last sound Maritza hears between the heartbeats that divide this stage of her life from her future is her own sharp, small, intake of breath.

"I HOPE SHE SAW THEM GO IN." SARITA PACES OUTSIDE OF THE auditorium doors, knotting her fingers together, pulling them apart, knotting them again. "I hope she knows they came back for her. Maybe I should go in." She starts forward, but Alex and Craig grab her and stop her in her tracks as Adrienne shakes her head.

"She's already dancing, Sarita." Adrienne taps at her earpiece. "Don't worry. This will be great."

"Great, or great TV?" Sarita hasn't decided whether or not she likes Adrienne. She decides to concentrate on what she does like: Adrienne is really hot. This helps her keep her smile on the warm side. "Never mind. Sorry."

Adrienne pats her shoulder. "You're funny. And you do have a point, but as I said before, this is my job."

"Yep. Yep." She keeps her smile on as she steps away, pulling Craig after her. "This is insane. I'm insane. She probably doesn't even want me here. I'm going to ruin everything. She's going to come out and either she's going to be happy and seeing me is going to wreck it, or she's going to be upset and seeing me is going to make it worse."

Alex has tagged along. "Didn't you say she was trying to talk to you all week?" he asks as he pokes a hand through his nearly upright hair. "Not the action of someone who doesn't want to see you. I mean, I don't think."

"I didn't answer the phone. That doesn't exactly engender goodwill." She spots a dancer in a floaty blue dress and bare feet gracefully prancing away from a chair and snatches it to sit down in, then props her elbows on her knees so she can cradle her head. "This is bananas."

Craig crouches next to her and puts a hand on her knee. "You're just in shock; this is what happens when you make major life decisions on the spur of the moment. It's all going to be just fine, love. Take some breaths."

"I *am*, it's not helping," Sarita snaps, turning her head to glare at Craig through her fingers. "I've had a really long fucking day, Craig, and it started last week. I have so, so much to process. I have had so, so not enough sleep."

Craig, unfazed by both her glare and her acid tone, opens his mouth to respond, but he is cut off by Adrienne. She's making incredible time given the height of her heels, and Sarita is surprised by the speed with which she finds herself snatched from her chair and hauled back across the lobby. "She's coming out soon," Adrienne says, brisk and smooth, not a single chestnut hair out of place. She hasn't broken the slightest sweat. "Go time, my girl."

Sarita can't catch her breath. "Do you do aerobics boot camp three times a week or what?"

"Crossfit." Adrienne beams and drops a wink. "Here we go!"

The auditorium doors burst open and Maritza explodes out in a cloud of chiffon and hair and unmistakably happy shrieks as she waves a strip of paper in the air. "I got it! I'm going to Los Angeles!"

Fred trails behind her, smiling and proud of his student. "She did a great job, just the best job ever," he tells Adrienne, who has stuck a microphone in his face. "I've never seen her dance so well, and it was an honor to partner her. I always knew she'd make it. It doesn't matter who she dances with, she's just that good, but I'm really honored I got to share this moment with her. She's always been a joy to teach." He is professional and cool; his voice is smooth, but he's beaming a huge, proud smile and can't take his eyes from Maritza.

Maritza jumps up and down, dashing over when she sees her family emerging from the auditorium behind her. She squeals again and throws her arms around Javi and Grace while Susana rubs her back. They're all smiling and happy. "You came; you made it, did you see? Did you?"

Javier laughs. "We saw. You were awesome."

"I got it; I got it; I'm going," Maritza says, and she breaks down to sob and laugh into Javi's T-shirt. "I did it, my God, my God, I did it."

A knot of emotions fills Sarita's throat: happiness, pride, fear, longing. Every bit of her wants to reach out and touch Maritza, pull her away from Javi and Susana and into a hug, whisper apologies into her ear. She is uncomfortably aware of the camera that focuses on her, watching and waiting for a reaction. She wants to run and hide. She shoves her hands into her jeans pockets, concentrates on her boots and the patterns in the theatre carpet and wishes desperately she could disappear. But maybe if she's not interesting, they'll forget about her, and that will be almost the same thing.

But no. Adrienne grabs Sarita's arm and pushes her toward Susana, Javier and Grace. "Maritza, there's one more person here for you."

Maritza turns, breathless and sparkling, eyes wide. "There is?" But before Adrienne can answer her, her gaze falls on Sarita. Her mouth drops open.

The moment is long, so very long, as Sarita waits, as Sarita aches.

"Sarita." It's an exhalation, the slightest of breaths, and no indicator at all as to what Sarita should expect next.

"Mari, I—" A lump rises in her throat to cut her off, and her heart freezes.

But in the next instant, Sarita's arms are full of Maritza, of laughter and tears and sweat and sweet jasmine perfume and chiffon. "Sarita, you came. I'm sorry; I'm so happy to see you. I can't believe; there's so much—" She can't get a single coherent, complete sentence out, and it's adorable, kick-starting Sarita's heart into action again.

It sets her off, and now she's a jumble of chortles and sobs herself. "Javi came for me; he said we had to make it right, and I want to. I miss you; I'm so sorry—"

"Nicky's an ass. I meant to tell you; I didn't know what to say, what to do—oh, Sarita."

"I know. I'm sorry, I should have let you try to tell me. I was just an idiot—"

"You're *my* idiot." Maritza pulls back to cup Sarita's face in her hands. "And apology accepted. I'm just so happy to see you."

"And you did it. I knew you would. I'm so proud." Sarita slips her hands around Maritza's sparkling maroon waist. "I wish I could have gotten here in time to see you dance. I'm so sorry, Mari, really."

"You will see it. Right?" Maritza cranes her neck around to face Adrienne. "Maybe they'll give me a copy?"

"And maybe it will be on the show." Adrienne's smile is big, a bright show smile, and Sarita is aware once more that the camera is on her, is on them both. "How do you feel, Maritza?"

"You can't tell? I'm on top of the world!" Maritza pulls Sarita close, squeezing as if she'll never let go. "Today is the best day. I just... I can't believe it."

"Well, believe it, baby, you're going to L.A.!" Adrienne smiles even more broadly before she slices her finger across her throat. The cameraman nods and turns away. "Okay, ladies, that's a wrap—so sorry, but we'll have more dancers coming out in a minute and I have to get them too. But thank you. Thank you for letting us film that. It was a really beautiful moment." She pats Maritza's arm, and her smile this time is softer, more genuine. "Good luck at callbacks. I'll see you in a few weeks."

That's enough to wipe the joy from Maritza's face. As Adrienne turns away, Maritza shakes her head. "Weeks. We only have a few weeks. Oh, Sarita."

Sarita glances at Susana and Javier, unsure if she should bring up the plan she blurted out to Craig. It's crazy, too soon after two months. But she wants to be with Maritza; she wants to see where it can go, and she wants her doctorate, too. Leaving the safety net of Seattle is the only way to make both things happen.

But does Maritza want the same thing?

Only one way to find out. "It..." She has to swallow hard to get the sudden lump in her throat to go away. "It doesn't have to be. It can be... it can be longer than that. If you want."

Confusion fills Maritza's eyes. "I don't understand."

Only a nod of encouragement from Craig makes Sarita go on. "Well. Um." She pulls her hands free, letting her fingers link and twist. "I've got a degree I want to get. And you're leaving. But your family, they can't go with you right away. Your mom's got her job at the hospital."

"Right..." Maritza nods, still not seeming to understand.

"And Javi's stuck in college for another couple of years at least, so he can't really pack up and go with you either." It feels so hard to breathe in this moment as she waits for Maritza to get it. "But

I can. I can apply to the PhD program at Berkeley. Or USC. My professors can give me references. I've got some great work done on my paper. I'm a great candidate; I think I could get in somewhere. And I could be near you."

The light of comprehension seems to be dawning on Maritza's face. "But the bakery?"

"Tash would be a better bakery manager than me. I just want to go to school and be with you. I can decorate cakes in L.A." She laughs and shakes her head. "I can go, Mari. I can go with you. If you..." Uncertainty unnerves her all over again. "I mean, if you want. And we shouldn't live together, I don't think, but you know, when we have free time..."

"I want! I want, I want, I want." Maritza starts bouncing in place, taking Sarita with her since they're still entwined in a snug embrace. "Sarita, I want it bad, but what will you do? The show is crazy. I'll be exhausted all the time, and that's just callbacks. If I make it to the top twenty I'll be in rehearsals all the time."

"It'll take me some time to get there. I have to get all my stuff in order, help my parents move." She spots Devesh as he wanders out of the auditorium with a bemused look on his face. "Oh, man, and my brother. I don't want to go before my brother and his husband have their baby." There's so much to do, yet her world seems so much more wide open than she had ever dreamed. "But I can do it. I can do anything, and I'll get to be with you."

Maritza's eyes are wide, so bright, so happy. "It's so much, it's too much, I can't..." She laughs and buries her head in Sarita's shoulder. "Oh, my God, and you don't know half of what's going on; I have so much to explain."

"Oh, I've got so much to tell you; you don't even know." How could it be just a week since she'd walked away from the dance studio, still reeling from Nicky's smug nastiness, with everything all wrong? "But we have time. We get to have time."

A sigh of what Sarita hopes is happiness warms her collarbone. "We have time."

They have time, and with her arms full of Maritza and her heart full of something that might have the chance now to become love, Sarita finally knows what she wants, every last bit of what she wants. Stepping back, she takes Maritza's wondering face in her hands for a kiss. "Here's to fresh starts," she murmurs, brushing Maritza's nose with hers.

"As long as you don't scream this time," comes the soft, laughing reply, and with it, a smooth, absolute certainty and joy that settles over Sarita and clicks into place like the last piece of a puzzle.

THE END

Sucre Coeur Signatures

S OFT ON THE INSIDE WITH A BIT OF A CRISP TO THE OUTSIDE, these bittersweet chocolate chunk cookies are a decadent treat. A dash of Bailey's Irish Crème smooths the edge of the chocolate, and a dash of sea salt lifts the flavors into a whole new realm of delight. Serve with ice-cold milk or a big cup of strong tea.

1 c. unsalted butter, room temperature
1 c. granulated white sugar
½ c. light brown sugar, packed
½ c. dark brown sugar, packed
2 eggs, room temperature
1 tbsp Bailey's Irish Crème
3 c. all-purpose flour
1 tsp. baking soda
2 tsp. hot water
½ tsp salt
1 pkg bittersweet chocolate chunks
Good, coarse sea salt
1 c. toasted almond pieces, chopped small (optional)

Preheat the oven to 350 degrees Fahrenheit (about 175 Celsius) and line your baking sheets with parchment paper.

In a large bowl, cream your butter and sugars together until smooth. Add the eggs one at a time; beat after each until fully blended. Add the Bailey's Irish Cream and blend well.

In a small bowl, dissolve the baking soda into your hot water. Tip the mixture into the batter and mix well. Add the salt.

Add your flour slowly, blending well. Fold the chocolate chunks (and almond pieces if you used them) into the dough mixture.

Using a dough scoop or spoons, drop the dough onto your baking sheets in walnut-sized dollops placed at least one-inch apart. Add a sprinkle of sea salt to the top of each.

Bake one tray at a time for 10-12 minutes, turning the sheet around once at the halfway point. When the edges of the cookies are nicely browned, remove them from the oven and allow them to sit for ten minutes before transferring them to a cooling rack.

Acknowledgments

As always, I must give my gratitude and love to the team at Interlude – from top to bottom, you're all lovely and wonderful and it is a privilege to publish with you. Annie, Candy, Choi, thank you for everything.

Lex, I wish you could be here. *Sic itur ad astra.* You're so, so missed.

Team Sucre Coeur, your support is invaluable. Love to Jessica, Paco, Angela, Aaron, the entire extended Thomas clan, Mom, Aunt Kathy, Dad, David and Elena, Drew and Nadine, Az, Will – so, so much love and thanks for your continued support. I could not get these books out into the world without all that you give me.

Ali and Alana, you're there when I need to cry and kick and fuss, and you're very tolerant of all the cat photos I send you both. I in turn am grateful for all of the pet photos you send back. I love you to pieces, my darling, darling ladies. One day... wine and cheese dates? Let's make a plan.

To Kat and Alysia and Rachel and CB and Nomi, my IP cheerleaders and friends. Thank you for every virtual hug and word of encouragement. I truly can't thank you enough for being there to help kick me in the hind end when I struggled. I needed it, and you're all just so grand. Thank you, thank you, a thousand times and still not enough, I love you.

To Lauren, thank you for being so excited for this book and for rescuing me from a sea of Pepsi Madness with a badly-needed Diet Coke. Bisous!

And love, all the love to my readers, and my eternal gratitude to go with it.

About the Author

LISSA REED IS A QUEER, NON-BINARY (SHE/THEY) WRITER OF fiction, blogs, and bawdy Renaissance song parodies. She traces her early interest in writing back to elementary school, when a teacher gifted her with her first composition book and told her to fill it with words. After experimenting with print journalism, Reed shifted her writing focus to romance and literary fiction and never looked back. She lives in the Dallas-Fort Worth area.

Certainly, Possibly, You is the second installment of her Sucre Coeur series, which also features *Definitely, Maybe, Yours* and *Absolutely, Almost, Perfect*.

interludepress™

 interludepress.com
@InterludePress
interludepress
store.interludepress.com

interlude  press™
also by Lissa Reed...

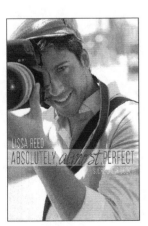

Definitely, Maybe, Yours
Sucre Coeur Series, Book One

Seattle-based baker Craig Oliver leads a life that is happily routine: baking cupcakes for an enormous family reunion, managing Sucre Coeur for its frequently absent owner and closing out his day with a pint at the local pub. He has a kind heart, a knack for pastry and a weakness for damaged people.

Habitual playboy Alex Scheff is looking to drown his sorrows, but instead discovers that he may have a weakness for Englishmen who carry cookies in their pockets. Can a seemingly incompatible pair find the recipe for love in a relationship they claim is casual?

ISBN (print) 978-1-941530-40-5 | (eBook) 978-1-941530-41-2

Absolutely, Almost, Perfect
Sucre Coeur Series, Book Three

Craig Oliver and Alex Scheff lead a charmed life. Craig is part owner of Sucre Coeur, the bakery he's loved and managed for years. Alex is an up-and-coming Seattle photographer. Their relationship has been going strong for a year, and everything is absolutely perfect—right up until Craig receives a wedding invitation from his long-estranged brother.

As Craig grows tense over seeing his brother for the first time in years, Alex can't control his anxiety over meeting Craig's family. At the wedding in an English hamlet, boisterous Scottish mothers, smirking teenage sisters, and awkward ex-boyfriends complicate the sweet life they lead.

ISBN (print) 978-1-945053-26-9 | (eBook) 978-1-945053-39-9